SHADOW RISING

By Peter Sartucci

SHADOW RISING

Second Edition

ISBN: 978-1-7335745-1-8

Edited by Kier Salmon

Cover art copyright by Claire Peacey, used by permission.

Solar system graphic by Gregory Sartucci, used by permission.

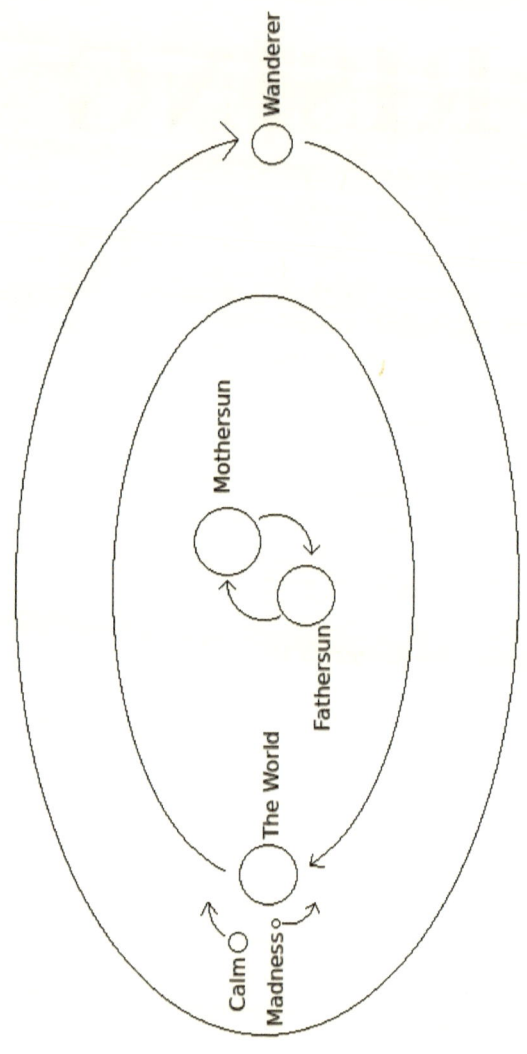

ACKNOWLEDGEMENTS

No author writes in a vacuum, we all receive help and support from countless others. I want to share a few of those names here.

To the members of my writer's group, Northern Colorado Writers Workshop, especially our late founder Ed Bryant and including Marie Desjardin, Ron Hosler, Dave Kilman, Ronnie Seagren, and Pat Smyth, my grateful thanks for many hours of combing over chapters and marshalling criticism. I am a much better writer thanks to you all.

To my First Readers, including Artis Aboltins, Markus Bauer, Scott Palter, Kier Salmon, and Lori Walker. Whew! Without you this text would have been a much bigger mess.

To Kier Salmon, editor extraordinary, for imposing necessary consistency and catching bloopers that nobody else noticed. Oops! Thanks tremendously, Kier!

To Stephen M. Stirling, for encouragement when I really needed it.

To Kevin Anderson, Dave Farland, Eric Flint, and James Artemis Owen, for organizing and running 'Super Stars Writing Seminars', which taught me about the business of being a writer. If you share my writerly ambitions, you need to get yourself to Colorado Springs for the first weekend of February and join your Tribe!

To my friend Brandon Slaten, for quiet support and encouragement over years and years. There were many times when I would have given up, if not for your unwavering confidence. Thank you.

All the dumb mistakes are solely mine.

DEDICATION

To my wife Elizabeth, who tolerated endless late-night typing and weekends spent in painful plotting instead of yard work, while I labored under the lash of my muse; all my heart's love.

TABLE OF CONTENTS

CHAPTER 1: KIRIN

Morning, First Day of the New Reign.

The flying carpet settled onto the wide ridgeline of the Sulfur Serpent Inn. Kirin DiUmbra scrambled off the undulating fabric, relieved to have the solid tiles of home under his feet once more. He could finally relax his terrified grip on the Shadow within him without fear that it would devour the magic in the carpet and plunge him to the cobblestones below.

The Master of the Air looked up at Kirin from his cross-legged position on the enchanted rug. "You are here, Prince."

Kirin flinched. "Please, Master, don't call me that." He hesitated a moment, almost afraid to ask, but he needed to know. "How much of what I did on the Hill could you see?"

"Enough to know who you must be." The gray-haired Ilvar clan wizard blinked owlishly at him, eyes deep-sunk in his wrinkled brown face. "I saw you lift the Amethyst Crown and stand unburned. Only one of the royal blood – one approved by the wight within the Stone Throne – can do that. You must be Prince Ryghar, thought dead these eighteen years. Amazing! You could be king at this very moment. Instead, I saw you reject the Crown and place it on Prince Terrell's head to make him King. Twice amazing! Still, you could claim a place at his side, wield power both magical and mundane in service to the Kingdom. Yet you fled the Hill of Sight like a man in disgrace, exchanging your opportunity for this squalid slum." He gestured at the blocks of four-story tenements and narrow courtyards surrounding

1

them, wrinkled his nose at the tidal reek of the nearby harbor. "Astonishing! I know not whether to be dismayed or awed by such – generosity." From the pause, that description hadn't been the mage's first choice.

"Neither." Kirin shook his head, wishing he could negate the other's words as easily. "This is my home. I don't know how to be a king, and I'm not a mage despite what you think. I'm an acrobat, a good one, and that's all I want to be. Please do not ever speak of this to anybody else." He put his palms together and bowed. "I beg you."

The chief of the Ilvar Clan stared at him with sadness in his old eyes. "My oath is to the King of Silbar. You could have become that and bound me with words stronger than chains. Yet you chose to pass any such decision to King Terrell. I cannot take oath to you in conflict with him – but unless he orders otherwise, or you take back your request, I vow that I will keep your secret."

Relief made Kirin slump; he converted it to another bow. "A thousand thanks to you, Master of the Air. You won't regret this."

The brown-skinned wizard smiled at him sadly. "But you may. A moth may not return to its birth-husk, nor a child to the womb. Fare you well, young Kirin DiUmbra."

The carpet lifted and sped away.

Kirin resolutely buried the wizard's parting words in his memory as he climbed down off the roof of the Sulfur Serpent. The familiar ladder tiles led across the vast slate surface to the exterior stairway at the north end. He swung down over the gutter onto the narrow platform, ignoring the four-story fall, and checked the back door to the attic.

Unbarred. With half the city and most of the Watch at the crowning ceremony on Aretzo's Hill of Sight, there were sure to be thieves about looking for opportunities like

2

this one. That anyone in the family could be so careless appalled him.

Then he remembered. Pieter had always been the one who locked up after everybody.

And Pieter was dead.

For a moment the loss hit him like a hammer. He leaned against the door jamb, remembering that whitewashed room in the mining hospice. Pieter broken and dying on the bed, still able to whisper encouragement even at Death's door.

Oh Father! What am I going to do without you? You weren't my sire, but you were Father to me in all ways that mattered. Kirin looked at the too-pale skin on his arms, touched his pointed ears. Both testified to the Gwythlo taint in his blood. Two days ago he had learned who that blood came from.

The Emperor of Gwythlo was my sire. The King of Silbar is my birth-brother. He buried his face in his hands and shuddered at the terrifying vistas that opened before him. Both sides would be against him, the barbarian pale-skinned point-eared Imperials of the North, and the brown-skinned round-eared civilized folk of the south. Palace intrigue, murderous nobles, assassins, and the Holy Inquisition itself, all directed at him. *I don't want this! Seraph Haroun, You who are mighty in the panoply of Heaven, intercede for me with the One God. I just want to be a DiUmbra acrobat.* He gazed up at the cloudless skies, pleading. *Please, Seraph, please.*

A pigeon winged past the balcony, then died with a puff of feathers as a falcon stooped on it. The falcon laboriously climbed again into the skies, its prey clutched tight as the killer screamed triumph. The omen was too pointed to ignore – or accept.

Kirin rubbed the heels of his hands against his eyes. *Seraphs, just leave me alone!* He peeled off his boots, went in and made sure to bar the door behind him.

The familiar attic loomed silent around him. Beams of sunlight slanted down from triple rows of dormer windows through sparkling dust motes. Ancient laws in the City of Aretzo forbid constructing any residential building taller than four stories. Pieter had told him that the Sulfur Serpent's builder had tried to get around that by adding three extra stories inside a high-arched roof. The City's Lord Warden had not been amused; he had forced the removal of the extra floors while leaving the roof. The resulting thirty-foot-high attic made a perfect practice room for a family of acrobats. The DiUmbra Aerialist Troupe had rented it ever since and lived in the fourth-floor block of rooms directly beneath.

Home.

He paused with a hand on the huge net hung under the double trapeze set. He had been the best male flyer in the family act and Pieter had been his catcher. Kirin's heart ached as he remembered the true star of the family, his wife Maia. Now Maia and Pieter were both dead, dead because of him. If only he hadn't fallen for Chisaad's lies. If only he hadn't been so stupid. If only.

He dashed fresh tears out of his eyes and shook himself angrily. It was done and he couldn't change it; couldn't give life back to the dead people in his wake. He could only pick up the pieces and go on. There was one very important piece waiting for him, his baby son Grigor, who he hadn't seen in almost twenty days. Somewhere a woman that Kirin didn't even know had been tending to the baby in his absence. Time to fix that. His acrobatic family would have to reassign roles and carry on, and he would have to learn how to be a father without a wife. He gripped the harsh hemp rope for a moment longer before he strode to the far end of the room and descended the stair to the DiUmbra family rooms.

He heard a stirring down the hall as he paused at the bottom. "Grandmother?" he called as he hung the battered pair of boots on the family rack, trying not to think of the dead soldier who had worn them and who now haunted his memories.

"Kirin?" her querulous voice answered, then she popped her head out the dining room door. "Kirin! Sweet seraphs be thanked, you're alive!"

The incredulous delight on her face warmed his heart. She started to shuffle towards him, so he bounded down the hall barefoot and saved her the trip. Her brown stick-thin arms embraced him as she sobbed, "Where've you been, boy? We've been so worried!"

Kirin swallowed a sudden lump in his throat. This wasn't going to get any easier if he put it off. "Grandma, I have bad news. I'm sorry to tell you, Pieter's dead."

The shock in her eyes hurt as bad as he'd feared. Hastily he added, "I went to Sulmona to rescue him from the sulfur mines, only he'd been crushed in a cave-in." He bowed his head. "I was with him when he died."

"Ah, my son, my son," Grandmother moaned softly. "I knew those mines were a death sentence for you. Seraph Haroun, curse those who put my son there, curse them to the hottest Hell!"

She wept then for Pieter, while Kirin tried to comfort her. Eventually she dried her eyes and demanded his story.

"I had to flee the city, Grandma." He tried to put the last eighteen days in as few words as possible. "Chisaad tricked me into doing something bad, and then he tried to kill me when I found out. He was plotting with Governor Ap Marn and that bastard Duke Darnaud all the time. Grandfather was right; the Duke hired us for that exhibition performance just so they could frame Pieter for murder. They wanted to make me mad enough to –" He faltered, still so ashamed that he could barely talk about it.

Grandma patted his hand and led him into the little dining room space that served the whole family. She sat him down on a stool next to the low table, poured him ale from the keg and shoved it into his hands. "Drink, boy, talking's thirsty work." She sat next to him and eyed him shrewdly while he drained half the mug. "Now tell me about it."

"I kidnapped the Prince, Grandma," he told her bluntly. "Right out of his bedroom. I just walked right through all the spells and crawled under the noses of the guards, not one of them saw me with my Shadow wrapped around me. The wizard gave me a drug to put the prince to sleep, and then I let him – Chisaad – in through a window. He drew a shape on the floor, a kind of star, and used it to whisk them both away to his tower. I had to sneak back out of the palace by myself because the magic didn't work on me. Once I got out to North Street, Duke Darnaud and his men and that damn Druid Boerga –" The fight came back to him as stark as if it had just happened. The growl of the Druid's wolf had practically turned his bowels to water. "They tried to kill me. I barely got away, and then I knew I'd been used."

Grandma nodded sadly. "Darnaud and Boerga came here after that."

"I know, oh Seraphs forgive me," Kirin whispered while tears leaked out of his eyes. "I saw Maia at the window. She floated Grigor down to me. I didn't know her levitation talent was strong enough to do that. Then I saw Darnaud kill her for it. Because of me." He rocked on his stool. "Oh Grandma, it's my fault she's dead."

She hugged him. "That Gwythlo bitch practically boasted about her plans. My granddaughter was no fool. She realized they were going to kill you and little Grigor too. She chose to save her baby at the risk of her own life. My brave girl!"

For a while they cried together. Then she said, "So where did you go, boy? They were turning the Old City inside out looking for you, quietly to be sure, but nobody here could miss it. What did you do?"

"I rescued Prince Terrell." Kirin skipped over the more horrific details. "They had him chained in some ruins to the north, it took me days to get there and break him free. Then we had to run into the desert to escape Ap Marn's guards and Ter- the prince summoned some flying wizards to get us away. After Sulmona, he brought me here with him on a flying carpet. We got to the Hill of Sight in time for him to claim the Crown, so he's King Terrell now. Chisaad tried to steal the Crown for himself, but I killed his magic with my Shadow and the Throne burnt him to ash. Terrell ordered Ap Marn arrested, but he forgave me for kidnapping him and let me go. And here I am. I guess everybody's at the celebration now, but I just wanted to come home. Tomorrow I need to mourn Maia and Pieter, but today I've got to make arrangements for little Grigor. I'll have to hire a wet-nurse until he's weaned."

She patted him again, her hands dark against the golden color of his halfbreed skin. "That's good thinking. Where is he anyway? I'd like to see my first great-grandson again."

Kirin shrugged uncomfortably. "I left him with Dona Abbie. She was going to find him a wet nurse for a few days. I'd better hurry over to her Temple and get the woman's name – what's wrong?"

Her eyes had grown huge at the mention of Dona Abbie's name. "Of course. You just got back to the city. You haven't heard yet."

"Heard what?" Kirin asked, cold prickles running down his spine at the expression on her face.

"Dona Abbie and Dona Zella were murdered the night you ran, and Duke Darnaud swore that you did it. The

Temple Inquisitors thought they might have been killed in a blood magic sacrifice and they've been searching for you!"

CHAPTER 2: INQUISITOR AND MAGE

Morning, First Day of the New Reign.

Dona Nivera DuNimes DiGallipo, First Inquisitor for the Sacred Office, surveyed the massive crowd thronging the crescent-shaped cemetery wrapped around Aretzo's Hill of Sight. She didn't approve of the festive atmosphere in this holy place. Death should always be a serious business. But one had to make allowances for the once-a-generation crowning of a new King. She had to admit that most of the partiers were decently behaved, at least here among the tombs of the aristocracy. Though she suspected that The One God alone knew what misbehavior might be going on around the back of the hill in the Poor Field. Since she couldn't do anything about that, she turned her attention away from the mob and onto a more accessible target.

"You're excited about something." She sniffed disapprovingly at her son-in-law Murror DuVaya DiGuile, also known as Mage Yellow of Aretzo's Council of Colors. The Council was currently embroiled in a struggle with the Temple Hierarchy over their respective shares of the City's magic supply, so she hadn't started her day very happy with him. Their present perch atop the flat roof of her family's mausoleum in Aretzo's cemetery was comfortable enough – she'd had her servants haul carpets and plenty of pillows along – but the space was narrow. And very crowded with the two of them, her daughter, both granddaughters, their governess, and a nurse caring for her daughter's latest addition to the family, a boy. The two servants had to climb up ladders from the ground each time they delivered a tray of food or drink.

DiGuile lowered the gold-chased cup of wine and fruit juice that he'd been drinking. He put on a look of wide-eyed innocence as he gestured with his free hand at the vast cone of the Hill of Sight in front of them, and the now-concluded ceremony taking place atop it. "Well of course I'm excited, dear mother-in-law. We just witnessed the most astonishing King Choosing in millennia! The Stone Throne has never before accepted a halfbreed as King. We live in remarkable times."

"Did we?" she snapped back in a stinging voice. "'Witnessed' is an overstatement since your clever little scrying spell failed to give us a close view of the Choosing until the end. We had to watch most of it with our unaided eyes like the plebeians. No, you're excited about something else." She frowned and added, "Something you are trying to keep secret from me." The glint in her eyes grew dangerous; the Holy Inquisition was not something to shrug off in Aretzo. "Is it that flying carpet? Or whoever was riding it?"

DiGuile sighed and dropped his pose. He gestured a servant to back away and then cast a privacy spell about his mother-in-law and himself. His wife Nina hastily slid farther away on the rug as the spell manifested into a watery-looking spheroid enclosing priestess and mage; the nurse squeezed herself and the baby behind it. When DiGuile had the spell completed he said, "The riders. Did you attempt to scry them yourself?"

"Of course not, they were even farther out of my range than the top of the Hill." Dona Nivera added a glower to the glint.

"Then trust me this much — that dark-haired passenger could not *be* scryed."

"Surely he wasn't out of your range too? Or did his magic defeat yours?"

DiGuile put on a formidable scowl of his own. "Dona Nivera, when I served the Navy I routinely scryed beyond the horizon, especially when our ship chased pirates. A mere mile, or the top of the Hill, should be nothing. Yet I couldn't get my spell to focus anywhere near the Throne once that carpet arrived, and when it left I could barely detect the Ilvar flying it. That was the Master of the Air himself, by the way, I've met him once and I remember his aura. The second carpet that delivered Sir DiLione to the Grey Fort was flown by one of the Master's sons or nephews, and I could scry it just fine. But the Master's passenger might as well not have been there at all. My spell refused to focus on him or even on anything close to him. Yet once he left the Hill I could scry the Choosing ceremony perfectly well, as I demonstrated. I suspect my scry spell failed solely because of that passenger."

Dona Nivera raised her eyebrows a fraction, demonstrating real surprise. "Was he another member of the Council? You're all fairly evenly matched. I'd not be surprised if one of them could defeat your spells."

DiGuile shook his head. "Give me credit for basic awareness. We're all here, gathered around the northeast quadrant of the Hill. Blue himself is only twenty yards that way," he pointed across the cemetery below the DuNimes mausoleum, "And Red and White are only a little farther away. I can tell where the rest are as well. No, that wasn't one of us on that carpet."

Dona Nivera's expression clouded. "Who, then?"

He darted a sharp glance at her. "I suspect Chisaad's apprentice. The DiUmbra boy."

"Ah." She fell silent and her gaze slid away from him.

DiGuile gave her a sour look. "Are you now going to pretend to me that the Inquisition hasn't been investigating him for more than a tenday?"

She responded with a withering glare. "Such investigations are secret until and unless charges are brought against the accused."

"Secret, ha," he answered, imitating her earlier tone of voice. "You can't ask questions about your target without revealing who it is, and you and your crew have talked to dozens of people so far. Do you seriously imagine all of them kept silence?"

"We ordered them to," Nivera muttered in dark frustration. She bit into a pastry and chewed as if intent on making it suffer for the sins of humankind.

"Might as well order back the tide," he stated baldly. "All of us on the Council knew by sundown ten days ago. Something about that boy scared Chisaad, scared him badly enough to turn against his own apprentice and call you in to capture him."

"It was Duke Darnaud who filed the charges," she corrected him.

"Darnaud's been thick with our thieving bastard of an ex-governor, Ap Marn. Every bookmaker in Dripwater Court would give odds that the two of them were up to something," DiGuile countered. "Which means our Acting Royal Wizard, Chisaad, was up to something too, and I use *was* most specifically."

Her eyes widened. "You think it was him that the Throne burnt to ash just before the Crowning?"

DiGuile gestured toward the Five Hundred Steps, where the rejected candidates and the new King Terrell were slowly descending the Hill of Sight. The long procession looked ant-tiny on the slope of the giant cone. "I'd know

Chisaad's aura at this distance, easily. He went up there, but he's not in the procession coming down. And as far as I can tell, everybody else who went up is right there. I'd bet both of my workshops and all my income that the Acting Royal Wizard is now dust on the breeze." He failed to conceal his vicious delight at that conclusion.

Her eyes narrowed thoughtfully. "Chisaad dead, and his apprentice leaving the Hill on a carpet flown by the Master of the Air."

"Who obeys only the King." DiGuile nodded. "Looks like maybe that apprentice is closer to being a Master than the rest of us suspected?"

"But a Master of what?" The Inquisitor's gaze was needle-sharp now.

Her son-in-law shrugged. "That would be up to the Sacred Office to determine, would it not? You have an assigned case, a defendant, and one of the accusers is suddenly dead for no clear reason. Perhaps this so-called apprentice has some explaining to do?"

Dona Nivera favored her son-in-law with an enigmatic look. "Perhaps. If he is truly back in the City, we will of course extend him an invitation to explain why his Magister would react so . . . forcefully, to him. If he has nothing to hide, he would be wise to appear willingly."

DiGuile snorted acidly. "If he has nothing to hide, where has he been for the last fifteen or more days? I'm not the only member of the Council who'd like to know that."

She looked at him with her eyes half closed, like a falcon contemplating some beast just a bit too large to kill. "If Chisaad is dead, then the boy is no longer apprenticed."

DiGuile schooled his expression into something very bland while assuming the stern pose of a Council of Colors Mage. "That will be a matter to be decided among mages."

"If he is indeed a mage," she pointed out. "Demons would come under *my* Office's jurisdiction."

"Only if you can prove demonic possession." Mage Yellow relaxed his face into an almost whimsical expression. "I am beginning to suspect that either of us will have a difficult time proving anything where this boy is concerned. He may be the most challenging new talent to appear in the last thousand years."

Dona Nivera, First Inquisitor, smiled for the first time that day. "Challenge accepted," she said, and dispelled the privacy bubble. "Nina!" she barked at her daughter. "Gather up the family, it's time to get back home and prepare for the Coronation Feast."

~ ~ ~

As his personal carriage rattled out of Aretzo's cemetery gates, crowded by the throng of others who had elected to leave a little early, Mage DiGuile let a pleased smile escape onto his face. Now that Nivera knew he was interested in the DiUmbra boy, she would surely increase her efforts to investigate his strange talent. That scrutiny would put the lad under more pressure, which could be used to render him more pliable to a determined will.

You humiliated me, boy, he thought, brooding on the ease with which Kirin had destroyed his spells in that alley thirty days ago. *That was a mistake as big as serving Chisaad. Ordinarily I wouldn't let a man live after that. But if you can do half what I suspect, you could be the most valuable tool in Aretzo — in all of Silbar. The new King doesn't understand that, or he wouldn't have let you go so easily.*

But I do. I've figured out what you really are — and who can crush you. Either you'll serve me, heart and soul, or I'll see you burned on Nivera's bonfire.

14

CHAPTER 3: BOERGA

Morning, First Day of the New Reign.

Boerga, the banished Druid who had been Military Chaplain of the Gwythlo soldiers stationed in Aretzo, impatiently stalked back and forth while she waited for her colleague Daugala, the Chief Druid assigned to this sweltering southern city by their mutual superior in the far-off Imperial seat of Gwythford. Even here in a windowless chamber deep inside the Wyvana, the chief fane of the Gwythlo religion in Aretzo, Boerga had to restrain her frustration. Daugala was supposed to be her equal on the civilian side of the Imperial presence here, but too often they'd been rivals working at cross-purposes.

Daugala came in and shut the door behind her, carefully reengaging the privacy magic that they both hoped shielded this chamber from the prying spells of the Silbari Hierarchy.

"Good to see you again," the Chief Druid commented, extending her aura to examine her military colleague critically. "And good to see that you are back to your normal capacities. That Silbari priestess came very near to killing you."

Boerga grimaced in silent agreement and endured the magical inspection. She had been carried here by Duke Darnaud's men after the debacle at that half-ruined Silbari temple in the Sump where Kirin DiUmbra's family worshipped, and where he had fled after Darnaud failed to capture him at his home. She knew perfectly well that she would likely have died within hours from the spawning destruction of Priestess Zella's last spell, if Daugala's subordinates hadn't taken prompt action to save her. A debt like that had to be respected even though it set her teeth on edge to be in such a position.

"So where have you been for the last three days?" Daugala asked probingly. "You left without explanation, still with incompletely healed injuries. Which are now healed."

Boerga was unsurprised by the question. She had taken herself off to a secret location for the last three days specifically to recharge her powers through a means that neither the Hierarchy nor her Druidical allies could detect, nor likely approve, though Daugala must suspect. Boerga deliberately dodged the question. "I was recovered enough to finish healing on my own, and the longer I stayed here the more likely it was that someone would betray my location to our enemies. Now I need to find out what's been happening for the last three days. Did Ap Marn and his pet wizard succeed? Is Terrell dead?"

"No." The word fell from Daugala's lips like a crushing weight dropped from on high. "The Royal Wizard is dead, Ap Marn is imprisoned, and the halfbreed Prince is King."

Boerga reeled at the shock. "But – Ap Marn was so sure – how?"

"Does it matter?" Daugala's voice was acid enough to etch stone. "He lost. There are a few details you may wish to know. That stone throne on top of the Hill of Sight not only killed Wizard Chisaad, it also burned up what we had thought was Prince Terrell, which turned out to be one of the wizard's golems. The real Prince returned to the city on a carpet flown by the senior Ilvar wizard, the Master of the Air, along with another person who subsequently left the Hill the same way. That stranger could not be scryed, but he had dark hair."

16

Boerga's mouth dropped open at this last entry in Daugala's catalog. "Chisaad's apprentice? The demon boy Kirin?"

"Quite likely, as they flew to the Old City and then the carpet flew away north, without a passenger." Daugala continued, watching her closely, "After the Stone Throne chose the real Prince Terrell as king, he immediately ordered Ap Marn arrested. The entire Gwythlo brigade has been placed under house arrest in the Gray Fort. Its leaders and I are ordered to present ourselves before the new king in less than an hour's time. I don't think he'll have me killed, but if he does, you'll be the ranking Druid in all of Silbar. I hope you have some ideas for just how we salvage something from this set of disasters, Boerga."

Rage flared anew in Boerga's heart. "We should overthrow him now! Raise the troops! Tell the believers to support them with every weapon! If we storm that cursed Palace before he can –"

"Don't be a fool." Daugala curled her lip at her sister priestess. "King Terrell controls the most powerful node in the known world, and he can cut off our access to the city's magic supply with a word – nay, with a *thought*. He has more Silbari troops in the city than we have Gwythlos, he can call on thousands of loyal mages, and their Temple Hierarchy outnumbers our sisters forty to one! We'd be slaughtered."

"But Osrick's the Emperor now!" Boerga appealed.

"And has a thousand issues clamoring for his attention, most of which he cares far more about than our problems in this foreign place." Daugala snarled. "Always you dream of the swift strike that carries all before it! But we're not fighting some bear or ice drake that can be killed by a stab to the head or heart. Silbar is a hydra that grows three new heads each time one is cut off."

"Then we must behead the entire beast at once. We must take control of the city node ourselves!"

"You have prated at me about that dream for a decade." Daugala's voice was bitter now. "With no result. The wight that sleeps beneath this city is bound deep, with spells far more powerful than anything we can cast – or break."

"I have finally found a way through them! All that is needed is to pour in enough life energy to waken it again."

Daugala snorted disbelief. "And you think these yellow-robed bitches will not notice us opening such a sluice, and interfere? To say nothing of what the new king will do?"

"His mage guild wrestles with this cursed Hierarchy for a bigger share of the power, and they all have been distracted by their ridiculous 'royal succession' ceremonies. I will begin now and have the wight awakened sooner than they think possible!"

"If we have that long before you are caught," Daugala grumbled. "But I can see that you will do as you want regardless of anything I say. I have no better idea, and I cannot stop you from trying, so do as you will. Now I must leave to present myself before the new King. If he does not kill me, perhaps I will see your scheme bear fruit."

"Say no more." Boerga smiled. "The wight will be ours."

They made their farewells, both too aware that this might be the last time they saw each other. Then the Chief Druid of Silbar left her sacred fane by the main door, with two sisters for company and a train of guards for swank. Boerga donned a disguise, the blue robes and face mask of a Herdae servant woman, and then slunk out of the building through a different hidden tunnel than the one she'd arrived by.

18

As she walked through the musty darkness below, a small spell lighting her uneven path, her mind raced across a fan of possibilities. She thought she was a stronger spellcaster than any other Gwythlo or Silbari priestess in Aretzo, but Daugala was right – the Silbari priestesses numbered in the thousands and would respond to any attacker in a thundering mass calculated to overwhelm by sheer numbers. Her faith had to have a lot more power than it did if the Druids dared stage any magical attack. The only way was to first wrest control of the magic-spewing node under the city, and thus fatally weaken their opponents while enormously strengthening themselves.

The Druids' tunnel soon connected to the old catacombs under the city at a point adjacent to the Southern Sewer. There was always a risk that a Hierarchy spell would detect her down here. The bitches knew the potential the old caves represented and were damnably thorough, but they did have their blind spots. She sorcelled her way through a locked service door used by the city workers to clean blockages in the sewer. Then she held her breath and walked two hundred quick paces along a raised walkway inside the stinking tunnel. She was near choked by the stench when she reached an even-more-secret door that let her out. She rested for a few breaths in a subbasement while tamping her light spell down to a bare glow. This building belonged to the Gwythlo lord who had been Count of the Harbor since the Conquest, but even here she might not be safe.

Boerga concentrated on her disguise, swathed head to toe in the blue robes that a Herdae woman would wear to conceal her tattoos from offended Silbari eyes. She made sure her face mask was secure and adopted the mincing walk of Herdae servant women. Two stairs and three doors later she was out in the service courtyard on the side of the Count's townhouse and moving sedately down an alley toward the Processional and then the Old City. She plunged into the unusually empty streets of Aretzo with barely a ripple. The few Silbaris about, warned by her blue covering and painted face mask, chose not to see her, turning their faces away.

Half of any disguise is the confidence with which one wears it, she thought.

A mile of squalid streets later she was deep in Aretzo's Old City and passing through a much smellier courtyard. The contents of too many chamber pots hadn't yet drained into a stone sewer grating clogged by the offal spilled from an indifferently maintained butcher shop. Black clouds of buzzing flies made her glad for the suffocating Herdae robes. The teeth-grating sound of a reed pipe drifted from a window. Tattered paper broadsides fluttered on a wall, an unwelcome reminder that even here in the Old City most people could actually read.

Foolishness, to draw the darkie peasants' minds away from their duties!

Her left leg, still healing, ached abominably from today's unaccustomed walking. She couldn't help brooding on the monstrous insult implied by her injury. Who could have guessed that the bitch priestess in that ruined temple by the harbor was powerful enough to hurt a senior Druid? The residual embarrassment still made her grit her teeth in renewed rage. Rage at this entire cursed country, this appallingly hot southern land of dust and disgusting practices. A land that never knew the clean scent of northern pines and the crisp air of a snowy morning. She dearly wanted to fling off the too-warm cloth that concealed her identity and bare herself to a cleansing sea breeze.

No, she reminded herself sternly. *That would be suicide.*

She paused to listen as a cheerful whistling came to her muffled ears, tried to gauge which of three possible alleys it might come from. The King Choosing had drawn many but not all of the Old City's folk to the Hill of Sight, which handicapped her ability to move without notice today. Worse, the City Watch was actively looking for her, a miracle of effort from that benighted bunch of drones. Though they were few and unskilled, most of them were also still on duty in these mean streets despite the coronation feast.

They are lazy but given enough time even a blind squirrel can find an acorn.

The situation was hideously fraught for her, for she was in no condition to flee the city unaided and wouldn't be for a while yet. If the plan that she concocted today failed –

I will not fail. The halfbreed prince is now King, and the cursed demon-mage helped him. Neither can be allowed to stand.

The whistling faded as the whistler turned down a different alley. A burst of children's grating laughter and the sickening scent of blooming jasmine sped her steps. A careful spell let her through a deceptively plain door into a dingy little alcove with a steep stair sloping down into a basement. A barrier spell at the bottom deadened sound and filtered out odors. Stepping through it returned her to the familiar sweet miasma of blood and pain that she'd left this morning to go meet Daugala. She bared her teeth and licked her lips. These darkies' suffering had such a delicious flavor.

And a crucial use. With the blood power of enough victims' deaths, I can awaken the sleeping wight. I will awaken it!

The Hierarch and her Circle might have numbers and ancient might, squatting here atop the giant Aretzo Node that the darkies prided themselves on controlling, but they did not realize their weakness.

I know what really controls the power you use – and how to take it from you.

She almost drooled in anticipation of the blood, and the deaths.

When she reached the cellar, her brother was manhandling a corpse into an open manhole in the floor.

21

Gorsyn had stripped to the waist and his pale skin sheened with sweat even though the basement was tolerably cool. He smelled of sex.

"Gorsyn! I told you to dispose of that right after I left!" Boerga growled around a sudden fury that nearly led her to clout him on the spot. He must have been rutting with his darkie paramour, a self-degradation that disgusted her. Boerga breathed deeply, mastered herself, and added, "You were supposed to be out fetching the next one!"

"I can't get him until tonight," he grunted as he maneuvered the mutilated clay of the dead man through the stone hole. It dropped with a splash into the sewer below and he wrestled a massive stone plug back in place.

"Tonight! What happened? Did you awaken his suspicions?"

"No, he's a pie-eyed little lamb, doesn't suspect a thing," Gorsyn answered placatingly. "I *was* going to bring the mark here while you were out, only I discovered too late that he'd got a job working the Feast. He won't even be home until the ninth bell, and then I'll have to get a drink into him before I enchant him here."

Boerga wanted to scream in frustration, but not in front of her sibling. She breathed deeply, throttled her anger and said, "Very well. Make sure your arrangements are secure when you fetch him." She added a glare. "Meanwhile you can explain why you were rutting with that filthy darkie woman again instead of doing the work your own sister assigned you!"

Gorsyn looked abashed. "I just went up to my room to fetch something, Sis, and she was waiting for me. She'd managed to get away from her husband earlier than planned. I figured an hour either way wouldn't matter." He stamped a foot on the stone plug. "That piece of fish food will still ride out on the tide. And the extra hour helps make sure none of the yellow bitches will be able to raise his ghost even if they find the body."

That last was a reasonable point, and the main reason that she'd already kept the body here for more than a day. Still. "Lame excuse, brother. Even in small matters, never put your lust ahead of your duty!"

"I am sorry, Sis, I won't do it again. But she also told me something important. The Inquisition is taking a fresh look at that little halfbreed you want. He's back in the city."

"Yes, Daugala already told me. But we have bigger concerns now. Our most important task is to take control of this Node through its wight, and as soon as possible."

Gorsyn brightened. "For that we'll need more than one victim. I think I can get us the third one of this set with a little work." He cast a spell to clean every speck of the dead man's blood off himself, then the more difficult spell to darken his skin and make his ears appear round instead of pointed. In perfect Silbari he said, "How do I look?"

"Believable," she admitted grudgingly; he really was very good at illusions, even down to his body scent. "Just remember to behave like one of them as well as look that way, and above all, do not get caught."

"I won't, Sis!" He happily went off to do her bidding. Boerga scowled at his disappearing back. If she had an abundant supply of pureblooded Gwythlo mages to choose from, Gorsyn would not have been on her personal list of most valuable. But their family link made him unquestionably loyal, he was practiced at moving wavelessly through this benighted city, and very skilled in administering torment. There were some acts of degradation for which a man was more useful than a woman.

She sighed with unhappy acceptance. Another lost day. At least she could use it to conduct a little spying. She trudged up five flights of secret steps to the top of the building. Spells denied roof access to anyone else – the darkie tenants could sweat in their overcrowded warrens below; the free air above was reserved for *her*. High walls and fences made a private space, as no taller building was close enough to this one to overlook the roof. She'd created a little garden of potted plants, a poor substitute for the deep cool forests of the north, but all she could do. One hemlock tree had managed to reach seven feet of height. She could even sit under it when she was most homesick.

Her pretties cawed and preened before her. Seven crows, the most she could manage, ready to be her eyes and ears in Aretzo. They lined up on a lath perch, jostling for attention and treats. After she had fed them and stroked their lustrous feathers, she activated her spells on them and launched them into the sky.

If Kirin DiUmbra is back in the city, he is sure to return to his home in the Sulfur Serpent. I need a closer look at that place, and at his family.

CHAPTER 4: YMERA

Morning to Night, First Day of the New Reign.

Madame Ymera, ageless ruler of Aretzo's Red Street, delicately drew her own scrying spells back from the crowd around the Hill of Sight and into the cupola of her House. She had been keeping an eye on all the Council members and senior Hierarchy of the Temple during the coronation, as had been her habit for the last nine kings. With so many Mages and Priestesses gathered outside the city walls, away from their usual protections, it was a perfect opportunity to study them more closely than usual. New schemes would always be hatched in response to a new King. The earlier she knew about them, the safer she would be from anyone foolish enough to try embroiling her in their own plots.

Terrell did indeed prove worthy of the Crown, she mused, pleased to see her expectation borne out. *I should offer him my oath soon. How public should I make it this time? I chose a private setting when Shyrill became queen, the better to limit any unpleasant Imperial attention. But for her son I think a time and place with more witnesses would be better. It will strengthen his control over the City to have my oath to him widely known, and he's certain to feel the need to assert that control as soon as he can. He clearly understands obligation and duty. I suspect that such a gift would gain me significant favor.*

There was no need for hurry, as the highly scripted Coronation Feast would consume the rest of the day. Tables in the Middle Court between the halls of Treasury and Justice, and the Outer Court where the Palace complex faced the Bazaar, were even now being set out for the plebeians and middle-rankers. Fancier preparations for the nobles and the high-ranking officials of Temple and government were underway inside the Palace itself. No departure from tradition would be tolerated for the rest of today.

For a moment she considered attending the noble's feast. It was her right, as a member of the peerage, albeit one with the smallest fief in the land, the few city blocks of the Red Street. But she had always declined those invitations, and already refused this one.

She set that thought aside and turned to the more interesting question of the mysterious arrival and departure.

I scryed the Master's nephew flying that carpet with Penghar DiLione aboard, she thought. *But the one flown by the Master of the Air himself was barely detectable. Something interfered with my scrying spells.*

That had to be Kirin.

Gee had told her about the murder of the boy's wife and his disappearance from the city. Ymera had watched from afar as Chisaad became more reclusive and strained as the King Choosing neared. While some strain was only to be expected, centuries of observing the once-a-generation change of Kings warned her that there was something extraordinary going on beneath the surface. When Gee apprised Ymera of the Temple's investigation and the conflicting rumors flying around about it, she had realized that Kirin had to be deeply involved – and therefore Chisaad. Even though the Temple made a valiant effort to keep the investigation subdued, Ymera soon knew Kirin had been accused of Blood Magic.

Ridiculous! She snorted to herself as she descended her private stairs to her third-floor bedroom. *I examined the boy thoroughly. The closest he ever came to Blood Magic was that disgusting mage that bought him.* It had taken a whole tenday of patient, unthreatening inquiries before her spy, Mother Gee, finally confided her palest suspicions about that bit of Kirin's past.

26

The long delay demonstrated how strong Gee's feelings for the boy really were.

Ymera had been impressed by Gee's resistance, but unsurprised by the information itself. In two and a half centuries she had seen plenty of human wickedness. And, she had to admit, enough countervailing virtue to awe her more than once.

Which will this Kirin prove to hold? Virtue or wickedness? She wondered. *And what would be the best way for me to get ready? For this looks to be another time of changes, and those are rarely smooth.*

A soft triple knock on the door to her bedroom let her know that one of her servants wanted her attention. They wouldn't disturb her for anything minor, so that meant something was seriously wrong somewhere.

"Enter," she called as she released the spell barring the door. It swung open to reveal one of the madams of the Red Street's lesser houses. "What is it, Eumita?"

Eumita bowed, nervous worry radiating from her like heat from an oven. "My Lady, the young halfbreed man I hired last Fourday for the Waterlily House guards, Rian Smithson, did not report for work yesterday."

Today was the eighth day of the ten-day-long Silbari week. Ymera nodded slightly.

"I sent a boy to ask where he was," Eumita continued, "But none at his rooming house could or would say, even when I sent another to inquire yesterday evening. This morning I checked the tracer spell you cast on him and, well, My Lady, it's been broken." She held out a small ceramic bowl.

Ymera deftly took it from her and peered at the locator arrow suspended within the bowl. It hung point downward and wiggled aimlessly when she turned the bowl. She examined the spells she had layered around the blond

27

wisp of plucked human hairs bound to the arrow. This end of the locator spell was secure, but it was not finding Smithson at its other end.

She drew upon her link to the Aretzo Node and cast a powerful searching spell through the locator, one that should have punched through any interference. If Smithson was anywhere within a dozen leagues, she should at least get a clear indication of his direction.

Nothing.

Ymera's eyes narrowed. There were only two likely possibilities. Either a powerful mage was actively blocking her spell; or young Smithson was dead. The possibility that someone might have murdered one of her servants, however lowly or newly hired, raised her hackles and made her instinctively bare her teeth, though fortunately her disguise spell concealed her very real fangs from Eumita.

"Do we have any of his personal effects?" she asked.

"Only this, My Lady." Eumita held out a battered leather pouch. It held a well-used whetstone in a chamois wrapper, a bone pick, a corked ceramic vial of mineral oil, and a bit of coarse sea sponge, all typical tools used by a sellsword to maintain the weapon that gave him his living. "He left it in his assigned cupboard at our guard station."

Ymera's attention went to the whetstone. It was heavily worn at one end, much less so at the other. Delicately she floated it up without touching the stone and magically probed at a pair of matched discolorations on the unworn end. Tiny flakes of skin had been ground into the porous stone by repeated gripping in the same place.

"You did well, Eumita. I will examine this further and determine what is to be done. Return to me in the morning."

The madam bowed herself out. Ymera sealed the bedroom door after the woman and hurried up the stairs to her aerie. Time was probably short; it might even be too late to learn what had happened to cause a hopeful young man to miss the start of an enviable advance in his life's station. Ymera had long ago learned that unexplained minor issues could conceal dangerous weaknesses, like a stomachache disguising a cancer.

She positioned the stone in a clamp that she kept for such examinations, and then drew heavily on the City Node again to power a waiting spell that she had crafted decades ago. The feather-fine wisps of magic brushed the whetstone's surface, dug in and seized those tiny fragments of Smithson's skin.

"Now, the other end," she murmured to herself, painstakingly linking it to the locator and then reshaping the joint spells to fit like a key into a lock. A lock shaped like the flesh of one Rian Smithson, who might be living or dead. It took several tries, for the requirements of this spell were far more exacting than the brute-force locator she had tried before, but at last she had it ready. A slowly spinning torus of light manifested around her and the whetstone, sharpened into a flat ring, and gradually shifted color. When it reached a deep indigo she launched the search with a word and a gesture.

The circle began to make small ticking sounds as it rotated, invisible spells sweeping in ever expanding circles out from the walls of her House to ripple across the Red Street, then the City beyond. The ripples skipped over the Palace and the Hill of Sight and steered clear of the Mother Temple, for the spells there were older and more powerful than her own, but everywhere else her magic's slow subtlety leaked through even the strongest of barriers. Nothing aggressive, nothing to alarm any mage, but absolutely focused on one target only: Rian Smithson. His plucked hairs in the locator spell gleamed while the spell compared them to man after man as it searched.

There were a quarter of a million people in Aretzo. She watched with the patience she had learned over centuries. Her ordinary hours of sleep passed, the deadly suns outside the louvered cupola of her House shifted from east to west, and afternoon waned into evening and then night. The dawn Temple bells rang and fell silent before her spell finally found its target.

A cold target. A dead body, already starting to rot.

"So," she muttered, scowling. "Now to find out why. Is this part of a plot against me? Or some simple mischance? Or perhaps, the tail of something deeper, but not connected to me at all?"

Smithson had missed more than a full day of work, time that should have been spent on her behalf. He might have been missing for thrice that without anyone on her Street the wiser. Anything over a day or two meant that the Inquisition wouldn't be able to raise his spirit for questioning. From the initial decay of his body, that deadline was past.

Nor could she raise him, not if he'd been dead for nearly two days. His spirit would have separated from his flesh and sunk through the Skin of the World. Once a soul left the surface of the World and began its voyage into the depths, no magic she had mastered would suffice to contact it. But she thought she might know someone who could empower her to talk directly to the poor severed spirit. Someone who could reach beyond the veil between Life and Death.

She glanced through the louvers of her cupola, through the twisting cables of her spells that extended her rule to every corner of the Red Street. In the early morning sky the Moon of Madness waned toward the brightening east. Calm had long set behind the western mountains. Did she dare try this? To invite him here again, to the very center of her power, now that she knew something of what he could do? If he lost control of his Shadow here, it could take her years to repair the damage – assuming she lived through the experience at all.

There is no gain without risk, and no safety this side of the grave, she reminded herself. *I'll send Kirin an invitation and see what he does.*

CHAPTER 5: KIRIN

Morning, First Day of the New Reign.

The old Temple of Heavenly Peace looked the same as when Kirin left it nearly twenty days ago. Collapsed dome, glassless windows in the long nave, the string curtain where front doors should be. He parted the strings and walked in quietly, made his obeisance to the altar and then went to the door to the Priestess' chambers. Nobody answered his knock, not the first time and not the fifth.

Oh, of course! He thought, feeling a fool. Any priestess in the city who didn't have a pressing duty was sure to be at the coronation.

He hesitated, remembering Dona Abbie's last words in his hearing. Something about taking Grigor to a woman who'd lost her baby. A woman named –

"Merria," he spoke aloud in relief. He knew of three different Merrias young enough to have a baby in this part of the Old City. There might be hundreds, it was a common name, but at least he had a place to start.

A candlemark later he dodged the contents of a chamber pot flung by Merria Cadie Rodum the fishwife.

"I'm a respectable woman, you halfbreed dog-on-two-legs!" she screamed in a voice fit to wake the dead. "I wouldn't have you if you came wrapped in silver! How dare you!" She shook a fist at him while her ample bosom heaved in outrage and two children clung to her skirts.

"Please forgive my clumsy words!" Kirin begged. "I didn't mean to imply –" He had to dodge again as she heaved the chamber pot itself at him.

"Get out!" Her bellow shook dust from the ceiling of this fourth-floor walkup.

Kirin hopped over the smear of urine and dung and leaped down the stairs, afraid she'd find something else to throw at his back while he fled. He made it to the street only to have to dodge the contents of another chamber pot dumped from her apartment window. Most of it splashed into the canal, angering a boatman poling his skiff. A new screaming match erupted and under its cover Kirin made his escape.

He stopped running a block away and blew out a breath.

"Okay, no baby there," he muttered to himself, and started working his way around the Pepper Merchants Canal toward his next candidate.

This Merria lived with her husband and child on the fourth floor of a worn old building a few blocks east of the Serpentine. He wasn't sure which room, so he started knocking on doors. Nobody answered the first two, their tenants had probably gone to the King Choosing, but a bar clattered at the third. The door opened to reveal a muscular youth his own age clad only in a damp loincloth and showing similar skin to Kirin's own, and the same pointed ears. The halfbreed stranger did a double take as he stared at Kirin and Kirin stared back.

"Woah, I thought you were Rian. You knocked just like he does," the young man muttered apologetically, then added in a hopeful tone, "Do you have news of him?"

"Sorry, no, I don't know that name." Kirin hesitated; the room's resident looked sad at the words. "Is something wrong?"

"He got a big hiring bonus for his most recent job and went out to buy a new pair of vambraces and then celebrate. He hasn't come home for three days. Jerril and me are both worried about him. But I'm forgetting my manners, would you like some fresh ale?" The stranger stepped back and waved him into the room. "Come on in. Don't mind all the clothes, I just finished doing laundry."

Kirin hesitated a moment, but the chance to talk to another halfbreed like himself decided him. "Sure, a drink would go down nice right now."

It was a two-room apartment like many others, a bare plank floor bereft of rugs under a raftered ceiling that was obviously the underside of the roof. Kirin glimpsed three pallets wedged into the adjacent bedroom, which didn't even have a curtain to separate it from this one. The main room had a couple stools and a sturdy bench for seats. A small, battered shield and a nicked sword leaned in one corner. Two freshly washed tunics had been carefully draped over lines to dry, other damp garments hung on strings tied across an open doorway. Through it Kirin could see a roofless balcony with a few bricks set up as an outdoor cooking hearth. Other than a wobbly table with a big wooden bowl and a bucket, and a shelf on one wall holding a few dishes and cooking gear, there was nothing else in the room.

The stranger poured ale from a pot into a mug, handed it to Kirin and waved him to the bench. The youth himself perched on one stool like a yellow-and-black cat, saying, "I'm Aeddan Soldierson. What's your name?"

Kirin answered as he sat. "I'm Kirin Sule DiUmbra. I'm sorry but I don't know anybody named Rian." He sipped – the ale was decent if not fancy.

Aeddan was staring at his face in fascination. "DiUmbra? I thought I recognized you. You're one of the acrobats who live in the Sulfur Serpent. Your family kept you."

34

"Kept me?"

"Gave you a real name, brought you up in their business. Kept you." The longing in Aeddan's voice was almost palpable. "I've seen you performing in the Bazaar. Once the merchant who had hired me stopped to enjoy your show and liked it enough to stay to the end, so I got to watch the whole thing. I'm sorry I didn't have any money to throw."

For a moment Kirin didn't know what to say. He'd occasionally seen other young halfbreeds around the city but never spent any time with them. It only now occurred to him how fortunate his own family situation must look to them. "Don't worry about it." A little embarrassed, he drank half the mug.

Aeddan fingered his own ears, as pointed on the top as Kirin's. "Your blood came out just like mine and Jerril's – black hair and pointed ears."

"Yeah," Kirin nodded. "People call me an Imp because of that. You probably get called that plenty too."

"All the time." Aeddan scowled at the balcony door and by extension the rest of the city. "A lot of Silbaris won't hire us because of our ears. I've mostly had to work for visiting merchants. Rian's lucky, his ears are almost round, and he tans well enough to pass for a Silbari if they don't look too closely. That works out for us, sometimes he can get hired and bring me and Jerril in on the contract as seconds. He was hoping to do that with his newest score."

"Is it hard work, being a bodyguard?" Kirin couldn't help asking curiously. "You have to fight much?"

Aeddan shrugged. "No, mostly I just look fierce at pickpockets and such, but I am pretty good with those." He pointed to the sword and shield and flexed his right arm to emphasize his obvious strength. "I've only had to use them a couple times. Once three dirtbags jumped my client and me, but I beat the snot out of them with the flat of the blade, to teach them not to try it again. Told them they'd get the sharp edge next time." He smiled in happy memory. "Haven't seen those three since."

Kirin whistled appreciatively. "Where did you learn to do that?"

"My uncle taught me. His wife and mother wouldn't have me in their house, but three or four times every tenday he picked me up at my mother's garret and took me to his gymnasium. He'd been a soldier and taught sword work to Silbari boys and offered training to bodyguards. He made me learn between paying customers. Said a sword would always keep me fed, and it has so far." He added proudly, "I was good enough to get accepted into the mercenary guild on my first try. Jerril and Rian were already in and needed someone to split these rooms."

Kirin waved at the little apartment. "That worked out well for you."

"For my mother too. I moved out so that my aunt and grandmother would let her live with them and Uncle again. We three get along good, only I'm wondering where Rian's got off to. I hope he didn't get grabbed by some foreign ship and made to work crew." Aeddan's bushy eyebrows knit together with worry. "Better he's drunk somewhere than that."

Kirin vaguely knew that such kidnappings occasionally happened down near the docks. The priestesses inveighed against it as a form of slavery and thus forbidden by the Holy Writ. If a captain was caught doing it the fine was severe, but desperate captains sometimes grabbed men anyway. He nodded agreement soberly. "I'm sorry I can't tell you. I haven't seen many others like us, and I've been out of town for the past couple tendays anyway. I'm here looking for Merria Chade Liber and her family, but I don't know which apartment they live in."

Aeddan had taken a swig from his mug. He waved it toward the south.

"Oh, they moved out five days ago. Her husband got a job working for a chandler near the Navy docks. Came with a place to live for his wife and kids and all." Aeddan sighed enviously at such an opportunity.

"Kids?" Kirin perked up. "Did she have another one recently?"

"No, it's been more like a whole season since she popped it out. Dotes on that little girl, let me tell you!" He grinned. "I think her husband would have been in trouble if their second one had been another boy."

"Oh." Kirin's hopes deflated. This Merria obviously wasn't caring for baby Grigor. "Thanks for the word." He gulped the last of the ale and prepared to leave.

"Any time." Aeddan took the empty mug and saw him to the door. "If you run across Rian Smithson, tell him to drag his drunken ass home, his roommates are worried about him."

"Will do. Pleased to meet you, Aeddan." Kirin was glad to be able to speak the truth.

"Same here, Kirin. Don't be a stranger. We halfbreeds need to stick together." The young man looked sad to lose what was probably the friendliest human contact he'd had in days.

They shook hands in the Warrior's Grip, palm to wrist, and Kirin clattered back down the stairs to chase his last possibility.

Half an hour of fruitless inquiries later he finally found the rooms where the third Merria lived with her husband and three children. It was a sagging third-floor tenement at the junction of the Charcoal Canal and its north fork. Several businesses had taken advantage of the strategic location to plaster the front of the building with handbills advertising their services. The family also had left home early this morning to watch the coronation and join the free feast, according to a garrulous (and blind) neighbor woman whose fingers never stopped weaving silk thread into ribbons while she talked. Kirin thanked her and left.

Discouraged, he stopped on a little drawbridge over the canal junction to think. His stomach growled, reminding him that he'd broken his fast in Sulmona before dawn and a couple small mugs of ale weren't enough to fill it. The long trip through the sky kneeling on the Master of the Air's flying carpet had been exciting and terrifying, which left him even hungrier. He searched his belt pouch and found half of a silver doba and two copper lepta. The coppers might get him a fried fish at a stall on the Serpentine.

Two boys on the shore were throwing bits of broken crockery in the water and shouting excitedly. Kirin glanced over the bridge balustrade to see what the noise was about.

A human shape floated face down in the canal. Drowning?

He vaulted over the railing.

The canal water was comfortably warm even this late in autumn. It was also filthy and shallow, his feet hit mud before he'd sunk chest deep. He took the impact on his knees and kept his head from going under. Two steps brought him to the body. He flipped it over.

And recoiled. The man was naked, horribly mutilated, and very dead.

He nearly pushed the corpse away and fled back to land. This wasn't anyone he knew, or at least, he didn't think so – the face had been so badly cut up that he couldn't be sure. One thing kept him there. The man had the golden skin color of a Silbari-Gwythlo halfbreed, just like his own.

This could have been me. Despite the warm water he shivered.

He pushed the body over to the canal side. The boys, who had stopped flinging trash when he jumped in, clustered near to stare.

"Stay back," he grunted at them as he manhandled the corpse onto the narrow street. When he was sure it wouldn't slide back in, he crawled out and fished in his purse for the copper leptas, held them up. "Bring back a couple Watchmen and these are yours."

They ran off eagerly.

Kirin tried to wring out his clothes, finally giving it up as useless. Aretzo in autumn was still warm enough that he'd dry eventually, and well before then he'd want a bath.

The corpse lay there on its back, naked and hideous. He couldn't help looking at it, at first with little darting glances that sheered off in horror. But as time dragged by waiting for the City Watch, he got used to the horror and began to look closer.

The man wasn't much older than himself, roughly eighteen years. His ears were almost round on top, and his beard had grown enough to tell the color, a pale brown or very dark blond. His head was hairless, his scalp shaved and then slashed and peeled. Kirin had initially taken the clotted black blood for close-trimmed hair. Scabbed chafe-marks on the wrists and ankles showed how the victim had been tied. The man's chest and belly were a mass of cuts, some deep enough to let out loops of intestine. His crotch –

Kirin shuddered and looked away. He didn't need to roll the corpse over and check the buttocks, he could guess that he would find. Blood Mages drew their power from degrading as well as tormenting their victims; first rape, then maiming, as prolonged a death as the mage could manage. Could this be the missing Rian?

This is what Gerlach had planned for me. His own gut churned in double horror, once at the sight and again at the memory of the blood mage that had bought him off the auction block. The dead spirit inside his memories awoke and he lived again his own torment – and how he had ended it.

You heartless bastard! Kirin swore at the shade in his mind. *May you and all your kind burn in the hottest Hell the Tormentor owns. Eternity in the Pit would be too good for you.*

The dead memories didn't answer, except with that cruel hunger for power that had ruled Gerlach right up to the moment of his death. Until Kirin's Shadow had ripped the blood mage's soul from his body and swallowed him whole, turning domination into ultimate helplessness.

Kirin found himself hunched against the brick wall of the building that hedged the west side of the narrow canal path. A young couple crossing the bridge stared at him and the body in shock, then hurried their two children away. Another man paused on the bridge long enough to spit at him. It felt like hours before the watchmen arrived.

The boys returned first, running back and forth around the corner like eager puppies. Kirin hastily drove his Shadow back under his heart before he paid them. Two beefy men strode up as the boys ran off with the promised coins, and Kirin's heart sank as he recognized the new arrivals. Watchman Kobbir DiJulin and Sargent Melghar DiCerat, two second-son drones from the petty nobility dispossessed by Silbar's Gwythlo conquerors. He had never had any run-ins with either of them, but they'd never been friendly toward the DiUmbras either. The two looked at the body, scowling, and then looked at him. Kobbir scowled harder and got a nasty glint in his eye.

"Why'd you do it?" He demanded. "Been drinking? Started fighting? Pulled your knife without thinking?"

He had his arms crossed while he spouted off, so Kirin guessed the Watchman was jerking him around rather than actually accusing. Though Kobbir stood a head taller than himself, Kirin knew he was strong enough to lift the lanky man overhead and pitch him in the canal. That didn't make the fool's words sting less.

"Don't be an ass!" Kirin snapped back, not about to grovel after all he'd been through. "I don't even have a knife on me! I saw him in the canal, thought he was drowning, and fished him out." His Shadow rippled inside his chest, but he kept it safely bottled up. The last thing he needed was to raise the Watch's suspicions with a glimpse of real darkness.

DiCerat had knelt down to get a closer look, now he whistled. "Look at this, Kobbir. Blood mage work, or I'm a monkey." He glanced up at Kirin, his face as unreadable as ever. "How long ago did you find him, DiUmbra?"

The Mother Temple's bells rang just then and all the other temples joined in, signaling the noon hour. Kirin waved a hand toward the sound. "A little after the eleventh bell. Look, I'm still wet from going in after him." He scratched where the canal slime had started to dry.

Kobbir sniffed elaborately. "So that's why you smell like such a blossom today?"

DiCerat ignored his junior partner. "Mmmm. Tide pushing him inland then." He stood up and studied the canal. "Only two hours since it changed. He could've either floated in from the harbor or come down the Big Asshole."

Kirin knew DiCerat meant the Big Drain, the city's north-side sewer that ran all the way from the Palace to the head of the Charcoal Canal. It added considerably to the stench that always hung over this part of the Old City.

"Unless juggler-boy dumped him in right here," Kobbir suggested helpfully, leering.

41

Kirin shot him a glare, but knew that without putting his Shadow into it, it came off pretty feeble. Kobbir just grinned, secure in the knowledge that his father and older brother managed one of Mage Red's workshops and thus had clout that an acrobat could never match. All three of them knew that Kobbir would never get called on the carpet for mere words.

"Watchman DiJulin, I need your magesight. Look at these wounds," the Sargent ordered. "And tell me what you see."

Kobbir left off taunting and squatted down, stared hard at the body. Kirin's own magesight could see DiJulin's activate and probe the dead flesh without physically touching. Kobbir's face grayed a little and Kirin realized that the junior Watchman had been verbally jabbing him just to avoid looking at the horror. Kobbir's face lost the grin and gave up a couple shades of color under his dark Silbari skin.

"Nerve-slaved," he reported in a much quieter voice. "Mage used some kind of focus aid. Probably amplified every cut to five or ten times the pain that a normal one would cause. The rags of the spell are still there, and sharp around the edges. Likely took a day and a half, maybe two, to kill the poor sod – he'd have been screaming every moment of it, but his vocal cords have been sorcelled mute. Not proof of demon summoning, but nasty enough – and not many other reasons to do this to a man." He stood up abruptly and stared out over the canal, looking at nothing and swallowing hard.

DiCerat nodded as if that confirmed his own thoughts. Kirin knew the senior Watchman didn't have any magesight, but he did have half again Kobbir's years, and had spent all of them in the Sump. He looked at Kirin, eyes flicking over his damp clothes.

"Thank you for calling us in right away, DiUmbra," DiCerat said in a calm tone that actually sounded a touch grateful.

42

Kirin battled surprise. City Watchmen weren't usually polite enough to say *thank you* for any damn thing, never mind for making them work harder. But DiCerat wasn't done.

"Come by the Tomb and give our scribe a formal statement of everything you saw," he ordered. "From the moment you first laid eyes on him. But first, go get a bath."

Kirin winced inside at the order. Wasting an hour repeating himself to the Watch did not appeal when his son was still missing. But defying the Watch was dangerous, so he nodded, pulled his forelock in polite answer, and got out of there. The rest of his searching for baby Grigor would have to wait until he got cleaned up anyway, unless he wanted to be showered with more chamber pots by outraged mothers just for stinking like the canals.

But even as he wended his way through the maze of streets toward the Sulfur Street Baths, his mind wouldn't stop turning over something he'd seen with his Shadow. It was a little thing. He didn't even know what it meant. But buried inside that body, like a string tied around the heart, had been a wisp of a broken spell. He'd accidentally let his Shadow drink it down.

It had tasted like women's magic.

CHAPTER 6: TERRELL

Morning, First Day of the New Reign.

"I'm going to do you all a large favor." Prince Terrell DuRillin DiGwythlo, now King of Silbar, smiled at the assembled officers of the Gwythlo Brigade, part of the Gray Fort's garrison.

One colonel, three captains, not-quite-a-dozen lieutenants, five mages, and the senior Druid of the local Gwythlo fane stared back at him from pale and worried faces. Despite Terrell's less-than-average height and genial demeanor, they gave him all the attentiveness that a wise man would provide to a large and very irate bear. They'd seen their ex-Governor arrested, the army's Druid Chaplain banished, and heard the rumors of a failed coup against the brown-skinned man standing before them. His Silbari bodyguard, Sir Penghar DiLione, waited at his right hand with the famous soulsword, Irreneetha, unsheathed. That ensorcelled blade glowed a stark white with flashes of red visible even in this sunlit courtyard. None of the officers had been stripped of their personal weapons before being ushered into this walled box, but none wore armor, and every one of them knew how poor their chances were against that sword. The sharp-eyed Silbari archers posted on the walls above, bows at the ready and arrows in hand, only emphasized the point.

"I am going to tell my Imperial brother, Osrick," Terrell continued speaking in Gwythlo, "That you were only following orders when your leader committed treason against me. That you had no part in the chain of theft organized by ex-governor Ap Marn, and you did not personally benefit from the stolen loot." Three men with especially rich garments tried to be inconspicuous while the others shifted away from them.

Terrell pretended not to notice. His reeves were already auditing the garrison accounts and a complete report on those misappropriations was also being readied, but these officers didn't need to know that yet. "In return, you are all going to take personal responsibility for escorting Ap Marn to the Imperial seat at Gwythford Castle and presenting him before the Emperor. Who will have already been informed of his guilt by me, through messages dispatched to him by five different routes." Terrell smiled again, briefly and sourly. "Though my brother has little love for me, he has quite a bit less for anyone he suspects of cheating him. A suspicion that will also fall directly on everyone associated with Ap Marn."

All four of the senior officers paled further under their southern suntans. Osrick had been widely regarded as unforgiving and harsh even before he succeeded to the Imperial Throne a few days ago. This morning's message constructs had mentioned several fresh bodies hanging from the gibbets of Gwythford Castle. The colonel uneasily stared at the silver Silbari crown on Terrell's head and swallowed whatever he'd been about to say.

"But with my report on the unfortunate occurrences of the past few tendays in your hands," here Terrell smiled again. "Your odds of surviving his wrath will markedly improve. All you need do is make very sure that your prisoners, and the tribute that I am sending with you, actually arrive. If they do, Osrick's unfavorable attention will be eased, or diverted onto someone deserving, and you may find your lives much less uncomfortable than they could be." The smile vanished as he finished with, "If they do not arrive, well, I doubt my brother will be understanding."

The colonel glanced around, realized that the rest were all waiting on him, and cleared his throat deferentially. "Your Majesty," he began.

"Highness," Terrell instantly corrected. "In deference to my Imperial brother's wishes, I will not use the title King during my reign without his expressed permission."

"Your Highness," the colonel corrected himself. "What route do you wish us to follow on our trip home?" From the look on his face, he was imagining the more than two-thousand-mile march from Aretzo to Gwythford laden with treasure and prisoners, and not liking the prospect of constantly discouraging the dozens of nobles along the way from getting tempted.

Terrell bestowed a pleased look on the man. "You and your forces will be loaded on three Navy ships, along with the prisoners and a set of chests containing Silbar's tribute to the Emperor. Due to the weight of that tribute and the crowding that will result from packing so many men on board, those three ships will be stripped of their catapults and arbalests."

The colonel's face sagged like fallen dough. "But, Your Highness, that would leave us nearly defenseless against attack at sea!"

"Oh, don't worry about that," Terrell told him cheerfully. "Your ships will be guarded by my eight biggest warships, accompanying you all the way to Klinto's port. From there it will be your own responsibility to cover the remaining distance to Gwythford Castle. Since you'll be passing through the most densely settled part of the Empire outside Silbar, I imagine you will manage that part without difficulty."

All of the men followed the logic. Their lives would be hostage during the sea voyage, for if they mutinied and seized their three ships, the other eight could stand back and pound them into submission. If the Silbaris were careful to throw mostly anti-personnel ammunition there would be little risk of sinking the tribute ships, while the packed Gwythlo soldiers aboard them suffered huge losses. But if some other sea power tried to ambush the flotilla, their overly large complement of troops would make the three treasure ships very hard for any boarders to take. Heads nodded in grudging respect, and some relief. From Klintoport to Gwythford Castle they would be passing through lands that were firmly under the control of the Emperor's strongest loyalists, the best assurance possible that they would arrive at their destination alive. For the first time since being ushered into this semi-prison, the Gwythlo officers relaxed.

"Thank you, Your Highness," said the colonel, sounding like he meant it.

Terrell noted that the leader of Aretzo's Druidic fane, Daugala, looked less pleased, and he could guess why. The Chaplain of the Gwythlo brigade, Boerga, had fled arrest ahead of Terrell's banishment order and dared not show her face. Now Daugala would have to send three more of her limited number of capable sisters along with the Brigade to provide medical care for the three ships. Her Aretzo fane was already understaffed and would be more so in the tendays ahead. Which was bound to please her hated opposites in the Silbari Temple and advance their interests in the long struggle between the two faiths. But she was smart enough to know there was nothing to be done about it. Terrell was gratified to see Daugala's mouth firm into an angry line as she held her tongue.

"You'll leave in five days," he told the Gwythlos. "Prepare yourselves and your troops."

Sir Penghar watched the Gwythlos file out. His sword faded to a simple clear white with no red flashes. When the last of the pale northerners had gone and the dusky archers above returned their arrows to quivers, he sheathed

Irreneetha and remarked, "A third of them wanted to kill you when you started, but only the Druid still felt that way at the end. That went well."

"Yes," Terrell sighed, speaking to his best friend and bodyguard. "Now for the nastier task."

They strolled through long marble halls of the labyrinthine Palace, busy with hurrying servants and functionaries preparing the ceremonies that would mark Terrell's first day as de-facto King of Silbar. It wouldn't do for the new ruler to look like he was in a hurry, unfavorable gossip could start.

But I've got a hundred things to do today and too little time for half that, he thought ruefully, and increased the length of his steps. Pen matched him without comment.

The Palace Guard had its headquarters in an older building close to the moat that separated the Royal Apartments from the rest of the complex. The guards' commander met them at the door with a bow and ushered them to a room where, a moment later, a man was hauled in and chained to a pair of rings in the stone wall.

Ex-Governor Ap Marn still wore the dress military garb that he'd donned this morning, but it was a little worse for wear. *Like the man himself. That's an impressive black eye, and those scratches really should be seen by a Priestess. Pen said he tried to fight his arrest,* Terrell recalled. *A desperate move, and from the look on his face he's even more desperate now. I may be able to use that, if I can prevent it from turning to despair. If I read him right, once he despairs, he'll turn obstinate and spit in my face.*

The former Governor glared at Terrell and rattled the chains. "Getting petty revenge?"

"You did have me chained to a floor for eight days," Terrell pointed out reasonably. "I've only had you chained to a wall, with two yards more freedom of movement than I had. Including your own chamber pot."

Ap Marn puffed himself up in mustered outrage. "I have strong allies at the Imperial Court. You'll regret humiliating me!"

"Unlikely, but possible," Terrell agreed equitably. "Or it was, as long as your stolen money kept flowing to those allies. But that's ended now, and everyone ever associated with you will soon be scrambling to save their own hides from Osrick's wrath. While spilling every damaging thing they can about anyone who has attracted it. You'll head that list. My reeves are preparing a complete report on your peculations, copies of which I will send to my Imperial brother by multiple routes to make sure that at least one gets through unaltered. Stealing from me was unwise; stealing from him was stupid."

"I never stole from my Emperor!" Ap Marn blustered. "It's all lies spread by my enemies!"

Terrell smiled pityingly. "I almost wish I could be there to see you say that to his face – after you collaborated with Lord Gwynned to steal a fifth of the entire output of the sulfur mines. Yes, Gwynned defied the Temple Truthtellers until we defeated Darnaud's forces, which broke his resistance. He talked for hours last night and gave us the location of his hidden account book, which documented your scheme in great detail. All of it is being copied as we speak. I've already ordered the arrest of the handful of your minions that we hadn't identified yet. Alas that your ally, my dear cousin Darnaud, insisted on getting himself killed before capture, but that does simplify matters for me."

Ap Marn's face had paled at the mention of Gwynned's account book. He visibly wilted at word of Darnaud's death, his bluster running out like wine from a broached barrel.

"But I must say, My Lord Ap Marn," Terrell continued in a friendly voice. "Your scheme was awe-inspiring in its scope. Such breathtaking nerve! I'm sure

Osrick will be as impressed as I am. Feel free to continue plotting and scheming as much as you wish, but if you have any scrap of wisdom left, you'll turn all your efforts to persuading my Imperial brother to leave your head on your shoulders and merely exile you to some place unpleasant."

Pen favored the ex-governor with a grin that had no humor in it. "Maybe you can convince His Imperial Majesty to make you his ambassador to some nomad tribe beyond the Ice Mountains. He might let you live in a skin tent and eat raw reindeer meat for the rest of your life."

"Which would be less unpleasant than having your belly slit and being hung on the wall of Gwythford Castle by your entrails," Terrell added. "Osrick's in a mood to make memorable examples out of people who anger him. If you'd prefer to not be one of those, may I suggest you consider cooperation, my lord?"

Ap Marn's face had congealed into a mask of calculation. "What do you want?"

"The locations of all your secret hiding places." Terrell eyed him coldly now. "Your wife and retainers and even your servants have been arrested, your house seized, and the officers of the Gwythlo brigade are working very hard at wining my favor. All your contacts in the merchant's guild and elsewhere will be weighing their chances of going undetected, and not liking the odds. You see, my lord, Silbaris are fond of the written word, and fonder still of written numbers. I have ordered that Lord Snowdon and his eager young reeves be given access to everything, so no one can be confident that somebody else's accounts will not betray their own secrets. Discreet offers have already been made by some surprising people, who are most loyally eager to assist the investigation. More will follow. Your chances of keeping any wealth successfully hidden are quite bad and getting worse.

"But if you cooperate, I'll leave you with your wife's inheritance intact. Your own will be forfeit to the Imperial

Crown, of course. As for everything you stole here, it will become part of my first tribute payment to Osrick."

Ap Marn gritted his teeth. "You'd leave me with nothing of my own."

"I offer to leave you with your life and your marriage in exchange for your cooperation," Terrell countered. "And will recommend to Osrick that he do the same, which is your only chance for survival. Choose as you will, my lord, but you do not have long to dither. Tomorrow I will ask again, and that will be the last time."

Terrell made a small sweeping motion with one hand and the Palace Guards hauled Ap Marn away.

"What do you think he'll do?" Pen inquired quietly.

"Spend a sleepless night thinking about it, then give in," Terrell answered, his face hardening. "I wish I could afford to make it eight nights, with him chained naked on a floor like I was, but I cannot spare the time. From my first day as King, I must be seen to reverse the corrupt traditions he imposed. The One God knows it will take Snowdon's reeves many months to unravel all the mares-nest of bribes and extortion, though I expect it will be impossible to undo more than half of it. Too much money will have changed hands again and again since the original crimes. The best I can hope for is to extract enough from Ap Marn to buy a grace period before the weight of Osrick's tribute falls upon Silbar's shoulders."

Pen grimaced. "Two hundred thousand pounds of raw silver. You think Ap Marn has that much hidden away?"

Terrell shook his head as they departed the room and headed for the exit from the Guard headquarters. "No, though I can substitute his hoard of stolen sulfur for part of it at the usual eight to one ratio. Precedent will allow that and Osrick won't complain. I'm going to have to make up the difference from the Treasury. I want that difference to be as small as possible."

Pen had received the same education as Terrell and understood the hard financial realities the Silbari Crown faced. He nodded soberly.

Terrell beckoned to a waiting secretary. "I hereby order Chisaad's house and tower seized," he told the man. "See to it. I'll want to inspect the place tomorrow."

The secretary bowed and hurried away as Terrell thought, *one more thing to handle tomorrow — but I really can't let it wait any later than that. I've got to figure out how he made the golem that he substituted for me. Before somebody else tries that trick elsewhere in my realm.*

Then Terrell composed his face into a blankly beatific mask before they stepped out into the Palace corridors. The usual mob of servants, spies, and sycophants waited to sweep him into the stifling embrace of tradition. *But tradition is a tool and a weapon as well as a cage. I'll just have to learn to wield it well. The kingdom is fortunate that Kirin doesn't have to do this, he'd be hopelessly lost.*

For a moment he felt for that shadowed mind, become intimately familiar despite such a brief acquaintance. *I've known him for less than a dozen days, yet now I miss his company nearly as much as I missed Pen. How strange.* Somewhere out in the city Kirin moved, feet treading cobblestones as he went about the daily details of his life. Terrell envied that freedom.

But his own work awaited. He turned his face toward it.

CHAPTER 7: KIRIN

Afternoon, First Day of the New Reign.

For more than half of Kirin's life, Silbari Priestesses had been telling him that cleanliness was a critical step on the path to godliness. He thought they must believe it too, for the Temple insisted that the Baths in any Silbari city had to be free, to encourage people to use them. But if he wanted to have his clothes cleaned, he would have to pay. To cut the cost of that, he stopped at the first fountain he came to. Like most in the city, it had a round pool of drinking water that spilled into a stone trough for doing laundry, which in turn spilled into a sewer grating where the neighborhood dumped their chamber pots every morning. He squatted under the trough's overflow until he had washed the worst of the stench out of his hose and shirt. His buskins would be harder to clean, but at least he got them rinsed off. Some women made unfavorable comments while they filled their water jugs in the pool, so he got out of there and hustled to Sulfur Street and the Warrior Baths.

He stripped in the Men's changing room and handed his clothes and his last coin over to the elderly clerks at the laundry desk. It made him self-conscious to walk around the Men's room naked. He couldn't help being uncomfortably aware of his slave tattoo. Luckily the only other patrons around were men who already knew him as part of the DiUmbra clan. They all studiously ignored his tattoo. He spent a while sweating in the Hot Room just to be out of sight, and then washed himself thoroughly. When he couldn't stand waiting around any longer, he reclaimed his freshly laundered clothing and got dressed.

The day was warm enough that the fabric would dry on him and he wouldn't get chilled. He thanked The One for Aretzo's balmy climate, strapped his damp buskins on and hurried away through the filthy streets of the Old City. Sargent DiCerat had told him to report to the Tomb, and there was no point in antagonizing the Watch by not obeying. Especially when DiCerat had been nice enough to let him bathe first. Though Kirin figured that was mostly to spare the Watchman's comrades from the stench of the canal water being brought inside their station.

The Tomb was still the same massive box that it had always been, its broad stone front looking across the Serpentine at the inland end of the Mustard Canal. One of Kirin's pedantic uncles liked to point out that the Tomb really lay just outside the Sump, like the Sulfur Serpent Inn, both being on the uphill side of the snaky street that ran along the high-water line of the harbor district. But since it was also the only City Watch post located close to the half-sunken district of canals and piers, everybody knew the Watchmen assigned there would always get the joy of dealing with the Sump.

Kirin wondered sometimes what the heavy building had been built for. The three-story cube stretched more than forty feet on a side, with a worn inscription over the entry arch that only had one word that could still be read: "Dead." So everybody called it the Tomb. He walked under the arch and into the front room with his chin up. There he found Sargent DiCerat right away.

The Watchman waved Kirin to accompany him upstairs. Kirin followed like an obedient plebeian, hoping to get this over with quickly. DiCerat ushered him into a room with a heavy door, where Kirin discovered another reason for the Sargent's leniency with the bath diversion.

The scribe that Kirin had expected sat at a slope-topped desk with quills and paper all ready. But a Priestesses in robes quartered black and yellow, and a man in trousers and tunic colored the same, were also sitting on wooden chairs. "Here he is," Sargent DiCerat said, and all three of them looked at Kirin.

He gulped. No wonder the Sargent had sent him to get clean. The Watch had used that time to call in the Inquisition.

The Priestess wore four silver stars on her starched wimple, which made her a Quartissima, a bit above middling in the Temple Hierarchy. She wasn't any taller than him, just under five and a half feet. She wore her brown Silbari hair in a bun on the back of her head and had enough wrinkles on her face to show she must be in her late fifties. The man was obviously a mage, probably her husband, with silver streaks in his own hair and his spell auras drawn in close to his brown skin. The two of them fixed him with mild gazes that didn't fool Kirin for a moment.

I'm in trouble. Kirin remembered grandma telling him the Inquisition was looking for him. His Shadow churned inside him, and he hastily corralled it under his heart.

"This is Dona DuVigo DiCerat," the Sargent introduced the Inquisitor, "And her husband, Mage DuVigo DiCerat."

Oh ho! This mage must be the Sargent's brother or more likely cousin. Kirin sensed string-pulling going on and gave the Watchman a dry look.

DiCerat put on a bland expression and said nothing.

Kirin bowed to the priestess and pulled his forelock to the Mage and the Sargent, ignoring the scribe who only ranked a notch or two above a plebeian like himself. Then he raised his chin proudly and said "Kirin Sule DiUmbra at your service, Dona Quartissima." He wasn't about to let them know how nervous they made him. He figured he could ignore the Mage, who would take his orders from the priestess. Besides, the man's magic couldn't hurt him unless he let it. Kirin doubted that the same was true of her.

The door closed behind him with a thump like a judge's gavel. Kirin had to suppress a start. The Sargent took up a parade-rest stance next to the scribe and gestured for Kirin to sit on a stool in front of the desk. He resisted the temptation to complain and just sat, tamped his Shadow down hard, and waited.

Dona DuVigo didn't keep him in suspense for long. She started out by asking him about the body he'd found. Kirin told her how he had thought it was somebody drowning, found out otherwise, and sent some boys for the watch.

"Kids shouldn't ever have to see such things," he finished, growling. If he could have strangled Gerlach's ghost at that moment he would have, but the mage was only a memory.

"You say that with great venom," Dona DuVigo observed. "Have you seen the work of a blood mage before today?"

"Once." Kirin frowned as he shoved Gerlach's memory back under.

"When?" The word was casual, but her steely gaze wasn't.

He didn't want to tell her about the monster haunting his memories, much less have her asking questions about what really happened to Gerlach. "A long time ago, Dona. I was a kid myself then. I saw a corpsetaker's cart with a body a lot like the one I found today. It was nasty. Not something I can forget, though I sure wish I could."

To Kirin's relief, she appeared to accept that, even commenting, "Yes, there are enough fools among the twenty thousand mages of Aretzo that one of them tries to make himself blood-strong every year, sometimes two or more."

"Leaving bodies in their wakes," her husband added, "And too much work for us."

"Who was he?" Kirin asked; the dead man's halfbreed skin still bothered him. Could it be Aeddan's friend?

The mage shrugged. "A bastard left behind after the Conquest." He gazed at Kirin with an enigmatic blankness. "A sellsword named Rian Smithson."

Kirin closed his eyes for a moment. *Damnation, I didn't want it to be him!*

"I see that you know the name," Dona DuVigo commented. "How?"

"We're both halfbreeds," Kirin reminded her tonelessly. "I know his friend Aeddan Soldierson, another halfbreed who shared a room and a profession with him."

"I see. Both mercenary guards." She made a dismissive motion with her fingers.

Kirin scowled. Every Blood Mage's favorite victims were always people from the Sump or the Old City, people who wouldn't be missed. The Temple claimed the Inquisition always tried to catch them as fast as possible no matter who the victims were, but he had noticed that it was never the rich and powerful who got tortured to death. There was no benefit to saying so out loud, so he gritted his teeth and said nothing.

He realized his Shadow was stirring again and quickly tamped it down. He hoped it hadn't been visible in his eyes.

Dona DuVigo peered at him oddly, and then abruptly extended her aura over him in a wave of golden light. Kirin cursed himself for not expecting that, she'd be a fool not to investigate him magically too. He barely prevented his

Shadow from swallowing her magic, but it refused to go into its cage under his heart. It obstinately stayed just below his skin and blocked her spells.

He got to see what surprise looked like on her face.

"The Mage Guild says you are merely an apprentice!" She glanced aside at her husband.

He nodded and extended his own aura at Kirin like a spear. The shadow blunted it too, and both of their auras seethed around him in a confused mess.

"Dona," Kirin said hastily, "I have an unusual talent. It makes me blank to spells. That's why Magister Chisaad took me as an apprentice; to see if it could be trained up to be useful." He grimaced and rolled his eyes, hoping he wasn't overdoing his reaction. "So far it hasn't been, but I had – have – hopes."

The priestess and her husband both drew back their auras. He looked utterly astonished, but her face was very intent now. "I had wondered how a plebeian from the edge of the Sump managed to be apprenticed to the Royal Wizard. Tell me more about this talent of yours."

Kirin shifted uncomfortably on the stool and wished for the gift of smooth talk. "You both just saw it. Spells don't work on me much; they either slide off or just go away. That was why Magister Chisaad took me on. He said my talent was unprecedented and he wanted to study it. I don't know how it works, though he claimed he had some ideas." Kirin scowled. "Probably just more lies."

"More lies?" Her eyes could have been needles.

Kirin sensed the attention from her husband and the Sargent grow sharper too. He let his scowl deepen. "Magister Chisaad was plotting against the Prince, and when I found out, he tried to have me killed. He did kill my wife." He stopped and did his best to swallow his rage.

She only asked, "What did you do?"

"Ran, of course," Kirin retorted. "What else can a man like me do when the Royal Wizard wants him dead? I was going to get my wife and our son and flee the city, only the wizard sent Duke Darnaud to my home to kill us. That thrice-damned Gwythlo got there first."

Sargent DiCerat shifted very slightly on his feet. Kirin darted a resentful glance at him and added, "The Sargent can tell you what he did."

The Dona looked at the man expectantly. The Sargent cleared his throat and stood stiff as a war pike.

"We were called to the Sulphur Serpent Inn, where the DiUmbra family lives, by a neighbor who came to the station a little after the fourth bell, eighteen days ago. We found a woman known as Maia Sule DiUmbra dead in the courtyard after an apparent fall from a fourth-floor window."

"Only falling wasn't what killed her, was it?" Kirin snarled, memory boiling over.

The Watch man continued as if he hadn't spoken. "She had been stabbed through the torso by a long blade, one that pierced her back to front below the ribcage and was then rapidly withdrawn; the entry and exit wounds were typical of a sword. From the blood marks on the floor of the fourth-floor room directly above, she had been standing at the window and was struck from behind. The family was very distraught and told a somewhat confused tale of a Gwythlo nobleman and his retinue invading their home in search of their adopted son, Kirin Sule DiUmbra." The Sargent made a little hand gesture toward Kirin. "The nobleman was identified as Darnaud, who is Duke of Guglione and a first cousin of His Highness Prince Terrell. A report on the incident was compiled the next morning and duly filed with our superiors in the central office of the City Watch. No instructions have been received since then."

His cousin the Mage had donned an extremely blank expression at the mention of Duke Darnaud. The Priestess closed her eyes briefly and her mouth twisted in silent words. Then she said, "I see. Thank you, Sargent."

When she looked back at Kirin her gaze was still sharp as an awl but there was a hint of sympathy in her face. "What did you do next?"

"Took my baby son to Dona Zella and Dona Abbie at Heavenly Peace. Dona Abbie took Grigor to be nursed by a woman who had lost her own baby that night, and Dona Zella helped me get out of the city without going through the North Gate where the Gwythlos were watching. I made it into the hills and hid."

Not the hills close to the city, and his hiding was mostly done while moving, but Kirin figured it wasn't a lie.

Dona DuVigo gave him a sharp glance. "Did you report the wizard's plot to the proper authorities?"

"Hel– umm, no, I told Dona Zella and Dona Abbie. I figured they would know who to tell." And Darnaud and Boerga had probably killed them for that reason alone, he thought leadenly.

"I see. So why are you back today?"

"I could see the top of the Hill of Sight from a long way away. When the Choosing started, I saw the spells go live and I watched. My magesight is almost as good as Sargent DiCerat's partner has, and I knew Chisaad's aura, even from miles away. I saw it turn black and disappear and then a big puff of black dust blew off the top of the Hill. I figure the Throne killed him, maybe while protecting Prince Terrell from whatever Chisaad planned. Then the Throne made purple fireworks and I knew we had a King again, so I risked coming back to the City." He shrugged and finished with, "And here I am. I was searching for my son when I found poor Rian Smithson's body instead. I'd like to get back to hunting for Grigor, please, Dona – unless you know where he is?" He wasn't quite begging on that last question, but it was very close.

She stared at him thoughtfully for a moment. "Alas, I do not. Are you aware that Duke Darnaud and Royal Wizard Chisaad accused you of murdering Dona Abbithana and Dona Zella as part of a blood magery attempt?"

Kirin's back prickled in fear. The Inquisition could put him on trial for his life. At the same time anger brought blood rushing to his face. That the teacher he had trusted could pile such a monstrous insult upon betrayal – "Lying bastards, the both of them! They tried to kill me to cover up their own treason. Anything they accused me of is a lie meant to confuse the Temple."

"I am beginning to come to that conclusion myself." She gave him a tiny nod. "The bodies of the good priestesses did not support the claim, as their death wounds were clearly given by sword and lightning strike. The coroner priestess concluded that the other disfigurements were inflicted after they were already dead. That is wildly inconsistent with the pattern exhibited by all previous blood mages."

Kirin relaxed a little. It looked like she was prepared to believe in his innocence. He was tempted to ask more about Rian Smithson's body but feared to press his luck. "Then may I go search some more, Dona DuVigo? I really want my son back."

"For now, you may." She pronounced this as if it were a pardon, and then spoiled it by adding, "I may have more questions for you later."

He promised to be around if she wanted him, made his goodbye bows and got out of there. It didn't seem to have gone badly. He hoped she would stop wasting time on him and go after the Druid Boerga, who was surely the real murderer.

It wasn't until he was several blocks down the Serpentine that it occurred to Kirin to wondered how long it would be until Dona DuVigo learned that Duke Darnaud was already dead. Followed by the sinking realization that he hadn't any way to prevent Sir Penghar, Terrell's bodyguard, from telling everybody just who had killed the noble. Or any of the dozens of Silbari soldiers who'd been in the courtyard at that moment and seen his Shadow dissolve to reveal Kirin standing over the Duke's corpse.

"Dung!" Kirin said aloud, stopping in his tracks. Dona DuVigo DiCerat would soon know that he hadn't been completely truthful. What would she do then?

CHAPTER 8: KIRIN

Afternoon, First Day of the New Reign.

Kirin decided to go tell Aeddan that his anxious wait for his roommate was in vain. The Watch wasn't likely to do it and the Inquisition would probably laugh at the idea. It didn't take long to find the fourth-floor apartment off the Pepper Merchants Canal. Aeddan was descending the stairs as he arrived in the building's cramped, pee-smelling foyer.

"Kirin!" Aeddan set down his shield and greeted him with a double handgrip. The young mercenary wore a thick cloth tunic, bracers and vambraces, a helmet with a riveted leather neck protector, and his sword. "On my way to work, but I've got time if you've heard anything?"

"Yeah, and I wish it was happy news." Kirin took a deep breath and blurted it out. "Rian is dead. I'm sorry."

Aeddan sagged against the wall as if he'd been clubbed. His stunned face stared at Kirin's. "Dead? Rian? Oh dung. Dung, dung, dung!" For a moment he shut his eyes and shook his head slightly, then let out a long sigh that seemed to shrink him by one-quarter. "You sure there isn't a mistake?"

"No mistake." Kirin shrugged awkwardly, wishing he had something to do with his hands. This was harder than any play the Troupe had ever done. "There's no doubt it's him."

"That stupid idiot. Brain-dead moron too dumb to climb stairs, piss drunk clumsy fall-over-his-own-feet stupid stupid *stupid* —" Aeddan paused for a breath that was suspiciously close to a sob, then panted several more while he beat his right fist into his left palm. "Damn him. What'd the jerkwad do, get drunk and drown in his own puke?"

"He was found in the Charcoal Canal," Kirin allowed, hoping not to have to give any more detail than that.

Aeddan frowned at him and asked, "Who found his body?"

Kirin sighed and leaned against the opposite wall. "Me."

"You!"

"I was heading home from trying to find my son – that's why I was here this morning, looking for your former neighbor – and I crossed the bridge over the canal's north fork. Saw what I thought was somebody drowning. Jumped in to haul him out. Too late, he was already dead." He tried not to shiver at the memory of the cold flesh.

Aeddan squinted at him. "It was bad, wasn't it."

"Yeah."

"Somebody knifed him?"

"Several times." Kirin fought down a shudder that wanted to claim his whole spine as he remembered Rian's wounds.

"Dung. He must have been drunk off his ass. He was really *good* with any kind of blade. Neither me nor Jerril ever beat him in a practice fight." Aeddan peered at Kirin more closely. "Oh, bugger. That's not the whole story, is it?"

"You're as sharp at this as an Inquisitor," Kirin grumbled, then wished the words back.

"My uncle says a sellsword has to learn early to watch and listen." Aeddan drew in a breath like he'd been punched. "Oh. No. The Inquisition? Why?"

Kirin sighed. "Why do they usually pay attention to one of us?"

Now Aeddan looked really ill. "A blood mage. A pig-humping dung-eating triple-damned *blood mage* killed Rian."

"Yes."

"The One God damn him to eternal fire. Salim eat him one thin slice at a time." Aeddan's words rapidly descended into an impressive level of inventive scatology and obscenity, a couple of which were actually new to Kirin. It took the grieved halfbreed a while to run down, roughly at the same time as the tears stopped leaking from his eyes.

"I'm sorry to have to be the one to tell you," Kirin told him, feeling as helpless as he'd ever been.

"Don't be," Aeddan sniffed and gave him a lopsided smile. "Better to hear it from one of us than some damn Watchman. If they even bothered to tell me."

"They probably wouldn't," Kirin admitted. "You'd have to hear it from a gossip. Where is Jerril?"

"Working for the Feast. Wish I was too, but I've got a contract with a Bhinnish merchant mage tonight. We'll both probably be home between midnight and dawn, only I'll get here after kicking my heels outside a House on the Red Street while my client humps himself silly. Then I'll have to guide the litter bearers to carry the drunk jerk back to his own bed." Aeddan made a dismissive gesture that took in all such clients. "Aw dung, the Feast will be lousy with gossip. Jerr's likely to hear about Rian before he gets off duty. What a hell of a way to have to learn."

Kirin shared the other's sigh at the brutal unfairness of life.

"Where's his body?" Aeddan asked. "I should tell the Guild so they can collect it. Our dues all pay into the funeral fund, looks like Rian will need it way sooner than any of us ever expected."

"The Watch has it over at the Tomb." Kirin stood up. "I'd better go."

Aeddan reached out and grabbed his right hand in the Warrior's Grip. "Thanks for telling me, Kirin. Better to know than to wonder."

Kirin squeezed back – Aeddans's grip was as strong as his own – and said simply, "You deserved to know."

He left the young bodyguard to his work and his grieving and headed home through the stink of sewage-laden canals where seagulls dived and bickered. On the way he detoured by the Temple of Heavenly Peace to see if the new priestess was there. He didn't have much hope of finding her yet, it was only the middle of the afternoon and the Coronation celebration wouldn't end for hours. But it was better than roaming the streets aimlessly or going home to tell Grandma he had no idea where his son was. The seraphs were kind, because as soon as he knocked on the office door, it opened.

A sharp-eyed old woman peered at him, her wimple starched and clean and sporting two stars like most parish priestesses. She wore clean yellow robes cut in the Orthodox style with beautiful embroidery about the neck and sleeves, and the thin black border that signaled she was a widow who had never remarried. Her glance started out cool and shaded over into chilly as she took in his pale skin. Her own was as brown as most Silbaris.

Kirin knew again the old pain of rejection. He swallowed it as he had done a thousand times before and put on a meek posture.

"Dona Duossima," he bowed, giving her title and rank with an extra flourish of courtesy. "I am Kirin Sule DiUmbra. My family has been longtime members of this congregation. I need your help finding my missing son." He stood with bowed head and downcast eyes to wait for her answer.

She shut the door in his face.

"Dona?" He called, resisting the temptation to pound on it. "Please Dona, I need help!"

Her voice came through the cracked wood. "You are the one accused of murdering my predecessors here."

"Dona, it's not true! The real murderers accused me to cover their own crimes." He threw everything together in one mad rush of explanation. "They were plotting against Prince Terrell, I found out, they tried to kill me and did kill my wife, Dona Zella helped me escape Aretzo, they killed her for that, probably because they were afraid I told her what they were up to, which I did."

There was a long pause while she unpacked that and thought about it.

Kirin rambled on with, "If you've met my family then you know we're just ordinary people. I already talked to Dona DuVigo DiCerat of the Inquisition, and she believes me!"

That last must have been the right thing to say, for to his great relief she opened the door a crack and peered at him. He put his palms together and bowed, then put on the best submissive posture he knew, and waited.

She took her time, looking him over carefully. He was glad he had washed himself and his clothes, and doubly glad that his curly hair had dried and fluffed out to cover his ears. After a while she welcomed him in, a little grudgingly, and bade him sit at the rickety table in the familiar room that had served Dona Zella as kitchen and office. It had a thick leather-bound book set on it, one that had adjustable pegs and a wooden frame binding so that new pages could be added. She pushed it aside, sat across from him and gave him a wary look that managed to combine severity with concern.

"I am Dona Sharra Pereto Lumin." Her voice at least wasn't too frosty. "Tell me what happened."

He gave her the same story that he'd given Dona DuVigo and dwelled on the details of how Dona Abbie had taken Grigor away to be nursed by a woman who had lost her own baby that same night. "All I know about the wet-nurse is that her personal name is Merria. Dona Pereto, please, I am hoping Dona Abbie or her superior Dona Zella left a note with the full name of this woman." He used the priestess' formal woman's lineage name with her title, wary of sounding too familiar if he used her personal name.

She frowned and pulled the big book in front of her, opened it. "I have only begun reading the Parish Register," she remarked as she searched through the back of it. "Here is the page that notes the birth of your son."

She tapped a line near the bottom of one page. Kirin tried to read it upside down and recognized Grigor's name written in Dona Zella's spidery hand. Dona Pereto turned two more pages and showed him the last entry Zella had made in the book, a note about an old beggar's death. The next entry was in a hand that he didn't know but guessed must be Dona Pereto's own; it was Maia's funeral and that of an unknown baby boy.

"That's not my son," he told her dully. "Dona Abbie delivered a stillborn baby from some woman she called Merria, which was why she knew the woman could nurse my boy. I don't know the dead baby's name, or even if he had one."

"I see." She scrutinized the last few pages again, reading selected lines aloud, but found no notes about delivering any babies.

Kirin's flickering hopes dimmed. His Shadow contracted to a cold lump under his heart.

"If Dona Abbithana brought your son to a nurse, her superior did not note it in the parish register," Dona Pareto declared flatly. "There were no notes left lying around these rooms. I have no way to know who this Merria is."

Kirin bowed his head, this time in pain as he finally realized. If there had been a loose note, Boerga and Darnaud could have found it when they killed Zella and Abbie, and then gone to the unknown Merria's home to murder little Grigor. Was his son even still alive?

Grigor, you're all I have left of Maia. Where are you?

The coolness of tears drying on his cheeks told him he'd been crying. He came back to himself with a start and swiped a hand across his face. His only hope was that Abbie and Zella hadn't had time to write any note at all. Grigor might be safe with some unknown woman that the murderers hadn't been able to find. "Th-thank you, Dona Pereto," he choked out.

She had sat there watching him weep for who knows how long. The frost had thawed and now she just looked like an old woman. Gruffly she said, "I'll look through the register and make a note of every woman named Merria for you. Come back at midday tomorrow to get it."

Kirin needed a moment to understand, and then he smiled like a giddy idiot and thanked her so profusely that she had to shove him out her door to get him to stop. He made his way back home to the Sulfur Serpent with a smile on his face. He could keep asking different Merrias until he found the right one. If he had to ask every Merria in the Sump, he would.

~ ~ ~

69

The central stairway of the Sulfur Serpent reverberated with excited voices and the tramp of many feet. Kirin could hear the hubbub all the way down on the bottom floor. He raced up the treads to catch the end of the family as they hung up their street shoes and crowded into their fourth-floor hallway.

"Change as fast as you can!" Grandfather's voice bellowed over the din, quieting it. "Get ready to do *The Three Brothers* and our large exhibition. Move it, people, we're expected back before the moon clears the mountains."

Kirin hung up his buskins and padded up behind the crowd attending to the words of the Troupe's leader. "Grandfather? What do you want me to do?"

Heads turned.

"Kirin!" Sevan the younger shouted, muscling his way past two of the cousins. "Thank the Seraphs you're alive!" Kirin's brother-in-law enfolded him in a mighty bear hug, which Kirin did his best to return. A warm feeling started in his heart.

Others gathered around and grabbed his shoulders, shook his hands, and demanded to know what had happened. "Where's baby Grigor?" several asked. Uncle Ger and two of the cousins were not smiling – and Attir's face might have been carved from stone. The warm feeling began to fade.

"I don't know yet," he had to admit. "I've been looking for him most of today."

"You!" Grandfather's single word hit like a stone in a still pond. It sent out ripples of silence as the venom seeped into everybody's ears.

The fury in the old man's eyes hit Kirin like the heat of a forge. He began to sweat as the old feeling of not being good enough welled up. *He blames me for Pieter and Maia's deaths – and he's not wrong.* He shrank inside his skin. His Shadow began to rise and he hastily wrestled it down, fearful of giving the old man any provocation. Uncle Ger, arms crossed on his chest, frowned at him.

"You look like you've missed several meals," Sevan-the-Elder interrupted. "Have you been practicing these last twenty days?"

"No, Papa," Kirin admitted, using the traditional form of address to his father-in-law. *Ex-father-in-law*, he remembered, and dropped his gaze in grief. Maia and Pieter had been his ties to the family, and now both were dead. Lamely he added, "I had to keep running." A yawning abyss seemed to have opened in the floor, one big enough to swallow him and all his hopes.

"Then you are not in adequate condition for a public performance tonight," came the firm answer. "Eat a good supper and get some sleep, and tomorrow we'll see, my son."

The emphasis on the last two words gave Kirin back his world. "Yes, Papa." He bowed his head in combined relief and shame.

Grandfather looked like he was about to explode, but Uncle Sevan clapped his hands and raised his voice to the family. "You heard my father's orders – get ready!"

Everyone scattered to their rooms, leaving Kirin standing in the corridor with the Troupe's two leaders and Grandmother.

"Sevan!" Grandfather spluttered at his eldest son, his attention totally ripped away from Kirin. "That – you – this is a blatant usurpation of my authority!"

"I have just saved you from yourself," Sevan the Elder replied with steel in his voice. "You are my father and I honor and respect you, but I told you I will no longer tolerate your abuse of my son – *any* of my sons. If Kirin, or anyone else, is to be punished, it will not be at the whim of your ire, but only after careful consideration and agreement by both of us." He stared into his father's eyes, and for the first time, Kirin saw Grandfather's gaze fall. The old man looked away.

The world should have trembled. Kirin couldn't understand why the floor remained still under his bare feet. His Shadow hunkered down in his gut, quivering.

Sevan took his father's arm and drew him toward the Attic stairs while asking several low-voiced questions about the coming exhibition that forced Grandfather's attention away from Kirin. Grandmother plucked at Kirin's arm and drew him into the dining room again.

Kirin trembled, staring at the empty doorway while the two men's footsteps and voices faded. His stomach ached and the room seemed unsteady under his feet. What had just happened?

Grandmother patted him, smiling tremulously. "Always knew my eldest boy would come into his own someday," she said to the air, then to Kirin: "You heard your Papa."

Kirin suddenly realized that there were piles of food on the long low table. Pocket meat pies, mounds of olives and fruits, braids of little onions, dozens of kebabs, waxed paper cones of spiced rice or fried polenta cubes, drumsticks of different fowl, and a heap nearly as big as all the rest combined made just of baked goods. Kirin stared, astonished.

Grandmother pushed him onto a stool and ordered, "Wake up and eat, boy. Everybody brought home all they could carry from the Coronation feast. I won't have to cook for days." She handed him a mug of ale. "Time enough for talking tomorrow," she added quietly, and hovered over him protectively as he began tentatively to nibble. Then his stomach remembered that he hadn't eaten all day and real hunger awoke. By the time the corridor filled again with voices and bodies, Grandmother stood firmly in the door shooing people away.

Most of the troupe hastened back to the festivities, garbed in new costumes or carrying different musical instruments or props. Sevan-the-Younger's wife Carlai bustled in and lit a taper from the night candle, making Kirin realize that the suns were setting.

"Finally!" She proclaimed cheerfully. "The little rascal whined a bit but at last she went to sleep." She plunked herself down across the table from Kirin and set the taper to shine on his face. "You really haven't been eating properly, have you? Your face is positively thin. You're sunburned too – were you outdoors that whole time?"

"Umm," Kirin tried to respond around a mouthful of chicken-turnip-and-herb pie.

"Let him eat, Carlai," Grandmother instructed.

Carlai obligingly switched to chattering about the Coronation feast and the money the family had made from their performances. "Grandfather wrangled us a decent spot in the Middle Court," she burbled thoughtlessly with details of the place and the competing acts, casting aspersions on the rival Suleimon family and shedding judicious praise on others. She concluded with the happy observation that, "Those middle-rankers threw plenty of money! I collected a good · hundred-eighty dhoba from passing the hat, maybe two hundred when all the copper coins are counted in. It would have been even better if we had you and Maia there. And the food!"

If we had you and Maia there . . .

Kirin stared at the remains of the small loaf in his hand, light bread stuffed with yogurt cheese and diced apricots. An instant ago it had been delicious. Now swallowing the lump in his mouth took an effort. His barely got it down while his Shadow churned unhappily in his belly. *Maia.*

"Two hundred dhoba's good," Grandmother muttered while packing parts of the food in crocks. "But we need four times that to close the gap on our rent, Carlai, and there aren't going to be any more coronation feasts between now and the day it's due. Still, every bit helps."

"Grandmother, may I be excused?" Kirin asked through his tight throat.

She gave him a sharp glance that softened immediately. "Of course, boy. Get some sleep."

Kirin hurried to his room and barely got the door shut behind him before racking sobs tore their way out of his chest. He fell to his knees on the pallet that had been his and Maia's marriage bed. The wall pegs that had held her clothes were bare. The room had been cleaned and his things hung up neatly, no blood smell lingered, but it was as empty as the bed. He fell forward and clutched the blanket to his face.

Maia! He screamed soundlessly into the silence of the night. He curled on the pad and muffled great heaving sobs in the blanket. It was a long time before he fell asleep, and then dark dreams haunted the night.

CHAPTER 9: TERRELL, DAUGALA

Evening, First Day of the New Reign.

The Palace staff could not know who would stride back down the Hill with Silbar's crown on his head, so they planned the celebratory feast to cover all possibilities.

I wonder how they'd have handled Kirin becoming King? Terrell thought whimsically as his valet finished dressing him. *Probably with serenity and some quick stitching to resize the wardrobe. And a quiet lesson in etiquette to save everybody embarrassment.*

Pen's own batman had already finished garbing him and left. Now the bodyguard surveyed his lord critically. "That overtunic will hamper your sword draw. And how can you move fast in those shoes?"

Terrell tapped his left foot on the floor; the bells on the curled-up toe of his slipper chimed madly. "I can't, which is probably the point of wearing them."

Dona Seraphina, who had just finished checking Terrell's health magically, snorted at Pen. "You're the one who's supposed to move fast if he's attacked."

Pen's left thumb flicked Irreneetha partway out of her sheath even as his right hand flashed across to draw her. The blurring motion ended with him threatening a painted gazelle on the wall of the King's Bedroom. He held the pose for a moment, then relaxed and sheathed the angelic sword again. "Hopefully I'm fast enough."

The priestess gave him a dry look and said nothing.

Pen went on to Terrell, "I'd still be happier if you were wearing something that you could fight in."

"This is the first time my nobles will meet me as their ruler by right, rather than as an agent of my Mother," Terrell answered. "The angry ones like DiSolera won't be won over no matter what I do, but most of Silbar's dukes and barons will simply be waiting."

"Waiting for what?"

"For a sign that I'm not going to upset their lives like a runaway horse-hitch."

"Or," added Dona Seraphina, "Given the power the Hill just conferred on you, like a volcano."

Terrell smiled. "That too. I need to calm their nerves, soothe their worries, and in general persuade them that their lives won't be any worse under my rule than they have been under Ap Marn's, and might be better. For that, I want as much help from tradition as I can get."

He touched the crown on his head but didn't change its position. He'd already noticed that it didn't shift or slide on his hair, staying always centered and comfortable. Mother's head had been noticeably smaller than his, but it fit him just as perfectly. "So tonight, I'm going to do exactly what they expect, right down to the tiniest traditions. Let's get started."

~ ~ ~

Hours later, after jugglers and bards, dancing and music, the fete had settled into serious eating and drinking in an enormous feasting hall built eight hundred years ago. Modern mage lamps lit it now and a chain of servitors paraded forty delicacies back and forth along aisles between the guests, pausing at each place setting to tempt the assembled nobility with fruit and pastry concoctions each more fanciful than the last. About half of the guests sat in formal Silbari fashion, cross-legged on cushions in half-circles around low tables. Some of the Gwythlos still looked uncomfortable with this dining style. The rest of the crowd, having had their fill and more, were milling about the hall and especially passing in and out of the arched doors. Those opened to ornately carved cloisters surrounding lush gardens on either side of the long hall. The scent of blooming flowers and rare perfumes drifted on the air, melodious with four different groups of musicians who miraculously coordinated their tunes into a harmonious whole.

A perfect arrangement to encourage clandestine assignations, he thought ruefully. *But my life is too scripted to allow that. At moments like this I could envy the freedom my nobles enjoy.*

Terrell covertly studied the crowd. Sixty-one dukes and barons comprised Silbar's landed nobility, those whose titles went with the terrain they ruled. Together they made up the working aristocracy of Silbar, men whose wealth came from the land and the actions of the people living on it. A wise and ancient law set their debt to him as a percentage of what they themselves received from their fiefs, so that building more farms, more towns, and of course recruiting more people, gave them, and him, more wealth.

They were joined by the five Counts whose fiefs were restricted to cities or parts of cities or mines; the sixth, the long-empty Countship of Sulmona, was now ruled directly by an Imperial appointee.

Who I've arrested for theft from the Kingdom and Imperial Treasuries, Terrell thought with a pleased smile. *I've got to find someone honest enough to take over the place and root out the corruption.*

He'd already made sure that the Royal Treasury had a phalanx of reeves and scribes empowered to descend upon any noble at any time and audit them. All but the smallest one, anyway; he was doubtful of the wisdom of auditing Madame (technically Baroness) Ymera, who in keeping with tradition was not here tonight.

Her taxes are the least of my worries. She simply doesn't rule enough people to matter financially. Her best payment to me lies in keeping the Red Street regulated and safe for my soldiers, and unavailable to plotters.

The crowd was thickened by the twenty-odd dispossessed nobles to whom his mother had given lifetime baronetcies, entitling them to mingle with their social equals. Sir DiNivir and Sir DiSolera were two of the most prominent and had taken themselves off somewhere after the initial stages of the feast.

To plot, no doubt, he sighed internally. *I hope my mages are able to overhear whatever they're getting up to, though in this mob it will be a serious challenge.*

Most of the crowd had spent the evening trying to curry his favor for their pet schemes, some of which even seemed to be good ideas. That new canal that Baron Terme wanted to build would add nicely to the prosperity of his fief and a neighbor's, and thus augment the Crown's wealth too.

If I fund a tenth of the cost, I suspect that will be enough to draw other supporters eager to look good in my eyes. But it'll have to wait until after I cover Osrick's tribute. I wonder if I can find another source of revenue? Mage Blue's proposal certainly implies an increase in taxes from the mages. But raiding the Temple's share of the City Node's output will reduce the healing and other good works that the priestesses do, with detrimental effects on the people of the city. Though if Mage Blue is right, the Hierarchy could simply become more efficient and accomplish as much with less.

All eight of the Council of Colors mages were here, and a dozen members of the Hierarchy's Inner Circle also; by long custom that did not include the Hierarch herself, since she was technically his equal. Terrell suppressed an amused smile at the way the Council mages and some of the senior priestesses maneuvered around each other in the throng while finding opportunities to exchange scowls. Some of the mages and priestesses who were married to each other were trying to soothe tensions between the clashing partisans of Council and Temple. They were clearly not enjoying the rancorous undercurrents as both sides' more extreme members treated the peacemakers with hostile suspicion.

Eventually I'm going to have to choose a course of action between their dueling petitions, and somehow reapportion the Node between Temple and Guild. Somehow. He resisted the temptation to sigh. *Just not tonight.*

~ ~ ~

In the east garden, shrubbery rustled. Daugala, the Chief Druid of Aretzo, looked up just as the Duke of Anagni, Roan Gryffud, stepped through an artfully vine-draped arch into the private little courtyard where she waited. The space was barely big enough for the four people now standing in it, surrounded by ancient cedars poking at the night sky. Baronets DiNivir and DiSolera immediately fawned on Gryffud in whispers, which she was glad to see the Duke cut short by holding up a blue-glowing rod.

"We have secrecy while this spell lasts, which won't be long. Cut to the chase, gentlemen and lady." He inclined his head to her.

She gave him a wintry smile, her pale skin matching his and contrasting sharply with the rich brown of the two dispossessed Silbari nobles. "As you will, My Lord. I believe you have reason to fear this new king's intentions toward you."

Gryffud jerked his head in a hard nod. "He's made his dislike plain, and openly supports his kinsman, my neighbor the Duke of Cerrai, in our boundary dispute. I foresee my realm being nibbled to death by a hundred contrary decisions as all my other neighbors pile on."

DiNivir and DiSolera had the grace to not smile. They had tried to dispossess other nobles of Gwythlo blood through an earlier lawsuit that Prince Terrell had emphatically rejected, winning the loyalty of most of the other twenty Gwythlo nobles who ruled Silbari fiefs. Two of whom claimed chunks of Gryffud's duchy and were no friends of his either.

Daugala continued, "The time to limit this new King's ambitions —"

"Prince," DiSolera interrupted with a note of self-satisfied outrage. "He himself said he will rule under the lesser title in order to please the Emperor!"

"This Prince's ambitions," she graciously corrected, "is now. But support is necessary to effect change."

"You want me to pay for a rebellion," Gryffud answered, waving the ensorcelled rod; almost half the length was no longer glowing. "One with no chance of success. Impossible, and I haven't nearly enough resources for that anyway."

"Oh no, My Lord. Success is measured in many different forms," Daugala continued. "Some forms are much less expensive. Such as induced public disgrace, and the loss of Imperial favor, through arranging a spectacular failure. All of which would be potent distractions keeping Prince Terrell's attention fixed on Aretzo and off your realm in the north."

"Understood." Gryffud plucked a ring from his finger. "This will open a secret account at the Herdae bank in Dripwater Court. Be sure you empty it before noon tomorrow, when I will discover the ring missing amidst much loud woe. I will deny ever meeting any of you here tonight."

He pressed the ring into DiSolera's eager hand, the rod into Daugala's, and left so fast that branches and vines swung in his wake.

Daugala smiled at her two patsies, who were visibly gloating over the ring. "I believe you have what you need.

Farewell for now." She followed Gryffud's example and left before the spell on the rod winked out. Whether those two fools succeeded or failed was of little concern, so long as they kept the Prince distracted for a few days.

Boerga, time is all that I can buy for you, she thought. *You had better succeed.*

~ ~ ~

Terrell stretched and groaned as his valet carried away the heavy over robe and other ceremonial clothing. "Glad to have that off." He peeled off the silk pantaloons and stood before his bedroom windows in his loincloth with both arms outstretched, enjoying the breeze on his bare skin. "I thought I was going to melt despite that cooling spell."

Pen still wore his pantaloons and formal shirt but had unlaced it to share the breeze. He cocked an eye at the windows, carefully checked to left and right and down and up. The moat surrounding the Royal Apartments plunged more than thirty feet below the sill and stretched as wide, and on the far side the towering cone of the Hill of Sight blazed in ghostly purple splendor. It would be possible for an assassin to fire a dart from the flagstone path circling the Hill, but the ward spells on these windows were strong enough to stop any arrow. Or a flung spear, or for that matter the biggest arbalest bolt fired point blank. The Hill itself didn't tolerate overt hostiles; more than one very stupid assassin had ended his days as drifting ash on its slopes. Only after Pen had contented himself that no possible assassin lurked out there in the night did he relax and take his hand off Irreneetha's hilt.

Terrell smiled indulgently at him. "Pen, I'm as safe here as I can be anywhere."

"I used to share that confidence until you were kidnapped right out of your own bed!" Pen shook his head and crossed his arms, frowned at his lord. "I wish you hadn't

81

let that kidnapper go. If you'd told me you were going to do that in advance, I'd have put up an argument!"

"The situation is complex," Terrell told him, honoring Kirin's desire to keep his parentage hidden and therefore choosing his words with care. "It may change without notice – but I am morally certain that Kirin will never enter my bedroom uninvited again. And I owe him my life and freedom for rescuing me from the conspirators. Debts must be paid, and some risks must be taken."

Pen started to open his mouth to argue but at that moment the valet returned with a bowl of water, washcloths and towels draped over his arms. Tacitly recognizing that this wasn't a subject to be discussed in front of even the most trusted servants, Pen bowed and retreated to his own room, pointedly closing the door after a glance that said clearer than words, *we're not done with this.*

Terrell twisted his mouth in a wry grimace. The price of close friends was that you had to listen to them even when you were sure they were wrong. He submitted to the ministrations of his valet and soon, garbed in fresh silk half-pantaloons, luxuriated in the sensation of being clean again. The valet bowed himself out with the bowl and damp cloths, and immediately there came a knock on the door from the concubines' rooms.

"Enter," Terrell called, and was promptly surrounded by Wren, Mist, and Rose, all dressed in their seductive best – which left little to the imagination.

"We were so worried!" Rose declared, embracing him with arms around his ribs and her body pressed against his. By some agreement known only to themselves the three took turns at his bed on any given night, rotating the opportunity among them equitably. But tonight they all crowded round him. Terrell inhaled the warm scents of perfumes and healthy young women, intensely aware of their presence and touch.

"You wouldn't sleep with us for night after night after night!" added Wren, gripping his right arm with unusual force and laying her face against that shoulder, and her hip against his.

"We were afraid you'd come down with some secret illness and the Healers were hiding it from us!" finished Mist, capturing his left side.

The press of three scantily-clad nubile bodies reminded Terrell that he'd been involuntarily celibate for most of two tendays. *From famine to feast!* He thought, and then realized the golem must not have been capable of sex. *Just as well, or it might have had to manage details that Chisaad probably knew nothing about himself!* He smiled tenderly at them, ignoring the suspicion that fear of losing their status really drove this ostentatious concern.

"The false usurper is gone, burnt to ash by the Throne," Terrell promised. "I'm back, I'm real, and I missed you all very much. Now, whose turn is it tonight?"

CHAPTER 10: MAGE, INQUISITOR

Morning, Second Day of the New Reign.

Mage Yellow began his day as usual, but his mind wandered far from his workshops and his duties as a Council of Colors Mage.

There must be a way to pressure the DiUmbra boy non-magically, DiGuile mulled. *But how? His wife is dead, his child is missing and probably dead — I can't imagine Boerga leaving the babe alive if she tried once to kill it. Pressure on his family? There are so many of them, nearly forty; how can I possibly pressure them all?*

His attention was abruptly yanked back to his meeting with DiMaritus, the manager of his firestarter workshop. "What did you say?"

DiMaritus patiently repeated himself. "The expansion of the Firestarter workshop into Lady DuMellito's building is ready to go, Magister. She even approved your proposal for an annual payment plan instead of a lump sum at the beginning, which frees up considerable funds that we now need no longer spend immediately."

"Property," Mage DiGuile cackled. "Of course! Excellent idea, DiMaritus."

The workshop manager blinked at him in confusion.

The mage made a dismissive gesture. "Stray thought. Never mind. You've done well. I'll sign the papers this evening."

The manager assented and left with his orders. DiGuile dropped him from his thoughts before he was out the door.

The DiUmbra family lost their place in the Bazaar due to Ap Marn's greed, the Mage remembered. *Then Kirin's strange talent caused a disaster during their performance at Millago's party. Their reputation took a big hit from that, so now they have got to be in financial trouble. The cocky little snot thought he was on the road to wealth with Chisaad, and* that *blew away like dust on the wind. They'll be hurting even more when they have to pay their rent — or can be* made *to hurt. That's my opportunity to persuade the boy to work for me.*

DiGuile rubbed his hands together happily. *Who owns the Sulfur Serpent? And will they sell it to me? And if they will, how do I pay for it? Lady DuMellito's mortgage won't free up enough money.*

"Magister?" said his personal secretary. "Baronets DiSolera and DiNivir wish to see you."

~ ~ ~

Dona Nivera DuNimes DiGallipo swept into her office like a warship entering a harbor, her thoughts just as filled with grim purpose.

"Bring me the file on the DiUmbra case!" she snapped at a secretary. "Then fetch Dona DuVigo DiCerat, and tell her I want a full report on her progress so far."

Half a candlemark later Dona DuVigo appeared at her office door. "First Inquisitor?" She bowed. "How may I serve you?"

"I've just read your notes on your interview with the DiUmbra boy." Dona DuNimes scowled. "I find this unexplained talent he manifested to be extremely disturbing."

"As did I, First Inquisitor." DuVigo shrugged her shoulders and held her palms up in a gesture of helplessness. "I could detect nothing at all beneath his skin. Nor could my husband."

"You're certain it was not an unusually strong version of Haroun's Gift?" The Inquisitor named the talent that gave its owner immunity to any hostile spell.

"Positive, Inquisitor. He had a scratch on his left arm, so I tried a small Healing on him. It should have worked; Haroun's Gift never blocks Healing. But I received the same result as everything else cast at him – complete blockage at his skin. We might as well be dealing with a marble statue as a human, save that he moved and talked as normal."

Dona DuNimes remembered the rumor that had raced through the coronation banquet. Chisaad had replaced the Prince with a golem so lifelike that even the Royal Healers couldn't tell – though thankfully the Throne *had* known. She shivered internally. The Mages were already too powerful and wanted more, curse all their pale souls to the Everlasting Darkness. "Are you certain that the boy isn't a construct instead of a man?"

DuVigo allowed herself a small but proud smile. "I thought of that, Inquisitor, and checked the things he touched. He had bathed and washed his clothes shortly before he arrived and as a result left damp marks. He not only dampened but also warmed the chair under his behind to precisely the same range as a living man would. I have good scent detection magic and had that spell going before he entered the room. He smelled of worried sweat while he was being questioned just like a normal man, though not like someone really frightened."

"Worried?" DuNimes gaze sharpened. "Then he had something to be worried about."

"Everybody above the age of childhood does, Inquisitor." DuVigo's smile turned melancholy. "The world is drenched in petty sinning."

DuNimes ignored the implied rebuke. Dona Celia DuVigo DiCerat had five cousins in the Aretzo Hierarchy, one placed more highly than the First Inquisitor, and wouldn't be shy about complaining if she felt poorly treated by her superior.

Instead DuNimes pursued a different path. "Very good, Celia. It's clear that he either has a new talent, or we're dealing with an extraordinary form of demonic possession. It's been more than a hundred years since we had either one of those, so we can dare to hope the latter is not the case."

DuVigo's lips moved in a silent recitation of the Inquisition's unofficial motto; "Do not hope or guess; be certain." The pride in her eyes drained away and a sliver of doubt entered.

"At least go through the motions on the remaining issues, so that we can render a complete report to Her Holiness," DuNimes continued carelessly. She closed the file as if her concerns were satisfied. "Dismissed."

Dona DuVigo DiCerat bowed with proper salutation and left, her face set in a mask that might have hidden anything.

Only I'm quite sure she'll brood over the possibility I just dragged across her path, DuNimes thought contentedly. *And therefore, choose to be just a little more thorough than she might otherwise be.*

I wonder what she'll find?

~ ~ ~

"You're robbing me," accused Bassir Goya Mareo, hunching in a shabby overstuffed chair in his shabby house. "My thrice-great-great-grandfather built the Sulfur Serpent, and you're stealing it from me."

"It wasn't me that gambled too heavily on the horses these past few years," DiGuile pointed out, leaning back in a companion chair that smelled of moth eggs. Absently he cast a small spell over his clothes to repel any importuning larvae intent on hitching a ride. "Nor was it me who borrowed from the Herdae moneylenders to buy controlling interest in a trade ship that sank five days later! Everyone in Aretzo knows a wise man spreads his money around among several different investments and doesn't bet everything on one."

"You bought up my debts," Mareo grumbled. "You saw I was vulnerable and now you're taking immoral advantage of me."

"Your debts are a whole season overdue," DiGuile reminded his target patiently. "You are hopelessly overextended. I can save you from impoverishment and even leave you with enough money to live respectably for the rest of your life. But the Sulfur Serpent Inn is the only unmortgaged thing you have left, and its rents can't cover what you owe. If I take you to the King's Court you lose it to me and have nothing. I'd rather not waste the time and expense on that, so I'm offering you a generous bonus for settling today. You can fight if you want, and be left with nothing but lawyer bills, or settle and still have some money. What is your choice?"

Mareo grumbled some more but eventually signed the papers offered by DiGuile's secretary. DiGuile managed to be civil as he took his leave amidst more self-pity while Mareo stared glumly at the mage's draft attesting to his canceled debts.

"Brilliant opportunism, Magister," gloated his secretary as they piled back into DiGuile's carriage. "And an excellent diversification of your own holdings. How did you know he was in such desperate straits?"

"I asked the Herdae bankers," Mage Yellow answered smugly, signaling to his driver. "They planned to do what I just did, but I pointed out to them the political unwisdom of foreigners conducting such a financial coup in Aretzo just when our new King is looking for ways to pay a hefty tribute to his half-brother. They settled for a comfortable middleman's profit and let me take the risk."

"You'll be well rewarded for it too, Magister," predicted the secretary. "Selling your money-losing device workshop to Baronet DiNivir provided just enough capital to cover this purchase. The rents paid by the tavern, the ground floor shops, and the middle two floors of tenants will carry the building easily. The fourth-floor and attic rent from those acrobats will be pure money in your pocket."

"Yes, unloading that failing operation on the Baronets was perfect timing," the mage answered. *And I don't want to know what those two fools plan to do with it*, he thought contentedly. *They can get into trouble without my help!*

"Get everything properly filed with the City Magistrate immediately," DiGuile told him as the carriage bounced over the uneven paving stones of the Old City with a teeth-rattling jolt. He hurriedly cast a gimbal spell on the carriage to make it float over the rough spots. "I must give thought to hiring a manager for my new acquisition." *And, more importantly, figure out how much pressure to apply to Kirin DiUmbra's family.*

CHAPTER 11: KIRIN, TERRELL
Morning, Second Day of the New Reign.

Kirin staggered through a red-lit darkness. Maia falling, baby Grigor falling, and himself unable to catch either one though he ran till his heart burst. The wet smacking sound as her body hit the pavement with Grigor close behind. Then the warm stinking water of the Charcoal Canal and mutilated Rian Smithson. Gaping wounds leered at him, spewing the wordless surety of just what the halfbreed had suffered. Lastly knives in the dark, held by no hands –

He shuddered, sat up, knuckled the sand out of his eyes, and swore. That dream had been far too vivid. He levered himself out of bed and went to his little room's lone window. Dawn sunlight flashed off the peaks of the Bright Mountains and lit the point of the Hill of Sight looming over the city. A white spot glittered – the Stone Throne. Every snowy angle of it shone in his mind's eye, and he remembered that brooding Voice.

SHOW ME WHAT YOU ARE.

The memory was a different pain, not eclipsing Maia's loss, but magnifying it. *It thinks I'm fit to be king. No! I just want to be an acrobat!*

He thrust both memories away with a gesture that bruised knuckles against his shutters. The weathered old wood banged against the brick wall and brought him back to himself. For a moment he panted, leaning on the sill. *I'm a widower now.* He had never imagined the status applying to himself. He squeezed his eyes shut again, opened them an uncounted time later to hear the fifth bell ring from the Mother Temple, followed by the other temples joining in. The Two Suns' light had crept far enough down the Hill of Sight to touch the Palace's tallest spire.

The City's cemetery wrapped halfway around the Hill's giant cone. Maia's grave would lay there, somewhere. There was a task that a new Silbari widower had to do.

He dressed in his Holy Day clothes, then padded next door to rap on Sevan and Carlai's door.

"It's Kirin," he quietly answered his brother-in-law's grunted question. "Sevan, can I borrow your spare knife? And will you show me Maia's grave?"

Sevan poked his head out the door, blinked at him, then his 'you-woke-me-up' scowl faded to a solemn look. "Sure." He closed the door again and Kirin waited while his brother-in-law dressed.

Another door opened and closed farther down the corridor. Sevan the Elder stepped out, also wearing his Holy Day clothing, and strode quietly toward him. Kirin saw something black fluttering from his father-in-law's hands in the dark corridor.

Black ribbons. The older man held one up and looked at him questioningly.

Kirin gulped and whispered, "Please," as he held out his arms.

By the time his brother-in-law slipped out to join them, Kirin and his father-in-law both had black ribbons tied around their upper arms. Sevan held out his own arms and they each tied one more onto him. Then he solemnly handed Kirin his spare knife in its shabby old sheath.

"Come," the elder acrobat said. Kirin belted the knife on and followed with Sevan at his heels. The three of them donned street footgear and padded down the echoing central stairway to Sulfur Street without saying another word.

The morning manure cart had already emptied the stables next door. Now it creaked up Sulfur Street ahead of them at a slow plod. They sped up their pace to pass it while trying to breathe as shallowly as possible. At Oldgate they turned onto the ring road around the Bazaar. The denizens of the tents were just starting to stir, bakeries giving off enticing aromas and breakfast sellers heating their oil pots and readying grilling plates over charcoal fires. A woman threaded bits of lamb and small onions onto iron skewers and laid them across flames while her husband tended a bubbling samovar of mint tea. Impoverished laborers patronized a standing-room-only caupona where lentil and fish stew was ladled into bowls. The buyers held the cheap crockery to their mouths as they shoveled with yesterday's flatbread.

Kirin looked away. There would be no eating before he did what had to be done.

They passed beneath the frowning walls of the Grey Fort, heard its sentries' cadenced call-and-response as predictable as the Mother Temple's bells, and passed the arched entrance to the Red Street. Last night's most stubborn or sodden revelers were being hauled home from their debaucheries by yawning retainers. Kirin remembered Darnaud's men in the fight at Sulmona and hoped none were back here yet to recognize him. As for the Red Street, his foray into Madam Ymera's domain still embarrassed him. She had captured him so easily.

But she said I'm not a demon or a vampire, and she would know. I believe her; I do.

He resolutely stared straight ahead and refused to look to either side until they had walked out of the City through North Gate, their footsteps calling echoes from under the drawbridge over the City's moat. The slaughter yards were calm in the predawn light, cattle and their butchers just beginning to stir. A breeze of drying flowers and verbena blew off the Hill to wash the smoke and manure stench of the city from his nose. Kirin gulped the cool air and faced the cemetery.

A yawning monk unlocked the gleaming bronze gates to admit them. His eyes acknowledged their mourning ribbons and then flicked uneasily over Kirin's pale skin. The monk sought solace in Sevan the Elder's gravitas. "Do you need help finding the right grave?"

Papa shook his head. Kirin followed him through the elaborate mausoleums of the nobility, then the less expansive but sometimes more gaudy tombs of the merchant class, and into the tidy realm of the plebeian workers' graves. Markers here generally lay flat to the ground in tight rows, small ones bearing individual names and dates clustered around large upright lineage stones.

Maia had been a Sule, the lineage of her mother. Papa turned left at a side path and followed it two lanes closer to the Hill. He stopped at a bulky stele carved with time-softened letters a foot high to proclaim the name 'SULE' and the glyph that signified a female lineage. Under that columns and rows of smaller letters listed the lineage through the generations. Behind the stele lay the stone-lined ossuary crypt where older bones had been dug up and stored so that their plots could be reused. Fading wildflowers hosted the last autumn butterflies.

"Maia Sule DiUmbra," Kirin read the last and sharpest incision set a few fingerwidths above the stele's base. The autumn breeze wasn't the only thing that made his mouth dry.

"Here she is," said Sevan from behind the stele. Kirin stumbled around the rock and found him at the south end of the plot, pointing down at a patch of recently churned soil shadowed by the Hill's immense cone. Closer, Kirin saw that the dirt had been inset with a gray marble square thrice the size of his hand. He knelt in the dirt to stare at it.

On the simple marker had been carved her name, her birth and death dates, and three lines of formal script below.

"Daughter of Carmella Sule DiUmbra and Sevan Sule DiUmbra," he read. "Wife of Kirin DiUmbra. Mother of Grigor Sule DiUmbra." Nothing else.

Papa sighed, staring down over his shoulder. "Dust to dust," he recited, absently adding, "In the end, we are all just links in the chains of our lineages." He put a consoling hand on Kirin's shoulder and squeezed lightly.

He doesn't know, Kirin thought numbly. *My lineage is cursed.*

He traced the sharp letters with a fingertip, slowly shaping each one. Every letter a memory. Maia dancing along the horizontal bar in the Serpent's Attic during rehearsal, her patched practice tights fit raiment for a queen. Maia teasing him when he missed Sevan's catching hands and fell into the net, a teasing he had eventually realized was always encouragement to try again. Maia embracing him in their bed, joyously giving and receiving pleasure with him. Maia's swelling belly as their child grew within her, and the total triumph on her face the day she delivered that squirming precious new being into his hands.

Maia! He wept. *You made me a husband and father! What do I do without you?*

A glassy veil seemed to have drawn itself between him and the world. Through it the Hill loomed above him, its flaming core constrained. Waiting. Perhaps watching. He looked blindly up at it as tears coursed down his cheeks. The white block of the Throne seemed to hover a mere arm's length away.

Do You know where she is now? he begged silently. *Will you tell me?*

THAT KNOWLEDGE MAY NOT BE GIVEN TO ANY MORTAL, the Throne's bodiless voice informed him. IN THE FULLNESS OF TIME, YOU WILL FIND THE ANSWER YOURSELF.

Kirin bowed his shoulders under the weight of that cool rebuke, then anger lit, and he fought back with defiance. *Then what of my son? Did Boerga kill him? Does he still live?*

YOU WILL ALSO FIND THAT ANSWER ON YOUR OWN, AND SOONER AS HUMANS COUNT TIME.

Something else underlay that cool distance, something Kirin couldn't put a name to. Pity? Did that mean the answer was bad? But the Throne withdrew into the distance once more and the glassy veil faded.

Humbled, twice bereft, he covered his face and sobbed. Great roaring gasps of grief tore their way out of his heart, again and again and again until the quiet of exhaustion settled over his shaking body. He finally became aware that Papa and Sevan knelt on either side of him, hands on his shoulders, quietly sharing his grief. It took him several tries before he found enough command of his voice to speak.

First he drew the knife. Sevan had kept it sharp – very sharp. Kirin turned it in his hands so that the point caught the suns' light.

"Papa?" he asked. "How do I do this?"

Sevan the Elder gently parted the curly hair of Kirin's sideburns with his thick fingers. "Cut a single line through the hair from front to back."

Kirin raised the knife, tried to position the point.

Papa helped set it against the skin at the front edge of the black hair. "Not too hard," he cautioned. "And not too far. Do not cut your ear too."

Kirin dragged the blade back, slicing through the hair and skin of his sideburn with a sharp pain still much duller than his grief. Blood welled. Sevan the Younger helped him with the other side. Then Kirin dropped the knife and groped for some dirt, rubbed bits of it into the bleeding slashes.

"Did I do it right?" he begged his father-in-law as blood dripped down his face.

"You did it exactly right."

Papa had brought some boiled rags and a long strip of bandage. Kirin knelt quietly while the two Sevans dressed his wounds and tied the bandage around his head. It was no sooner settled in place than his Shadow fretfully surged into the wounds. Kirin managed to hold it there, hidden within the bandage, while he cleaned and sheathed the knife with trembling hands and held it out to Sevan.

"Thank you for lending it to me," he croaked.

"Keep it," Sevan said firmly, pushing it back toward him. "What happened to your own?"

"Chisaad turned it to dust," Kirin waved at the Hill. "While he was trying to kill me – well, I was trying to kill him, too."

His brother goggled at him. "What!"

Papa glanced around; nobody was visible in this part of the sprawling cemetery. "My mother told Father and me a little of what you told her yesterday, Kirin. I think it would be wise for me to know the whole of it."

And so, kneeling on Maia's grave, Kirin poured out the story of how the wizard had fooled him, used him, and discarded him, and how he had redeemed himself by rescuing the prince he had kidnapped. He kept back the secret of his bloodline, unable to share that deep shame with the two living men he loved most. The sunlight crept down the Hill and across the gravestones while he whispered, throat dry and eyes red as he recounted Pieter's final words.

"Then Prince Terrell summoned a wizard who flew us both back here in time for the King Choosing. Chisaad tried to kill Terrell and usurp the Crown, but I stripped his magic with my Shadow and the Throne burnt him to ash. Terrell forgave me for kidnapping him and sent me home." He gusted a sigh.

Papa gave his shoulders a squeeze. "Bravely done, Kirin. I confess, the ease with which the Royal Wizard took you on, and his generosity toward you, made me nervous. I talked to Pieter about it. But we both knew you had a unique talent and we both told ourselves not to worry, that uniqueness was the Wizard's only reason." He sighed. "We both should have known better. The powerful are rarely generous unless they see a gain for themselves."

"I know that now," Kirin muttered, knuckling his eyes. "And I'll never forget it."

Papa eyed Sevan, who was staring at Kirin in open-mouthed astonishment. "Sevan. Do not speak of this to anybody. It could endanger Kirin, or the family."

Sevan shut his jaws with an audible clack. "I won't, Father. But Kirin, you – you really killed men in Sulmona? With your own knife, in your own hands?"

And a little help from my Shadow, Kirin thought as he nodded. "It was easier than I expected." He shuddered. "It scared me; how easy it was. I hope I never have to do it again."

"I hope the same, for both of you," Papa told them. "But it is good to know that you can, if a time comes again when you must."

97

Kirin's brother and his father helped him to his feet and all three of them bowed to the Sule lineage stele. Kirin walked unsteadily back to the main path, but when Papa would have led him toward the gate he resisted.

"Papa, Sevan; take me to the DiUmbra graves, please?"

They did. It was a smaller stele but a second and taller one stood behind that, and a third, cracked and nearly illegible with wear, behind that; two ossuary crypts lay between them. An owl perched atop the tallest stele and blinked at them slowly in the brightening daylight. Blackeyed daisies clustered around the gravestones and lined the little paths of cracked flagstones. Their bright yellow heads nodded in the breeze.

"Papa?" Kirin asked, looking over the homely but cheerful place. "Where should Pieter be buried?"

Both Sevans looked at him with surprise.

"Kirin," Papa said gently. "His body must have been buried in Sulmona by now."

"If I can get him cremated and his ashes sent back," Kirin answered stubbornly. "Then where should he be buried?"

Papa raised an eyebrow; such an effort would cost far more dhoba than Kirin could earn, or the family afford. But he led them both around behind the first stele. A flight of steps sank down into the ground to the massive stone door of the ossuary. Stone grilles set into the wall on either side offered glimpses of the interior. Papa pointed through one toward the back of the room.

"My brother would not be the first of us to be cremated. There are twelve niches in the wall for urns; eight are filled. The ninth one would be Pieter's."

Kirin pressed his face to the cool stone, stared through the grill into a dim interior. He called his Shadow into his eyes and details appeared. Stone walls were stacked high with bones. At the back a clear space could be seen, with six niches one above the other and a second column like it. The topmost four niches in each column were filled. A dry scent of old death tickled his nose. He withdrew before it made him sneeze.

This is where you belong, Father, Kirin thought. *I swear I'll find a way to bring you back here.* For a moment he thought of Terrell, who could order such a thing done on a whim, but his heart hardened against that choice. *No. I want to make this happen myself. Somehow.*

"Thank you, Papa," Kirin said. "I'll find a way."

Papa smiled wryly. "Don't be in a hurry. First we need to raise enough money for our rent. Then we still need a patron, and a place to perform. My brother will be patient."

The family was breaking their nightly fast when the three of them tromped back into the fourth-floor corridor. Grandfather glanced up sharply, saw the black ribbons and the fresh bandages on Kirin's head, and closed his mouth with a snap. When Kirin came back out of his room after shedding his good clothes in favor of practice tights, Grandmother promptly corralled him and Sevan and sat them down to eat more delicious Feast food. Kirin was surprised to find his appetite good.

A knock on the family's front door echoed down the corridor. A few moments later Uncle Ger appeared with a strange expression on his face.

"Kirin," he said in a stilted voice. "There's a messenger for you." He stepped aside and let a man dressed in formal livery into the little dining room.

The stranger wore a Heralds' Guild tabard over a bloused particolored shirt and elaborate diamond-patterned tights. The herald-for-hire removed the curl-topped hat of his profession with a sweeping bow made directly to Kirin. "Have I the honor of addressing Kirin Sule DiUmbra?"

From the way the man's brown eyes stared at him, Kirin guessed the herald already knew there weren't two pale-skinned halfbreed sons in the DiUmbra family. "Umm, yeah, that's me," he mumbled, while everyone else in the room gazed in frank surprise from him to the herald and back. "What do you want?"

"To deliver this message to you." The herald struck a formal pose and recited, "To Journeyman Mage Kirin Sule DiUmbra from Baroness Ymera, greetings and salutations. It develops that I have need of your special magical talent to solve a problem that cannot be solved by other means. Time is of the essence in this matter. I offer one hundred silver dhoba in compensation for your inconvenience if you will provide your aid to me this morning. The favor of a prompt response is requested."

The herald fell silent and gazed at him expectantly.

Kirin gulped. *Oh dung!*

"What in the Nine Hells?" Sevan said, staring at him.

Attir burst out with a snigger. "Kirin! You dog, you!" and began laughing. Two of the cousins joined in.

Kirin felt his face grow hot. "That's not what she means!"

"Then what does she mean?" asked Grandmother with some asperity.

"When did you become a Journeyman? I thought you were still an apprentice!" blurted Aunt Silla.

"We could really use that money," Carlai suggested practically while nursing her baby.

"Everybody pipe down," Grandfather growled. "First things first. Kirin – does this have anything to do with your stupid invasion of her garden?" He glanced at the herald, standing there with ears wide open.

Kirin grimaced. "Probably." He wondered if the herald reported the things he heard to Mother Gee for her information business – or if not her, then who else.

"She didn't fry him then," Papa pointed out. "This probably isn't some complicated punishment for his, ah, youthful daring. It's likely a real work offer."

"And at that price, it surely must be a very dangerous one," Carmella added worriedly.

That stopped everybody's words for a moment. Kirin remembered the little room at the top of Ymera's House, the portal through the Skin of the World, and the slick touch of its edge – the edge she had as much as said she could not go beyond. *But I reached right through it with no trouble, and there were souls beyond. Souls of the recent dead . . .*

"I think I know what she wants me to do," he said slowly. "It wouldn't be very dangerous – well, for her maybe, but not dangerous for me. And if I'm right, it probably wouldn't matter to anybody else but her." *And maybe it could show me to a way to get rid of Gerlach? Would Maia be there? Or Pieter?*

Grandfather stared at him through narrowed eyes. "If you're right. If." He let the damning word hang there in the air.

Kirin bowed his head for a moment, shamed by the memory of his clumsy stumble at Millago's house, Dona Keldra's destroyed dress, and the ruined play. Then he raised his eyes to meet Grandfather's gaze squarely. "I can learn from my mistakes, Grandfather." The old man's eyes were the same deep brown color as the rest of the family but buried in wrinkles. For the first time Kirin noticed the bags under those eyes and the way the white hair had receded across Grandfather's parchment-like skin. His beard was as thin as an over-used washrag.

Grandfather held his gaze and nodded grudgingly. "If you do this, boy, you'd better not bungle it. Powerful people like Madame Ymera don't want to hear excuses."

Kirin jerked his head in a silent assent.

The old man's gaze slid to his eldest son. "Sevan? What say you?"

Sevan the Elder blew out the breath he'd been holding. "I don't like the idea of Kirin having anything to do with her. But with his previous Magister dead, he has to establish himself somehow, and doing an important job for hire is one way to do it. She's made this offer openly using a public go-between and in front of the family, so she she's dealing above-board." His attention shifted to Kirin's face. "Son, if you want to do this, I won't object."

Kirin turned to the herald. "Tell her 'Yes.'"

The herald held out a bulging pouch of fine blue-dyed suede. "Half in advance, half upon completion," he recited. "Do you agree?"

"I, Kirin Sule DiUmbra, do agree," Kirin answered formally, binding himself with his word. He took the pouch and passed it to Grandfather who immediately opened the drawstrings and spilled it onto the table. Grandmother deftly counted it and stated, "Fifty silver dhoba."

"Then let's go," Kirin told the herald.

"You should put on your good clothes first!" Carmella objected. "You want to make a good impression."

Kirin looked at the Herald, who repeated blandly, "Time is of the essence."

102

"Thank you, Mama Carmella, but I better go right now," Kirin answered her, and left.

CHAPTER 12: TERRELL

Morning, Second Day of the New Reign.

Terrell awoke with a pleasant lassitude weighing him down. Last night with his concubine had been delightful, and the slight soreness lingering from it served as a pleasant reminder. He luxuriated in the feel of clean silk sheets and inhaled the sweet-scented morning air drifting through his windows from the flower-covered Hill. Polished floor tiles reflected sunlight, which meant his servants had let him sleep late.

Even though I promised Osrick I'd not use the title publicly, inside my head I can say it. I really am the King of Silbar, just as I meant to be, he thought triumphantly. Memories of the feast last night, with a hundred nobles and mages and priestesses all currying his favor, warmed him like a banked fire.

But underneath lurked a sorrow that chilled his heart.

Am I mourning Mother and Father's deaths? But he had been expecting those for many tendays and done much of his mourning already. There would be a formal grieving ceremony later today for his parents – it would be publicly focused on his mother, since most Silbaris still had no love for the Empire. It wouldn't be politic to remind the people today just who his father had been.

No. This is something else. He became aware of a faint prickling sensation on either side of his head, but when he touched his sideburns there was nothing there. The sensation seemed to come from within – but not from him.

I'm feeling Kirin's pain. This is very strange.

It took him a moment to remember. When a man's wife died, the custom in Silbar was for him to cut himself on either side of his head deeply enough to leave scars, as a public sign of his widower status.

Kirin must have done it this morning, while I slept. But why am I feeling it? I didn't feel anything like this when we were fleeing through the canyon.

Oh. I was the one in pain then, after eight days chained to a floor. Was he feeling my pain then? Now that I look back on it, he flinched several times when I was hurt, but he never complained. Mother Umana forgive me, I was blind.

Terrell almost reached out to his twin in that moment, then hesitated. He could tell that Kirin was walking, bound on some errand.

This sharing of our minds upsets him. I should keep some distance between us; I certainly owe him that much. I'd have died in Sulmona if he hadn't killed Chisaad's spell at the right moment. Not to mention freeing me from Ap Marn's prison in Silbariki and stripping Chisaad's magic on the Hill. I owe him a great deal of discretion.

I wonder what Osrick would think if he knew my twin was alive?

The thought started out amusing, but it didn't stay that way.

There's no oath binding Kirin to Osrick. From Osrick's point of view, Kirin's another claimant to his throne — one over which, unlike me, he has no hold.

That could not be a good thing for his half-brother's peace of mind. The more Terrell thought about it, the worse it looked. *He'll think Mother kept Kirin's survival a secret deliberately, which means he'll be looking for a threat from Kirin — and I know what Osrick does with threats. He's already hanged a dozen men from the gibbets of Gwythford castle, while Father only used them twice in my memory.*

If Osrick learns Kirin still lives, he'll kill him. And he'll never believe I wasn't in on the secret all along. I don't think our oath would hold against that.

It was, Terrell decided, a very good thing that Kirin had refused the crown and asked him to keep their relationship secret. *And a good thing I didn't tell Pen, either. Or anybody. This is a very dangerous situation.* He thought of half a dozen actions his half-brother might take against both him and Kirin, each more worrisome than the last.

Then the memory of Kirin offering his life in expiation for the kidnapping came back starkly. Terrell felt again the knife in his hand, saw Kirin's bared throat before him.

No. If I'd killed him then, he wouldn't have been there to save me from the Duermus, or help me save Pen during Darnaud's ambush, or to save me from that arrow. Chisaad would probably have just killed me on the Hill before I touched the crown again. That kidnapping, miserable as it was for me, set things in motion that are still moving in this world. I cannot see the end of them — but fratricides are surely despised by God.

I will not kill him, nor allow others to do so in my name.

A quiet knock echoed from Pen's door.

"Enter," Terrell called, and stretched under the sheet.

Pen poked his head into the room and said, "Has the weight of that feast still got you nailed to your bed? Past time for your exercise this morning."

"Agreed," Terrell answered, levering himself up. "Let's get a little riding in, then some wrestling and sword practice. While we're out I need to think about how to word my formal message to Osrick about Ap Marn's conspiracy, and then make some progress on the pile of petitions on my desk. And this afternoon I need to find out what's inside Chisaad's house."

His valet bustled in with shaving gear and a selection of garments, and Terrell the First, Prince (*but really King,* he thought proudly) of Silbar, got ready to face his day. But all the while that awareness lurked at the back of his mind, and occasionally he found himself touching his unscarred sideburns.

Two hours after rising he and Pen reined in their horses at the base of a marble balcony built into the hillside above. They were several miles west of Aretzo, within the vast royal riding park that ran from the city to the foothills.

"So this is King Chaghar's Portico," Terrell said, admiring the graceful columns and the zip of exotic hummingbirds. Rarely seen in Gwythlo, the abundant southern varieties reminded him of flying jewels. A huge mass of red and orange trumpet flowers buried the roof and made the air heady with scent. "Let's take a look at the view."

He dismounted and left his horse to the care of a groom, Pen doing the same, and they raced up the long marble steps. Age had pitted the stone and worn off its former polish, but the vast panorama of meadow, forest, and distant sea, with the city set like a jewel in the middle, still testified why a long-dead king had commanded stonemasons to build here.

Pen glanced around, determined that they were alone, and said, "Terrell. About our conversation last night."

Terrell sighed. "I've thought about what Kirin might do or say and what trouble it might cause for me. Though not all of my decisions and actions in the desert were flattering to me, there's little he could tell people that I would care about. His use of his rather – unusual – power of illusion was witnessed by both Darnaud's troops and your own, and when they return to the city there will doubtless be entertaining rumors running around." He shrugged. "That's more likely to complicate his life than mine."

"He could tell someone how he got into your bedroom to kidnap you," Pen growled. "And an assassin could repeat the trick."

"No," Terrell disagreed patiently. "No one but him can do that. Given all the losses he suffered the first time, with his wife being killed, I'm quite certain he'll never do it again."

"Maybe not willingly, but he could be coerced," Pen argued. "He's got a family; they could be threatened."

"True. I should give some thought to ways to protect him from that when the knowledge becomes public. Right now, only you, he, and I know it."

"Your trip back here was seen by thousands," Pen warned. "Some are certain to recognize him since all he had to hide himself was a hood. People are going to figure out who flew here with you, and then they'll make guesses about why."

"Let them. I intend to refuse all questions on the subject. As, I suspect, will he. Eventually speculation will wear itself out and the gossips will find fresher meat."

"You are taking this much too calmly," Pen accused. "Terrell, he can walk right through your guard spells as if they weren't there!"

"Aha." Terrell gazed at Pen closely. "That's what's really bothering you, isn't it? You think he's something that neither you nor Irreneetha, nor all my guards and mages, can protect me against."

Pen looked away for a moment, and then his face hardened as he uttered a curt, "Yes."

"I agree."

Pen looked up hopefully.

Terrell reached up and touched the Crown on his head. He had worn it all the way up here, his hair unbound and flying in the wind, and it had not budged a fingerwidth the whole ride. "And this tells me I don't need to worry." Terrell put his hand down and pointed to Irreneetha. "What does she tell you?"

Pen had kept a hand on the soulsword's pommel ever since getting off his horse. Now he drew the blade and gazed into her white depths. The light of the sword stayed muted and clear.

"She doesn't have anything to say, yet," he reported. "But all the time the three of us were together in Sulmona, she *watched* him."

"Really!" Terrell was intrigued. "Irreneetha has found someone who she considers interesting enough to truly watch? Does she do the same to me?"

"No," Pen admitted uncomfortably. "Just him."

Terrell blew out his breath and laughed. "I wonder if I should be jealous."

"This is not a joking matter," Pen said pompously, a little hurt in his voice.

"I wasn't joking. Just marveling at The One God's mysteries." Terrell touched his forehead, lips, heart and groin in the manner of a pious Silbari, while thinking *Strange are your ways, O God!* "I think that's your answer. We wait and see what God and the Seraphs and Angels decide. Until then, Kirin shall be allowed to go about his business undisturbed by us, and we will not speak of him to others."

Pen looked unhappy, but he sighed and bent his head obediently. "You are the King; you get to make the decisions."

"Yes, and I thank the One God every day that I have you to make me think hard about them. Especially the ones that need time to find the truly right answer. Meanwhile, let's head back down and get some wrestling and sword practice in before I have to bury myself amidst petitions."

Pen brightened at that. They leaped down the steps together and raced to their waiting horses.

CHAPTER 13: KIRIN

Morning, Second Day of the New Reign.

The newly washed Red Street shone in the morning light. A phalanx of men with scrub brushes and buckets had already worked their way down the flagstones as far as Ymera's House when Kirin arrived at the little ornamental gate. The guard captain greeted him with the same punctilious courtesy as when he'd left the last time – less than fifty days ago? To Kirin's surprise the man did not ask for his belt knife or comment on his ragged clothing, but instead ushered him directly inside, down a corridor and up two flights of a familiar back staircase. A door at the top opened as they arrived and before he quite knew where he was, Kirin found himself in Madame Ymera's bedroom again.

Attir's mocking words at breakfast echoed in his ears. Embarrassment flashed through him and he felt his face heating. Before he could say or do anything more, she beckoned to him from the little stairway that led to the top of her House.

"Time is short," she said. "I need your talents very soon, or not at all."

He stumbled up the narrow treads into the square room with its louvered windows. The silver bowl and its pedestal had been moved into a corner and a waist-high bracket installed in front of the north window. One clamp on the top held a miniature arrow and another held a whetstone. Spells wrapped both. Kirin stepped carefully away from the stair and the swarming spells in the walls, trying to find a spot as far as possible from any magic. His Shadow churned inside, hungry and unhappy. It filled him to his skin but did not fight his grip.

"Lady Ymera," he blurted out. "Just what is this task you need me for?"

"To reach where I cannot reach, and hopefully touch what I cannot touch." She raised a hand and slashed a clawed finger down across the north-facing window.

The World split.

Kirin gulped as once again the impossibly vast space under the Skin of the World revealed itself beyond the weirdly bent window frame. The opening now looked across and down at the lip of a vast crimson well with walls as slick and pulsating as a living throat. A vast rolling plain ringed the giant hole and extended out of sight in all directions, including right under the window. His shadow pushed him toward it but this time he planted his feet and refused to move. He'd seen this view before, but that familiarity did not lessen the spectacle – or the horror.

Ymera had busied herself with the arrow and whetstone. The arrow suddenly flashed and floated free of the clamp as it turned crazily, and then settled to point toward one of the gray streams. A thin ray of light stabbed from the arrow's point into the dimness beyond.

"Good, it is not too late," she murmured, then fixed him with gaze that stopped the questions on his lips. "One of my men has been killed, long enough ago that his spirit cannot be raised, but not so long that he is lost to the Well. With this spell I can identify him, but I cannot reach him. You may be able to."

Kirin felt his eyes go wide. "You want me to reach in there and grab a *soul?*"

"Precisely. Bring it to the opening, but not through, so that I may question it." She looked expectantly at him as if

112

she had just asked him to move some furniture, and took up a post on one side of the beam of light. Waiting.

Something invisible seemed to have grabbed his throat from the inside. He swallowed with difficulty. *One hundred silver dhoba — and we need eight hundred more to pay our rent. I reached in there once before and it didn't hurt me. I can do this.*

He pried his feet from the floor and took three steps to the edge of the gaping hole. The beam of light passed through and bent to point sharply downward. He leaned forward to look where it led. His head passed through the gap with no sensation at all. He found himself looking straight down at the rolling plain under the World.

Gray wraiths flowed like water across an uneven and glistening floor that slowly *heaved*, as if it were the belly of some great breathing beast. The wraiths flowed toward the Well's rim, pooled in some places or swiftly rushing in others, but all eventually reached the huge opening. All slipped over the rim and fell down, down, impossibly far down toward Hell, and the Door into Heaven.

The light beam pointed to one misty cloud slowly swirling in a pool almost under his feet. He leaned on the windowsill – it was as cool and slick as a fish, so he gripped it tightly – and reached down. The tips of his finger hesitated just above the mist. Was it blasphemy to touch a soul? Would it hurt, possibly burn, maybe even maim his hand? But his own soul was in constant contact with his flesh, and that caused no discomfort.

He plunged his hand into the gray cloud and closed his fingers.

Cool as spring water, the taste of apricots, the smell of steel, and the touch of lightest thistledown. The soul rose with him as he straightened up and held it out at arms length, careful to keep it beyond the window. If he brought it through, he wondered if it would it try to fill a body again –

maybe take his? The misty gray mass roiled as if agitated; the light from the arrow shone unerringly on its coils and billows.

Ymera hurriedly triggered a spell and then snapped words at the mist. "Rian! You gave your oath to me as your Lady. I hold myself honor-bound to find your killer. Tell me who slew you!"

The mist threshed in Kirin's hand, unpleasantly like a snake, and he barely resisted letting it go. Instead he grasped it with both hands. Then the air in the cupola vibrated.

"I know not names," a voice declaimed, as dramatic as a poet busking in a public square. "They did not use them in my hearing. The man cast a spell on me that made me feel drunk, then all went dark and I knew no more until I awoke strapped to a rack in a windowless room." The spirit sobbed with a wrenching grief that clenched Kirin's gut. "The evil things he did to me! And her, the pale-skinned magic-woman-but-not-a-priestess who directed him!" The voice dissolved into gut-tearing sobs.

"Rian, help me find your tormentors," Ymera pleaded, hands casting new spells as she spoke. "Describe the man!"

The spirit voice described a Gwythlo man of medium height and age. A mage, clearly, for he cast spells, but a brute as well for the fragmentary mentions of tortures and rape.

Ymera patiently led it on to descriptions of the woman – also pale and northern, with pointed ears. Kirin wanted to cringe with shame and cover his own, but the soul slithered in his hands and he had to use every grappling trick to hang onto it. He hoped he wasn't hurting it worse with his grip – how tight was too tight to hold a soul?

Finally, Ymera seemed satisfied. "Rian, I will find them. Be at peace." She signaled for Kirin to release it. The pathetic wounded thing fled his hands and Kirin pulled them back to the living side of the opening. It had already begun shrinking. As soon as he stepped back from the frame, shaking a not-quite-imaginary chill from his fingers, she closed the hole and shut down the spell. The window became just a window, looking north toward the distant peak of God's Mountain.

"Lady Ymera," Kirin said deferentially as she furled the spells on the arrow. "You called him Rian. What was the rest of his name?"

Ymera gazed at him with keen inquiry. "Smithson. He did not use his mother's name like Silbaris do, but styled himself in the Gwythlo fashion. I see that you already knew that name, too. How?"

Kirin closed his eyes for a moment of grief. Aeddan and Jerril deserved to know what had happened, but he couldn't tell them this. "I dragged his body out of the Charcoal Canal yesterday."

"Did you now," she breathed, and for the barest moment she glanced north toward the distant Mountain. Then: "Do tell me about it."

Kirin rubbed his hands as the strange sensations of that place beneath the World faded. "I thought he was a drowning man, so I jumped in to save him. But he was already dead – tortured, like the blood mages do to people. I pulled him out and sent for the Watch. They took his body and called the Inquisition. Later they asked me questions and told me his name. He –" The memory of Gerlach churned his gut and made his fists clench as he burst out, "He was a halfbreed like me! That could have happened to me!"

"Mmmm, no doubt. Blood sorcerers do like to find their victims among those not protected by either the ward spells of the Hierarchy or the bindings of the northern Druids." She tilted her head, owl-like, and changed the subject so sharply he blinked. "It took me some time to persuade Gee to tell me what she knew about you. She very much wanted to protect you. It is rare that her loyalty to me is so compromised, so rare that it has never happened before. You touched her heart in a way few of her boy spies ever have."

Kirin paled, feeling colder as he stared back at her. Her fangs were very sharp. "She told on me?"

"She told me a name," Ymera corrected. "Gerlach, a Fehdaran mage. I searched from there. It took me quite a bit of effort to get a copy of the Inquisition's full report without them knowing. They conducted a detailed examination of the ruins of his house, but they never determined what exactly killed him. Despite trying to raise his soul for questioning, which should have worked given how freshly dead he was when they dug out his charred corpse. But it did not."

Kirin clutched his chest, and then knew it for a betraying gesture when her eyes narrowed.

"You said – grown folks' memories pile up until they drive your kind mad. If I'm like that too . . ."

"Ah. Follow me to a safer place to talk."

She led him back down the narrow stairs, opened a door to another room entered through her bedroom. It seemed a backward way to organize her living space, until he realized there was a second entrance to this room that must open onto the top of the grand staircase. She waved him to a plush chair and he gingerly sat upon the edge of its silk-covered perfection, embarrassed by his sweat-stained and none-too-clean tights and shirt. His grubby practice garb was as out of place in this luxurious room as a cow in a coracle. *I should have changed clothes like Mama Carmella said!*

She settled herself on a sofa halfway across the room from him. Kirin realized she had moved them here to get away from the vulnerable spells above, and to give herself space from his Shadow. *She knows I'm powerful and that makes me dangerous – only my power might be more dangerous to me than to her.*

"Was Gerlach your first?" she asked him, as calm as if they were talking about the price of fish instead of murder.

"Y-yes. He bought me off Ap Marn's slave block. I wasn't even eight years old. He chained me to a wall in his basement and . . . told me what he was going to do to me." The monster's memory clawed at him and he forced it down again, shuddering. "When he started doing it, my Shadow came out and killed him."

She raised one exquisite eyebrow, and her claws flexed slightly. "How did that *killing* feel?"

His face twisted in memory. "Like sucking an oyster out of its shell. His soul came out, and his body fell down dead. It was very fast. Then his soul – went somewhere. But I still have his memories. I can remember what he knew, how he felt at that moment. It's like a horrible voice in the back of my head."

"I can imagine." Unexpectedly she added, "I have one a bit like that myself."

"You do?" His gaze turned hopeful. "How do you make it shut up?"

"Mmmm." Her face became introspective. "Long practice and much else to keep me busy. I haven't thought about him in a century. Pardon me if I don't thank you for the reminder."

She glanced at the claws on her left hand as if looking for something that was not there.

The prospect of having to wait decades for Gerlach to fade offered Kirin no cheer. He slumped glumly. "It's been ten years and he's as, as *sharp* as ever. Sharper than the soldiers, and they're a lot newer."

117

"After Gerlach there were others?"

He hung his head. "Chisaad tricked me into helping him against the Prince. Then he betrayed me. He sent Duke Darnaud and that druid, Boerga, to kill me in North Street. I got away and ran. They got to my home first and held my wife and baby son hostage against me, but Maia floated little Grigor out the window to me. Duke Darnaud killed her for that." His hands went to the bandages at either side of his bowed head for a moment, but he mastered his grief and continued. "Then a bunch of his men jumped me, and the only way I could get away with my son was to kill one of them. With my Shadow. Later I had to kill another the same way." He tapped his head. "They're both in here too, but not nearly as hard to bear."

"Three?" She regarded him critically. "You have three sets of memories in your mind in addition to your own?"

"I guess." He squirmed uncomfortably on the edge of the cushioned seat. "But Gerlach is the one that's been hardest to live with. Is there any way to get him out?"

"None known to me, alas, or I would long ago have excised the one I carry. That does not mean there isn't a way known to others. But I would be very cautious about revealing your problem to the Hierarchy, and as for the Druids, well."

Kirin cringed inwardly at the thought of sharing his story with Dona Pareto, or worse yet the Inquisitor Dona DuVigo. That one would probably just burn him, the Temple's usual solution to anything smacking of demonic possession.

"But I'm not a demon," he muttered aloud. "You said so."

"Quite correct." Her expression grew somber for a moment. "Once one has met the real thing, it's impossible to forget, if you have powerful talents. I have seen eighteen

118

possessed men – and five women – burned during my time here in Aretzo. When the flames at last drive the demon from its host, the scent, the sound, the very sight of the thing, those are unmistakable to my senses. What dwells in you is not like any of them."

"Then I'm not possessed by one either," Kirin went on with a wave of relief that nearly made him babble. "I'm just haunted. Haunted by other men's memories."

"That seems to describe it reasonably well." She studied him with that same piercing look she'd used on his first meeting with her. "Though whatever *does* dwell inside you is very strange indeed. Strange and deadly. You would probably confound the Temple theologians at least as much as you confound me." A brief smile flickered across her lips. "If you ever do reveal yourself to them, I would dearly love to watch, from a safe distance. If there is any such thing as safety around you, Kirin DiUmbra."

That made him hunker down on his seat. "Lady Ymera, I just want to be an acrobat! I'm a good one, too. I don't want this thing inside me!"

"Yet it is there, and it apparently grants you unheard-of capabilities."

She tapped a finger on her chin thoughtfully and again changed the subject so sharply it made him blink.

"Your troupe is very good. Eventually they will find a new place to perform, or a patron to support them. Their challenge is to survive until then. Your power can help them do that. I promised you a hundred silver dhoba for aiding me today, which you have done."

She plucked a purse out of somewhere and tossed it to him. It clinked solidly in his hands, a weight equal to the fifty dhoba the herald had provided. Kirin bowed his head and tugged his forelock in gratitude before he tucked the money inside his shirt.

119

"I'll pay as much again for your help tracking down my man's killers. The pale witch his soul referred to was most likely a druid, but who was the other, the mage? Without a physical link to them I cannot trace either of them, and certainly cannot identify them magically."

A hundred more! That would put the troupe closer to what we owe. For a moment he was tempted. *But I need to find my son, get back in shape to perform with the Troupe – I don't have time for this.* Kirin tried to sidestep the offer by asking, "Would Rian's body be a good enough link?" Then she could find her targets without him.

"Not normally." She pursed her perfect lips in a grim frown, a disturbing sight when he could also see her fangs. "Although in this case there is a small chance that his killer might have been careless enough to leave behind something that *would* provide such a link."

It took Kirin a moment to realize to what she referred, and when he did his whole body tensed involuntarily. Blood mages degraded their victims by many means, including rape . . . For a moment he was almost ill with remembrance. Gerlach's ghost sent a memory of its last savage glee to compound his misery.

"The problem with that approach," Ymera continued as if she had not noticed his reaction, "Is twofold. First, the Inquisition. Having taken charge of Rian's body, there is no chance that they will permit *me* to examine it. They would have to be persuaded to attempt the deed themselves – and I doubt that the Inquisitors are skillful enough to succeed at such a trace. Even the Hierarch wielding her Orb probably wouldn't be able to identify Rian's tormentor. And secondly, if that druid is who I suspect –"

"Boerga!" Kirin said, loathing the name as he finally caught the connection. He had avenged Maia by killing Darnaud in far-off Sulmona, but Boerga had almost certainly killed Dona Zella and maybe Dona Abbie too, and still roamed free.

"Yes." Ymera gave him a sharp nod. "She is more than clever enough to have cleaned up any trace that could be followed back to her or to her companion. She has been successfully hiding herself somewhere for twenty days now since Prince Terrell banished her. Three days ago she murdered my man and later dumped his body for you to find. Banishment or no, I doubt she has left Aretzo at all, nor intends to do so."

Boerga still here – is she still hunting my son? Kirin's blood pounded in his ears until he barely heard Ymera's next words.

"So, young Kirin Sule DiUmbra; we share a hope for vengeance upon the same person. Will you accept my commission to find her, and if possible, also find her co-murderer?"

"Yes," he growled.

PETER SARTUCCI

CHAPTER 14: YMERA
Morning, Second Day of the New Reign.

After the black-haired acrobat had left with a second fifty-dhoba pouch tucked inside his shirt, Ymera returned to her aerie. She put the whetstone back into its pouch – Rian Smithson had no living relatives, or none who would acknowledge him, but his kit could be sold to help buy him something better than the minimal marker in the Poor Field that his Mercenary Guild dues would cover. If necessary, she would make up the difference in cost out of her own pocket, which her other guards would notice and appreciate. When she returned the silver soul-catching bowl to its normal place in the center of the room, all was as it had been before.

No. Nothing is as it was before. She stirred the shining life sparks collected in the silver bowl. After the heavy casting she'd done today she would need to feed more than normal, but not yet. *Kirin DiUmbra can reach into the outer plain of the afterlife and seize a soul. He can hold my window open – perhaps even tear a new one with his bare hands. Surely the new King does not yet grasp this possibility, else he'd never have let the boy go so easily. Should I tell him?*

She had not yet met young Terrell beyond their brief ceremony on his arrival. But she had gathered every scrap of information about him that she could find, using not just Gee's services but every other resource she had. Terrell would have been astonished at what she had already deduced – and the reports of his kidnapping tied all the pieces together.

122

I watched the movements of Darnaud's household very carefully, she thought. *I am certain that Chisaad set up a hidden bolt-hole in Silbariki using the Duke's fast couriers.* That was unusually daring of him, as the maimed wight imprisoned in the corrupt node under that ruined city would eventually have awakened to the sudden traffic. *Then the Royal Wizard would have found himself in a fight!* The only possible purpose for such a risk was to have a place he could be absolutely sure would not be interrupted by anyone. After all, one of his Royal tasks was to recast the imprisoning spells every seven years, and the most recent time had been barely two years ago. The Chief Inquisitor herself had signed off on the sealing, with all due pomp and bureaucracy. Nobody would bother to check Silbariki again for years.

She was sure Chisaad must have brought Terrell there somehow, perhaps using a flying carpet and some form of concealment spell. Kirin was clearly involved. He could have walked right through every spell in the Palace with none the wiser, hogtied Terrell in his own sheets and handed him over to the Royal Wizard. *And why didn't I think of that potentiality when I sent the boy to Chisaad? All I saw then was the need to control Kirin's frightening talents. I must be growing careless.* The murder accusation against the boy's adoptive father was plainly a means to get Kirin to do what he normally would have refused. *If Gee is any judge of character, and she is. But Chisaad goaded him into helping to commit treason.*

And then Chisaad, knowing how dangerous the boy must be, tried to have him killed, but squeamishly delegated the job to minions. *Fool! When murder is needful, always do it yourself!* After which Kirin disappeared for nearly two whole tendays.

There is a wide streak of romance in that boy's soul, she thought. *He cut his sideburns in grief; he is desperate to get money for his family. He would not have simply hid. He would have tried to undo his part in the plot by freeing Terrell.*

Silbariki wasn't terribly far away. A strong young man could walk there in less than a tenday. Terrell had been artfully nonspecific as to how he escaped. By any reasonable assumptions Ymera could calculate, the two of them had to have spent days together. Time enough for a young halfbreed Prince with, and she thought this a critical distinction that too many would overlook, Shimoor-taught empathy, to perhaps have become friends with the miserable but uniquely powerful young acrobat.

That must be it. Terrell forgave him for the kidnapping, grateful for the rescue and, I suspect, genuinely fond of another halfbreed so different from himself. The fight in Sulmona sealed his sense of obligation. He told himself that honor required that he let Kirin go free.

And now Kirin plainly wanted to go right back to being an acrobat, and help support his family as if nothing had changed. *Oh, you romantic child! It will never be allowed.*

The situation was still very fluid, and she could not see all the actors and forces pressing upon young Kirin. But the logic of Kirin's predicament and her vast experience both said they had to be there. Dozens of influential people would eventually bring their power to bear on the boy, trying to push him into doing what they wanted.

After all, he was easy enough for me to manipulate into doing what I wanted, she thought, tilting up the north-facing louvers to gaze across the sun-washed city toward the distant Mountain; it was not yet noon. *Too easy. And that coincidence, that he was the one to find Rian's body?*

She fixed her gaze on the blue-white triangle of God's Footstool jutting up from beyond the curve of the northern horizon. The Mountain was so tall it could still be seen here, more than a hundred-and-fifty miles away.

I have learned to distrust your ways, you God of Silbar. You are no friend to me. Are you friend to him? Or merely another slave master, forcing him into a mold you design?

The thought galled her. She had always despised those who had to control others, enslaving and appropriating all free will solely for the pleasure of the master. It was such a one that she had slaughtered so long ago, slaughtered and drunk his life-force to gain the power to break her chains and escape. She had never looked back – and never followed in his footsteps.

She glared at the distant peak and growled silently, *If you make of that boy a tool, may he turn in your hand and gouge you for your arrogance.*

A wind high above the world plucked pure white snow from the top of the Mountain. The glittering flakes streamed briefly eastward into a miles-long banner that swelled and then faded. A response? Another coincidence?

You are not going to manipulate ME! She fumed. *I will have no hand in this!*

Belatedly she remembered that she had already hired Kirin to look for Rian Smithson's killer. She growled aloud this time and closed the louvers. Two days without sleep would be too many, though it was going to take discipline to achieve any rest today. The life sparks could collect in her silver bowl for a few more hours, tonight would be soon enough to feed again.

She turned her back on the Mountain and descended the stairs into her House.

CHAPTER 15: INQUISITOR

Morning, Second Day of the New Reign.

"This is all the direct documentation we have about Kirin Sule DiUmbra," the most senior priestess of the Temple Archives insisted.

Dona Celia DuVigo DiCerat stared at the annoyingly small array of papers, no bigger than it had been last time. The two of them sat side by side at a round table examining what the archivists had managed to find concerning the accused youth. "Still no birth record?"

"None," the Archivist replied, unintimidated by a mere Inquisitor and visibly annoyed to have her realm of paper and ink slandered by implication. "Approximately two hundred halfbreeds were born in the year following the conquest, but most were never registered. Family shame, of course – the Gwythlo troops were not very restrained at first and there were at least a thousand rapes of girls and women. The Gwythlos learned better after a dozen tried to rape priestesses and we stopped their hearts for their effrontery." She smiled unpleasantly and Dona DuVigo guessed that one of those incidents was very personal for the woman. "We only have records of eighty-two such births in that year, and he is not one of them."

Dona DuVigo hummed to herself thoughtfully, and then said, "That means his soul isn't protected by the birth-registry spells. Which would make him more vulnerable to demonic possession, and more useful to a blood mage who didn't want to fight our protective spells while slaying his victim."

126

"None of the missing ones are protected," the other shrugged. "But now and then one comes in voluntarily to get registered and sealed in the Faith. It's been happening more often this year – six just since Prince Terrell arrived. But most of the rape children are still unaccounted for. Even the total number I gave you, two hundred, is a very rough guess."

"The adoption you showed me last time is the oldest thing we've got on him?"

The Archivist hesitated, grudgingly added, "Possibly not. Your earlier dissatisfaction got me thinking, and over the past several days I've been checking other records from the last two decades." She produced a slender volume of four pages, water-spotted and creased. Carefully she opened it to the second page. "Your description of the boy reminded me of this. It's a record of the fifty-four unregistered halfbreed boys that Ap Marn rounded up from the streets ten years ago; the ones he sold into slavery." The page was organized in columns and lines indicating each boy, his height, how much was paid for him, and who bought him. She pointed to a line. "Here it references a short boy, one of five in this record with no given name. He is simply referred to as 'Black Eyes'."

Dona DuVigo's eyes widened. "In Old Silbari the name 'Kirin' means 'black eyes'."

The Archivist moved her finger down the line to tap the last column. "The buyer was listed as Hartimor Gerlach of Fehdar."

"That damned foreign blood mage!" Dona DuVigo's brown face paled in memory. "His inquest was one of my review cases as a new investigator. When was this list made?"

"Ten years ago. The day after the auction. The day before Gerlach's house burned."

"So the fire was two days after he bought a halfbreed boy with no proper name. The Inquisitor in charge found three skeletons in the ashes besides the Mage's own. All three belonged to young boys, but I remember that she was able to identify two of them as recent kidnapping victims, both halfbreeds."

"Yes, one was among the eighty-two registered, the other an unregistered child traced to a woman in the Sump; the third was never identified. Gerlach apparently had a taste for halfbreed boys and learned with his first victim how difficult it is to overcome our soul-protecting spells. After that he evidently switched to unprotected boys." The Archivist set another book on the table and opened it to the Inquisition's formal report of the incident. "Here are the descriptions of the corpses. Note the height of the third skeleton."

"Taller than the boy he bought off the auction block. So the slave boy was not one of the three skeletons." Dona DuVigo frowned. "Why didn't the Inquisitor make this connection during the Gerlach inquisition?"

The Archivist shrugged. "This list of the sold boys was kept by Ap Marn's reeve. We didn't even get this copy until this year, long after we forced him to stop enslaving children. And with so much other mischief going on back then, halfbreed boys just were not – a priority."

Dona DuVigo sighed acknowledgment of the unspoken point. Few in Silbar had ever spared much care for halfbreed bastards, often not even their families. The ones that survived to adulthood were usually reduced to taking the meanest and most dangerous occupations, like working in the sewers or becoming mercenary guards.

She pinched her lower lip in thought. "We have an unknown halfbreed boy with no name nor description beyond his height and black eyes, who was sold to Gerlach two days before the fire, who then disappears and apparently is not seen again. But –" she checked the adoption form. "Less than a tenday later Pieter Ille DiUmbra adopts a halfbreed boy that he identifies as simply 'Kirin,' who has no previous records in the city. And according to Kirin DiUmbra's marriage certificate nine years later, he claims to have come from the eastern isles."

"Where we have only indifferent records and more than a quarter of the people are not properly registered," the other woman pointed out. "We're lucky to get reports from some of those isolated priestesses once a decade. Half of them have never attended seminary, only got their training through books and from their predecessor's tutelage."

"And he lists no relations except a mother who died several months before."

"I found a mention in the cemetery records that appears to be her." The Archivist produced a copy of a funeral roster for the Poor Field. "Virtually no details at all, not even a lineage name. Only the personal name of 'Ena,' which just means 'woman' in Old Silbari. Which is still spoken on many of the eastern isles."

"Hmmm." Dona DuVigo read over the sparse entry. "Her cause of death is listed as a severe beating and its location referred to as the Sump. That would tend to support a background from outside Silbar proper, but she could have come from Haresalaam or half a dozen other places too. If this Kirin was sired during the Gwythlo Conquest, which fits with his apparent age, then he would have been roughly seven years old when she died."

The Archivist harrumphed and said, "He was probably living on the streets as a pickpocket or something similar. Which explains why he was swept up in Ap Marn's child slavery scheme two seasons later."

"But it leaves so much else about the boy unknown," fretted DuVigo. "Was he the one bought by Gerlach? If so, how is it that he wasn't killed in the fire or murdered by the mage? That monster kept his victims in cages in his basement! And how did the mystery boy go from being a blood mage's slave to an acrobat's adopted son less than a tenday later?"

"I checked the DiUmbra family's records, and they all seem to be in order. But note an interesting fact – Pieter DiUmbra, the man that adopted the boy Kirin, was recently accused of murder by Duke Darnaud. He was convicted and sentenced to ten years in the sulfur mines."

DuVigo's eyes narrowed. "Duke Darnaud filed the charges of blood magery against Kirin DiUmbra."

"Yes. A coincidence?" the Archivist asked drily.

"A very disturbing set of mysteries," Dona DuVigo grumbled. "Is Kirin DiUmbra the same boy Gerlach bought? The Inquisitor found plenty of evidence that Gerlach attempted demon summoning the day his house burned. We have assumed that he failed, but what if he succeeded – and instead of using the boy as a sacrifice, used him as a vessel to hold the demon?"

"That's been tried by other blood mages, dozens of times," the other priestess countered. "We have several scholarly works analyzing that disgusting practice in the Collegium library, with extensive lists of past victims. None of them lived more than twenty-eight days before the chaotic auras of the demons killed them. If your theory is correct, this Kirin has survived over ten *years* with a demon inhabiting him – utterly unprecedented!"

"Which means it is not likely," Dona DuVigo admitted. "But not impossible either. I remember that eccentric priestess at the Collegium who kept a captured demon alive in a flask for two years by feeding it pigeons. Perhaps Kirin DiUmbra found a similar method that let him survive."

"She was proving the theological point that there is more than one demon in the underworld," the other priestess answered primly. "With the approval of her superiors, I might add. And the daily renewal of the imprisoning spells, at a significant cost to the Collegium's power allocation from the City Node – much more than a mere acrobat could pay."

"Yes, yes." Dona DuVigo picked up the last two documents in the pile. "This Kirin also won a wife and they then had a child."

"That also seems highly unlikely for a demon-inhabited man," the Archivist noted. "What records we have of blood mages using pregnant women all end quite rapidly with the deaths of both mother and child. I cannot imagine a demon restrained enough for its host to have sexual congress with a woman, get her pregnant, and not give in to the chaotic urge to devour her life force or at least the child's. But the midwife priestess for DiUmbra's son reported a normal delivery and a healthy baby boy and mother."

"His wife was murdered," DuVigo responded. "Two tendays ago. Based on his family's account when I questioned them, by Duke Darnaud. Another coincidence? I saw the report filed by the City Watch. I wonder why there has been no follow-up on that?"

The Archivist made a dismissive gesture. "Civil law enforcement is a right of the Crown, not the Temple, and with the expected coronation, I would imagine it got set aside for a time. I do expect a report from my opposite in the Crown archives eventually."

A younger priestess bustled into the room, handed a stack of pages to the Archivist, and left. The Archivist glanced at it and her eyes grew wide. "Well. You may find this relevant."

She spread the papers on the table where they both could read; there were two copies. DuVigo discovered they were transcripts of a message construct from the Temple in Sulmona. Her eyebrows climbed as she read. "Kirin DiUmbra was with Prince Terrell in Sulmona two days ago? He killed

Duke Darnaud! And what's this reference to a Living Shadow?"

"I haven't the faintest idea, but I suspect you have a whole new line of inquiry," the Archivist smiled wryly. "Until the Inquisition needs my office again," she stood and sketched a polite bow, taking one copy, "I'll leave you to it."

Dona DuVigo barely noticed her depart. She read through the lengthy dispatch twice, and then stared into space as her thoughts raced. One thing was immediately plain.

He lied to me. Something deep is going on, involving the Prince at least. Should I stop prying?

She thought about it. The new King-who-goes-by-Prince might be covering up something questionable. There could be unpleasant repercussions for poking into Royal business, even for a member of the Inquisition.

Or this could be part of a diabolical plot on the Crown. Has a demon gained influence over not just the halfbreed boy, but over our new ruler himself? Terrell is also a halfbreed.

The Hierarchy must know — and it is my appointed task to answer such questions.

She carefully gathered up the document copies for her file, keeping the Sulmona transcript on the top, and went to see her husband. Message constructs were definitely going to be required for the next step.

CHAPTER 16: BOERGA

Morning, Second Day of the New Reign.

Boerga descended the five flights of stairs from her rooftop aerie as quietly as a cat. Sleeping in a tent surrounded by evergreens under the stars, even one pitched on a rooftop in Aretzo, always felt better than using a bed inside four walls. She had nibbled a breakfast of a little dried meat and some nuts – the benighted darkies raised only almonds and cashews and similar alien things, so her favorite chestnuts had to be imported from Gwythlo at substantial expense. It wasn't enough food to completely kill her hunger, which was all to the good. What she was about to attempt was chancy at best and being a little hungry would keep her sharp.

As she passed through the veil spell at the bottom of the stairs and entered the basement again, a fresh aroma assailed her nostrils. Her minion had brought in the new halfbreed last night, drugged and staggering as if he were drunk. The pawn had vomited against the outside wall before passing out on her doorstep – she would make Gorsyn clean that up today. But having the youth limp as a dishrag had been useful while they strapped him into the rack.

Boerga turned up a mage lamp to illuminate the room, and then checked his bonds. The leather cuffs were still just the right tightness, not enough to cut off his circulation but more than enough to secure him. He hung limp, spread-eagled in the frame and snoring like a banshee. Well-muscled, his body full of promise at roughly eighteen years old, with black hair and the golden skin typical of his kind. His ears were distinctly pointed like the noble houses of

Gwythlo. All in all, a veritable mockery of true Gwythlo features.

As ugly as that Kirin. But good enough for my purposes.

She slapped the youth's face hard enough to cut the insides of his cheeks against his own teeth. A gasp and his eyes fluttered open to stare at her blearily. She could read his first thoughts in his face. Shock at the harsh awakening, sudden realization that he was bound, and then another shock at realizing he was naked and a pale Northern woman stood in front of him wearing unfamiliar but ceremonial-looking robes. He flexed all four limbs, trying to pull free, and also tried instinctively to cover his exposed genitals. "Let me go!" he demanded.

"That I will do, but not the way you want," she told him. "Don't worry, you filthy breed, you aren't going to die today, though before night returns you may wish you had."

He fought his fear with bluster. "You can't do this to me! I've got friends! Aeddan will be looking for me! The whole Mercenary Guild will look for me!"

She chuckled. "Your guild does not care about breeds." She gestured to activate a prepared spell.

He tried to speak again, discovered his voice had been sorcelled mute, and looked wildly around as though hoping to find rescue. Boerga inhaled the delightful scent of his first flush of desperation. This one would surely attract many demons, which she could enslave to her purpose. A newly awakened Great Wight would be hungry enough to devour half a dozen demons, and thus let her bind it to herself.

She readied the polished instruments, lovingly laying each out on a table where the sacrifice could see them. At first her victim didn't comprehend, but soon he realized what they were for. A wild threshing followed as he fought to break free of the rack. He was impressively strong despite being underfed. He struggled until his wrists and ankles bled. The heavy frame rocked but did not yield.

"You are wasting your efforts," she told him pleasantly. "But feel free to continue."

She activated the spells set into the rack and the surrounding room by feeding power to them from hoarded scraps of silver. It would have been much simpler to draw on the Aretzo Node itself, but that would be detected by the Prince's mages and eventually traced to her location. She didn't know how long she would need in order to accomplish her goal, so she couldn't risk compromising her secrecy until success was firmly in hand.

Then she selected a set of charming little clamps with needle sharp inside teeth. "I like to start with the extremities and work my way inward," she explained to the youth's frightened face, and knelt to affix the clamps to his toes. His mute mouth mewled in pain and a sheen of sweat started on his bare chest. His fear-stink grew stronger as it was joined by fresh blood dripping on the floor.

"Good!" she said cheerfully. "We're just getting started but you have a lovely sharp pain sense."

Then she bustled about, setting up preparations for a very special summoning. Calling on the land-wights back home was easy. They were accustomed to heeding the commands of generations of Druids, who kept them well fed with sacrifices – deer and aurochs, bull and horse, and on high holy days a man. These southern wights were long sublimated into the net of power tapped by Silbar's priestesses and mages. Most were outright comatose, so accustomed to their subjugation it was nigh-impossible to rouse them anymore.

But she thought she might have found a way to wake the biggest one. *I have found your Name. You will answer to my call!*

"Awake for me, oh mighty spirit of this alien soil," she murmured as she cast a new and very difficult spell, the capstone of the long sequence she'd been preparing ever since the halfbreed Prince humbled her. "Too long these yellow-robed bitches have kept you confined. Too long these darkies have milked your power as if you were merely a cow. But I understand your true worth! I shall give you the respect you deserve! I shall feed you the meals you require – meals of blood and pain. Wake for me, oh mighty Obilochithlone! Wake!"

The faintest of stirrings touched her extended awareness. Far, far below her feet, in the deepest depths of the Aretzo Node, a faint thread of – not yet awareness, too soon for that, but a pulse throbbed once. Something that had not lived in a very long time was no longer dead, and had accepted her initial offering. The halfbreed jerked in his rack and rolled his eyes as a sucking sensation latched onto his life-force. From the cords standing out in his throat, he was screaming. If she had estimated the spell correctly, he would scream for a whole day and possibly more.

Boerga wiped her sweating forehead and resisted the temptation of triumph. There were many more steps to go, and this young breed would not be enough sustenance to achieve all of them. She would have to shield the awakening wight from the Silbari priestesses, which would require subordinating at least two demons and still more blood.

She checked the surrounding space under the Skin of the World. Already the demons had begun to gather, drawn by the halfbreed's pain and now linked to her driving purpose. They circled slowly, keeping their distance for now, but eventually they would grow tempted enough to come within her reach. It merely required time, and pain.

For a moment she wished she had the demon boy himself here, Kirin. There was a delicious symmetry in the idea of using him to feed the great wight. His dark chaos would be a fitting meal for the new stamp of order she would impose upon Silbar.

His son is still living, somewhere, she thought as she banked her spells, letting the tortured man's pain and fear do the work of preparing for her. *If I can find DiUmbra's baby, I might be able to use it as bait to capture the sire too. The pair would make a perfect offering.*

She went back upstairs to see what her crows could tell her about that. In the basement, the hapless victim writhed and screamed silently.

On the other side of the World Skin, demons gathered.

CHAPTER 17: KIRIN

Morning & Afternoon, Second Day of the New Reign.

The shortest route home from the Red Street took Kirin through Oldgate and past the edge of the Bazaar. The two pouches weighed on his mind more than they did on his shirt. He had never had so much silver in his possession before. When he reached the Serpent he charged up the stairs as though pursued. It wasn't until he shut the fourth-floor door behind him and stripped off his boots that he relaxed again. The familiar thumps of the troupe at practice came through the ceiling from the attic above.

Grandmother stuck her head out of the little boys' bedroom and called to him. He hurried over and found her and Aunt Silla combing the hair of an unhappy Berrin. The six-year-old squirmed and whined, "Morri just let me try on his hat! It had feathers!"

"And lice!" his mother snapped, crushing a nit between her fingernails with a frown of distaste. "What did I tell you about sharing hats?"

"Kirin," Grandmother ordered. "Clean this fool child's hair of these damned nits. Berrin, hold still!" She gave the lad a glare that could have curdled milk. Berrin stood still and pouted.

Kirin obligingly ran his hands over the boy's scalp, letting his Shadow ooze out into the brown hair as he had done for the family members for the past decade. Only Grandfather ever refused the treatment, and he had so little hair left that it didn't matter. Kirin felt the tiny life sparks of dozens of baby lice clinging to the roots of Berrin's shaggy brown hair. With a single thought he slew them all. The tiny wisp of life-energy flowed across his soul and into the Darkness. Berrin tried fruitlessly to watch without moving his head.

"There. I'd better check his bed too," Kirin told the women.

They took the boy and he shut the door behind them, then let his Shadow pour out. It took only a moment to fill the little room, penetrate the bedding, and slay several more lice in Berrin's sleeping pallet. He made sure the other pallets and the hanging clothes on the wall were all clear as well, then withdrew his Shadow and went out into the corridor to rejoin the women.

"No more lice," he reported dutifully.

"Thank Mother Umana for that," grumbled Aunt Silla, tugging on Berrin's ear. "Come, naughty boy, I'm going to scrub your head in the laundry trough."

She grabbed a bar of lye soap and dragged the whining boy down the corridor and out to the exterior stair that led down to the inn's courtyard.

Grandmother blew out a breath as she led Kirin into the dining room. "Glad we caught that before it spread to the other boys. Thank you, son."

"Of course, Grandmother." A little glow of pride warmed his heart.

She plunked herself onto a stool and picked up a mending project as she casually asked, "So how did it go?"

In answer Kirin pulled the pouches out of his shirt and emptied both onto the table. Silver glittered and winked.

Startled, Grandmother dropped her sewing project and fingered the coins. "This is much more than that herald promised. Did she pay you a bonus?"

"No, she hired me for a second job." He started to explain, but didn't want to tell her about grabbing a soul for Ymera to question, so he skipped to, "I helped her trace her murdered man to the body I pulled out of the Charcoal Canal yesterday. She hired me to look for his killers too, which I can do while I'm searching for baby Grigor."

She gave him a sharp look. "Son, hunting for a murderer is like running to join a fistfight. You never know when it might turn into a *knife* fight!"

"I won't be looking for a fight at all," Kirin protested. "I'll just be looking for some clue to the murderers. I'll tell her what I find and that will be the end of it."

Grandmother gave him a magnificent snort in response to that claim. Then she shook her head. "I should know better by now than to tell a young man to avoid trouble. Just be careful and don't let that," She pointed to his crotch, "overrule that," and she pointed between his eyes. "Now you better get upstairs to practice."

What Kirin wanted to do was get back to searching for his son, but he had to admit that it was much too early to ask Dona Pareto for the list of women named Merria. He also missed acrobatic practice with the family the way Uncle Ger complained about missing the tooth he'd lost last year. Kirin went upstairs.

Grandfather was out visiting the Guildhall so Sevan-the-Elder directed practice. He gave Kirin a sharp look as he asked, "How did the job go?" There was a general pause in the whole room as everybody else listened.

"Good. I traced the dead man she was looking for right away." Kirin answered loudly so all could hear. "He turned out to be the body I found in the Charcoal Canal yesterday." He figured that wouldn't end the questions, but it would keep the younger members of the troupe from badgering him for a while.

Papa grunted and immediately put him to work stretching and then ran him through the usual practice routines. After a quarter-candlemark of that the Troupe's assistant leader shook his head disapprovingly. "Your movements are erratic, and your timing is off. You need to rebuild strength, but even more you need to rebuild your coordination. No trapeze work for you today, Kirin. I want to see you on the bar and the rings."

"Yes, Papa," Kirin sighed. It had been twenty days since he last practiced, and even he had to admit the time had done him no favors.

He spent the rest of the morning at boring repetitive exercises while Sevan and Attir practiced on the trapeze. Kirin couldn't help the occasional envious glance as Attir soared through the routines that he himself was used to doing. The younger man's growing skill impressed him. Once he thought he caught Attir giving him a smug look.

Well, he's earned it, Kirin told himself. *He really is getting good, almost as good as I am.* Then a heartbeat later he admitted, *As good as I was.*

The thought made his back prickle. He returned to the parallel bars with doubled determination.

All the attic windows were open to catch the sea breeze, but the vast room was still stuffy. After a while Papa called a general break and the acrobats went out onto the exterior landing to get fresher air. Kirin finished his routine on the rings before he snagged a damp cloth from the washroom and joined them. He came out into the bright sun just in time to hear Attir saying, "What about that girl we saw perform last night at the Middle Court feast, the one named Joli? She could do Mercia perfectly."

That's Maia's role! He almost objected, before realization hit. *She'll never do it again. I'll never dance with her again.* He dropped to the floor of the landing cross-legged and buried his face in the wet rag.

"Who's Joli?" asked Stettir, Uncle Ger's younger brother. "You got your eye on a girl you ain't told us about, Att?"

Stettir's two sons began chanting, "Attir's got a gurl-friend, Attir's got a gurl-friend!" in their not-yet-broken voices. Their father and Sevan-the-younger swatted them into giggling silence. From the corner of his eye Kirin saw a couple of crows perch on the railing to watch the show, but Attir had all of his attention.

"Her name is Joli Melgara Talliber,' Attir answered Uncle Stettir, with a side glance of lofty disdain bestowed on the chanters from his almost-seven-year age advantage. "She's in the troupe that performed next to us; she did the third solo during their Dancing Flowers act. I sat next to her during the breaks. You were right there, Stett!"

Kirin thought he might be overdoing the umbrage.

"Oh, her." Stett considered, rubbing sweat off his head with brawny arms as large as Sevan's. Stett was the troupe's third catcher, but with Pieter dead Kirin realized Stett would now be the second after Sevan. "Well, she was pretty enough, and she moved well. Who was that guy she did the Dying Swan routine with? Those were some great lifts."

"Her brother," Attir answered. "Who's almost exactly the same height and build as me, so I know I could handle her lifts for *Malik and Mercia* just as well."

"Hey, that's my role!" Kirin objected in outrage. "You're just my understudy!"

"I'm ready to play it right now," Attir shot back. "You're not. And without Maia, you'll have to learn it all over again with someone new anyway."

"Enough, Attir," Sevan the Elder said firmly as Kirin bit back a hot retort and seethed silently. *My role!*

"Attir has a point," Uncle Ger argued. "The only woman in the family who's the right age is Carlai, and right now she's not in good enough shape for it and won't be until her little girl is weaned."

"By then Sevan will have her pupped again," Stett commented, to general laughter. Sevan the Younger looked annoyed and proud at the same time. Kirin remembered his son with a pang. *Where are you, Grigor? Please be alive!* More crows joined the first two on the railing, evidently drawn by the laughter, but Kirin ignored them. One of the cousins broke up a bit of stale biscuit to feed them.

"But seriously," Ger continued. "We need to be thinking ahead, and we need another young woman who can handle the role. Two would be even better. The Tallibers have a lot more daughters than sons, and Attir's nearly marrying age, with my Habbir coming along right behind him."

Habbir, Ger's eldest, blushed, turning his brown skin mahogany.

Kirin remembered that the boy was less than a year younger than Attir, the two of them bracketing age sixteen. He was shocked to realize that Att's seventeenth birthday would be in less than ten days. The younger members of the troupe were growing fast, which made him vaguely uneasy.

"I don't disagree, Ger," Sevan the Elder answered. "But these things can't be forced." He turned to his youngest son. "Attir, if you are truly interested in her, I'll approach the Tallibers about having Joli practice with us. If she's skilled enough for the role and wants it too, then we'll see.

Meanwhile," he turned his gaze on Kirin. "Kirin will get back into shape. But until we have an adequate Mercia, we won't be doing *Malik and Mercia* again anyway."

Attir bowed his head, smiling, and answered, "Yes, Father."

Kirin stifled the temptation to protest. "Yes, Papa." He reserved a dark glance for Attir.

"Now," Sevan the Elder continued. "We have that short exhibition job this afternoon. Sevan, Attir, Stett, and Ger, you wash up and get ready. Use soap and then put on that lavender perfume, we're performing for a minor lord and his lady and word is they're the fastidious kind. Kirin, you go see the new priestess about finding baby Grigor. Make sure you wash first; the family needs to keep up appearances with her. Everybody else is on cleaning and repair duty here. Hop!"

Kirin and the men designated for the exhibition went to the attic's tiny washroom and swabbed themselves off with sponges dipped in the rain barrel. Then they took turns two by two crowded onto the tiled part of the floor to soap up while a third poured dippers of water over them. The tiles drained through a hole in the wall into the building's gutters, then down into the midden outside the ground-floor tavern's kitchen. Uncle Ger directed Kirin and Attir to wash first.

Two men trying to slather themselves with soap in a space barely big enough for one required care to avoid jabbing each other with elbows and knees. So the third time Attir smacked him in the ribs without an apology, Kirin's resentment exploded. He jabbed back hard. His younger brother-in-law swung a fist and an instant later they were pummeling each other. Attir slipped, grabbed him, and they both fell hard onto the tile, still hitting each other furiously.

"What in the Nine Hells?" Uncle Ger snapped, while Sevan, who had the dipper, threw water at their heads. Stett grabbed the nearest foot, which happened to be Kirin's, and hauled him bodily out of the bathing nook. Along the way Attir's knee connected with Kirin's face.

Kirin saw stars. For a moment his Shadow roiled and filled him to the skin.

That killed his anger and turned it to fear. His Shadow could slay as fast as thought. If it had gone for Attir or Stett – his heart hammered in his chest even as his eye throbbed. He drove the nightmare back down under his heart and locked it away.

Attir, his face twisted in rage, scrambled up off the tile to lunge for Kirin again. "Stop it, you two!" Ger ordered, grabbing Attir's arm and twisting it behind his back. Sevan reinforced the command by tossing another dipper of water into his brother's face, half soaking Ger at the same time. The older man sputtered and glared at the suddenly shamefaced boy in his grip. "What's gotten into you?"

Stett hauled Kirin to his feet and pinned him against the wall to make sure he obeyed. "Doesn't take a priestess to figure out what's going on, Ger. Attir's feeling his oats and wants Kirin's role in our best play. Kirin doesn't want to give it up."

"Idiots!" Ger snarled at them. "You'll both do what's best for the family, and you'll damned well *like* it. You hear me?"

Attir mumbled assent, eyes cast down resentfully.

"Yes, Uncle," Kirin panted, trying to manage more dignity despite his throbbing head. Stett outweighed him by at least three stone and stood a hand and a half taller, so Kirin knew he wasn't going anywhere until the burly man let him. He drew a long shaking breath and tried to will the anger out of himself. *That was way too close!*

Stett held him two breaths longer before releasing him, then pushed Kirin's mop of black hair out of his face and studied the left eye critically. "You are going to have a big ugly shiner, cousin."

"That's just great," Ger declared in disgust. He shook Attir to emphasize the point, then set the youth back on his feet. "What about you? Any black eyes or bloody nose?"

"No," Attir answered defensively.

"I didn't hit him in the face," Kirin protested.

"I wouldn't have hit Kirin's eye if Stett hadn't dragged him away," Att argued. "Besides, he hit me first!"

"After you jabbed me in the ribs three times!"

"Enough!" roared Ger and Stett simultaneously. More quietly Ger added, "Attir, finish washing. Sevan, you take a turn with him. When he's done, and it better be quickly, Attir's out and Kirin goes back in, then both Sevan and Kirin come out and Stett and I go last. We've got work to do."

They all moved very cautiously after that, finished up and dried off. Sevan the Elder brought dry tights for everybody, the quality type used for shows, and bestowed a tight-lipped gimlet-eyed stare on the two youngest men while they dressed.

Kirin didn't know whether to be relieved at his father-in-law's silence, or worried. He put on his good shirt and belt with the knife Sevan had given him, then donned street shoes and clattered down the back stairs at the north end of the Inn. Dona Sharra Lumin Pereto had said she would have a list of all the Merrias in the parish ready for him after lunch, but right now he felt too impatient to eat. When he reached the Serpentine, he hastened off toward the Sump while crows wheeled in the sky.

By the time he got to the Temple of Heavenly Peace he regretted that choice, but without a coin in hand he couldn't feed himself. The priestess welcomed him civilly enough and sat him at her table where a sheet of parchment waited. Kirin was dumbfounded to see that the list of names covered the whole front and continued onto the back side. Many names had addresses with them, but not all.

"Fifty-seven women named Merria," Dona Lumin declared. "Those are just the ones of childbearing age. I omitted the elderly and the children. You are going to have a difficult time visiting all of them and that's no mistake."

"The sooner I start, the sooner I find my son," he answered, then thanked her and got busy looking.

Three hours later he had collected eight rejections, about half of them reasonably civil and the rest variations on *hell no* and slam the door. Trying not to feel discouraged, Kirin went back down to the entrance of the latest four-story tenement. He reflected that at least his legs were getting a good workout. He sat on the front step to mark another name off the list with a bit of charcoal. Then he rested for a few minutes, his black eye throbbing, and thought about Madame Ymera's remit.

She wants me to find a blood mage. They do powerful magic, and I can see spells even through walls. He called his Shadow into his eyes and looked at the buildings around this little square for traces. His memory of the magic stain left by Gerlach was still so strong that he didn't think it would ever fade; now that vivid memory was an advantage. He filled his eyes with Shadow to pierce the solid brick fronts of the other tenements and spy the magics inside.

At first he could barely see behind the outer walls, but with a little practice he was able to look all the way through each building. There was magic aplenty even in this poor neighborhood. Household tools, healing spells, purification spells, spells on animals and clothes. He got used to sorting out dozens of small magics and dismissing them at a glance.

Nothing like Gerlach's poison lurked in any of these buildings.

For a moment he put his head in his hands and kneaded his aching forehead. There were thousands of buildings in Aretzo. Boerga, if it was even her who had murdered poor Rian, could be anywhere.

A crow flew up and landed on the cobbles a yard away from him. It peered at him as if looking for a friend or a handout. After a moment it hopped closer and stared at him through one beady eye.

A faint blue glow surrounded that eye – a spell on the bird.

For a moment Kirin merely wondered who would put a spell on a crow. Then the way the bird stood there, so still and patient, raised the hairs on the back of his neck.

It's looking for somebody. Looking for me?

But spells couldn't detect him. He'd proven that and Chisaad had verified it with his tests. Then it hit him. *I must have dung for brains. The bird has eyes, and they can see me just fine.*

The crow pecked at something on the cobbles, then the shadow of another bird passed over it. The crow startled up and flew away. As it left Kirin saw a small and very tarnished silver ring encircling its left leg.

The ring is holding a spell. But it's still a bird. If some mage put a spell on a crow to spy on me, it's not gonna let him see me – but the bird itself can see me, and then it can follow me. But crows get distracted easy – this one just did! Who would sorcell a crow in the first place?

The possible suspects were too numerous. Ymera might be checking up on him to see if he was doing her work. One or more of the Council Mages might be watching him because he had been Chisaad's apprentice and now had no

148

Magister. A lesser mage might simply be practicing animal control spells.

He wondered if the Inquisition might be watching him. But they'd probably just summon him for another interview if they wanted something.

Could it be Boerga? I'm looking for my son — if she doesn't know where he is either, maybe she's watching to see if I find him, and then she'll attack us both?

He had a vision of trying to fight a powerful druid while carrying baby Grigor to safety. *But she knows where I live!*

He got up and headed home. Before he'd gone ten blocks, he was sure someone was watching him. At least three crows were always in view. One had a missing feather on its right wingtip; another had a single gray feather in its tail. Both of those had rings around their left legs, as did others that he saw frequently.

By the time he reached the north end of the Sulfur Serpent he had stumbled three times from trying to watch the sky and his footing at the same time. Crows followed him the whole way. He raced past a man pasting a handbill to the alley wall and ran up the exterior stairway to the family's floor, to find two of the little cousins playing on the platform.

"What are you doing?" he asked, more sharply than he'd intended. Two crows perched on a railing, both with rings around their left legs. They bobbed their heads as the boys tossed them crumbs from a bit of stale Feast cake. The two crows that had followed him the longest settled on another railing, watching.

"Playing!" answered little Berrin. Seeing the frown on Kirin's face, he added the clinching argument. "Mama said we could!"

Kirin almost threw his Shadow at the birds, but long habits of secrecy held him back. He was outside, it was afternoon, and people in the streets below and at the open windows of surrounding buildings could see him. Instead he grunted, pulled off his street shoes, and went inside.

To find the family in an uproar and Mage Yellow standing in the middle of their hallway. Four burly men stood at his back with cudgels in their hands.

CHAPTER 18: KIRIN

Afternoon, Second Day of the New Reign.

"What are *you* doing here?" Kirin demanded.

Mage Yellow smiled; his thugs leered over his shoulders. "Informing my tenants that I have bought this building."

"What!"

Grandfather physically put himself between Kirin and the Mage. "Magister, please! This rent increase is impossible! We can't raise that much money by the end of autumn."

"That would be disappointing," Mage Yellow sighed. "I suppose I'll just have to find tenants who can."

A dozen family members tried to talk at once. Grandfather overrode them all. "Magister! Can we negotiate an alternative? We could perform for your family, entertain your clients, and promote your firestarter workshop."

The mage pursed his lips and looked thoughtful. "None of those are particularly useful to me, but the idea of supplementing your former payment with service in kind is an appealing alternative." His gaze travelled to Kirin. "Perhaps the service of one member of your troupe would be adequate."

Kirin clenched his fists and glared. "You bastard!"

The thugs growled and shook their cudgels. Mage Yellow tut-tutted while his smile blossomed anew. "Such poor manners. Is that any way to talk to your new landlord – and employer?"

Papa and Grandfather looked at each other, then looked at Kirin. Grandfather growled, "So you're what this is all about!"

"It's just business," purred the Mage. "A few tasks I need done. I'd consider them adequate compensation for waiving the additional rent. If the tasks are performed well, I could even agree to discount the rent for your practice space." He pointed at the attic over their heads. "By half. What do you say, young Kirin DiUmbra?"

Maia's father's face turned beseeching. "Son," he said, then fell silent.

Kirin gulped. The whole family was looking at him. That big a discount would bring the rent down to something they could already afford with the money in hand. The wave of hope in their eyes hit him like a hammer blow. Those eyes could mold him into their savior, or with equal ease, into a scapegoat.

Mage Yellow looked like a sleekly satisfied cat. But his eyes were cold.

Kirin's Shadow stirred within him. He could just reach out and drain the life from that smiling bastard –

And then I'd have him inside my head like Gerlach. One crock of slime is bad enough! How long before two of them drove me mad?

Kirin took a deep breath, let his Shadow rise into his eyes and held it there.

"I'm already doing a job for Madame Ymera," he told the Mage. "I can't start anything for you until I finish hers."

Yellow nodded slowly. "I wouldn't dream of interfering with her business – but my tasks will be simple and quick. I have a task I need done tomorrow night. If you finish it for me, I'll waive the increase. Finish a second task that I have in mind by the end of this coming Holy Day, and I'll halve the attic rent."

"What kind of tasks are they?" Kirin let his Shadow ooze out through his skin and wreath him in darkness. The four thugs lost their grins and two made the Sign Against Evil. Sevan and some of the cousins gained savage smiles. They knew his Shadow could kill lice; perhaps human lice were not too big for it to hurt.

Mage Yellow didn't even blink. "Nothing I'll speak of here. Nothing that will harm anyone physically. Simple tasks, really." He eyed Kirin's shadow. "Tasks that you are very well suited to perform, I see. Excellent. Do we have a deal?"

"Yes, Salim damn you," Kirin growled. "We have a deal."

~ ~ ~

After the mage and his thugs had left, Kirin shoved his Shadow back down under his heart and sagged against a wall. The family crowded around him.

"Kirin!" Sevan muscled his way to the front as his voice overrode the babble of twenty others. "That son of a bitch came here just to flex his power over us. Don't trust him!"

"I don't," Kirin answered frankly. "But what choice is there? If I don't do what he says, he'll raise the rent until we can't pay it, and then throw us out on the street."

"Mentioning Madame Ymera was wise," Grandmother put in. "That'll make him cautious. Nobody wants to anger her."

"Is she willing to lend you support against Mage Yellow?" Carmella asked.

Kirin thought about it and the brief hope faded again. "I don't think so. She wants me to help find her servant's killer, but when I've done it, I think that'll be the end of her need for me. She's wary of the Council and the Hierarchy and wouldn't tangle with either of them if she could avoid it. There's no way she'd pick my side in a fight with a Council mage."

"I read the situation that way too," Papa agreed. "But Mage Yellow is a clever man for all that he's got the morals of a pig. He'll try to trap you into doing something that'll get you into worse trouble, just to get a better hold over you. You've got to do everything you can to avoid that trap."

Papa's warning conjured ugly possibilities in Kirin's mind. What if the mage wanted him to sabotage a rival's spells? Or steal from somebody? Or murder? *I'd be damned before God. But if I don't? What happens to the family?* Maia's fear of having to live on the street loomed unpleasantly close now.

Ger and Stett were looking around at the familiar walls of their home. Kirin heard Stett mutter to his older brother, "DiUmbras have lived here for a hundred and fifty years."

"Every man in the family was born here," Ger answered, nodding.

Except me, Kirin thought.

"There's a little time," Carmella pointed out. "It's thirteen days until Solstice."

"But only three until this Holy Day," Grandfather spoke up, staring at him. "And Mage Yellow wants something tomorrow night. Can you get clever enough by then, boy?"

A familiar tightness closed on Kirin throat. *Why do I always feel so small when he talks to me?* He had to force words out as he met the old man's eyes. "I guess we're going to find out, Grandfather."

Sevan the Elder broke their locked gazes. "The exhibition went well today, so we may have a contract for a real performance soon. Everybody go upstairs and practice before we lose the daylight. I want to see sweat rolling off every performer in the Troupe. Hop!"

Kirin took to the rings and the parallel bars again. This time he pushed himself until his arms and legs started trembling. Papa called a halt just as the sixth bell rang and the men took a breather on the back stairs before supper. Calm and Madness dueled in the sky as the last rays of the Two Suns lit the sky behind the peaks. Overhead, stars appeared.

Kirin gladly dropped to the worn planks and flopped back against the railing with his legs stretched out. The railing creaked.

A crow landed on it and stared down at him. The ring on its leg caught the last light of setting Mother Sun and glinted silver.

"To the Ice Hell with you, Salim-cursed bird," Kirin growled. He filled his hand with Shadow and threw it like a black ball. But a tremble in his arms betrayed him and he missed. The Shadow splashed against the underside of the roof and vanished into the larger shadows already there. The bird fluttered up, then landed again a little farther away, and continued looking at him. "Damn it!"

"Why are you pestering that crow?" asked Attir, flopping down beside him. "Did it dump on you?"

"No. It's a damn spy," Kirin answered tersely, not wanting Att's company right now.

"Spy?" Stett repeated, propping himself against one of the uprights. "How do you know?"

"Because crows just like it followed me around all afternoon," Kirin growled. "Six or seven of 'em, all with rings on their legs and spells on their eyes." He made another ball of Shadow and pegged it at the crow, this time hitting it square. The ring's glow died. The bird squawked and flew off.

"Whose spy is it?" Attir demanded in an alarmed voice.

"That damned mage?" Sevan asked, leaning on another upright and scowling.

"I don't know," Kirin admitted. He flung another Shadow ball and hit a ringed crow that had just landed near Sevan. It too flew away as if Salim himself were after it. Kirin sat up and craned his neck but didn't see any others lurking in the twilight. "I think the rest have wandered off."

Uncle Ger chuckled. "Whoever it is, they're done spying now!"

More seriously, and tacitly acknowledging Kirin's abilities, Attir added, "Really, Kir. Who do you think it was?"

Kirin shrugged. "Somebody with a beast-talent. Mage or priestess, not sure which." Then he remembered Boerga's wolf, the one he'd mortally wounded in the Bazaar. Gossip had told him that the Watch had found the body there the next day and the Druids had claimed it for their rites. He wondered if they had raised the beast, or skinned it, or maybe even eaten it. Boerga must have had powerful beast-talents to tame a wolf. Crows seemed simple compared to that.

"You don't guard your face well enough," Papa commented. "You just thought of somebody, didn't you?"

"Yeah," Kirin admitted, glancing furtively around the alley. "But I don't think I should say it out loud."

"Then don't," Papa said firmly. "Time to get washed up for supper."

As everyone else headed for the tiny washroom, Papa pulled Kirin aside and took him to the far end of the net under the trapeze set. The big room was dim around them, familiar and strange at the same time. Kirin scanned the rows of open dormer windows, wondering which hosted a listening bird.

"We're about as far from a window as we can get," Papa whispered to Kirin. "Tell me who you're worried about, son."

Kirin sighed and whispered back, "That druid who killed our horses, Papa. The one riding the wolf. Boerga. The Prince banished her, but gossip says she's still lurking somewhere in the city. I think she's trying to find baby Grigor before me, or maybe waiting for me to find him first so she can swoop in and grab him."

Papa was silent for a moment. "Why would she want a baby?"

"She killed that man whose body I found, Papa," Kirin told him. "The solstice is coming soon, and Druids make sacrifices then. Sometimes even human sacrifices. And she called me a demon. Maybe she thinks I sired a half-demon baby on Maia. What could be a better sacrifice when it's time for a druid to drive away the demons who eat the year?"

Maia's father's breath hissed. "That pale bitch. All right, son. Wash yourself, eat a good supper, then do whatever you're going to do tonight. Just please, be very careful out there in the dark. The streets are dangerous at night."

"Not for me, Papa," Kirin told him, feeling oddly relieved to have such broad permission. "If I need to protect my son, I can be the most dangerous thing in all of Aretzo."

CHAPTER 19: TERRELL

Afternoon, Second Day of the New Reign.

Terrell and Pen had barely finished cleaning up after weapons practice when a messenger appeared in the Court of Arms. Pen buckled on his sword belt as Terrell shrugged into a shirt.

"Majesty." The messenger went to one knee and bowed his head. The lad wore the general Palace livery with the badge of the Glass Office, the Royal Wizard's operation.

Titles are going to be a problem, Terrell thought as he held out his arms for his valets to tie the elaborate ribbon sleeves in place. He gently admonished the boy, "Address me as 'Highness' until Emperor Osrick allows me use of the higher title."

"Highness," the boy repeated, then in a rush, "There is a problem at the Glass Office and the duty mage begs you to visit at your earliest possible convenience."

"I bet that's how mages call for help," Pen commented as he plucked Irreneetha's point out of the stone where he had placed her and slid the soulsword into her sheath.

"No bet," Terrell answered Pen, then told the boy, "Now will do. Lead the way."

~ ~ ~

"Highness! W-w-welcome to the G-glass Office!" effused Nortin DuBir DiTellio, the senior assistant mage, with much bowing and a notable stutter. "Th-th-thank you for res- resp- for answering my p-p-plea!"

Nortin appeared to be perhaps thirty-five, Terrell judged, thin and willowy. The expression on his face reminded Terrell of a man expecting his own execution. Nortin and the other two assistant mages left behind to run the office of the Royal Wizard after Chisaad's death were all native Silbaris in their mid-to-late-thirties, established men with wives and children. They had been thoroughly vetted by the Council of Colors, and all three were members of multiple powerful Aretzo mage families. They'd been deliberately hired because of their conflicting web of relatives, on the theory that somebody beholden to three or more rival patrons would cling to the most powerful one in any conflict.

Which, Terrell thought, *would hopefully be me. But today he's almost incoherent. If I want to get anything useful out of him, I need to calm him down first.*

Terrell made the gesture that meant *no formality* and said, "Your message was not specific, Mage Nortin. What is wrong?"

"The b-b-black lines! Th-th-three of them now! Running the wrong way!" The man wrung his hands. "I've never seen this b-before, Highness!"

"You'll have to explain a few things to me first, Nortin," Terrell told him patiently. "Lines? Wrong way?"

"Y-yes, Highness," Nortin answered apologetically. He pointed and, without actually touching Terrell, drew him toward a huge rectangular crystal pane dominating the high-ceilinged room. It stood more than ten feet tall and stretched at least fifty feet long, braced in a wooden base that held it two feet off the tiled floor. The pane glowed with colored lights, which resolved into vertical lines when Terrell got close enough. Hundreds of lines.

"This pane is the device by which we in the Glass Office monitor the flow of magic power, what some call 'mana,' out of the Aretzo Node," Nortin nervously explained. "I believe Mage Shimoor showed it to you shortly after you first arrived."

Terrell nodded, glad to see Nortin's stutter had gone. Pointing a bureaucrat's attention to something he knew how to do was often sufficient to ease panic, his teacher Shimoor had once told him. Terrell gazed on the enormous pane and wondered how it had ever been made. He'd never seen so much glass in one place. It looked thicker than his arm. "Yes, I recall that conversation. He said it tracks a thousand of the City's mages."

"At one time," Nortin amended. "We do track most users of magic in the city, but only one thousand at a time can be displayed on the pane. Every quarter-hour we examine a different group."

A loud chime sounded and the curtain of lines within the pane rippled and rapidly slid to the right, then steadied. Terrell realized that half of it had disappeared off the right edge of the pane and new lines appeared on the left. Behind the glass a line of twenty mages with goggles over their eyes were studying the lines. Ten of them wore black badges and ten wore white badges. They all held small devices up to the glass and called off names and numbers. A row of scribes sitting at a long desk behind them industriously jotted down the information.

"The duty mages are tracking the individual users of the Node's power," Nortin explained. "All mages are required to register with this Office before we let them draw from the node. They pay a tax to the Crown and we track their use. If they repeatedly exceed what they are allowed based on their license, we fine them, or they can apply to reclassify their rank upward and then we charge them a higher tax for that bigger license. We even cut them off from access entirely if they become repeat offenders."

"How do you know how much power any single mage uses?" Terrell asked, staring at the broad sheaf of colored lines.

"The thickness of their line changes." Nortin pointed to a broad blue line that had a sudden bulge about a foot above the bottom of the crystal pane. "Blue is for Silbari mages. This is Mage Red of the Council, who has been working on the wards for a new hull being laid down in your naval shipyard. This morning he sealed the various wards that he's been casting on it and bound them together, which is the bulge you see there. Shipbuilding often has sudden bursts of power use between many small castings."

The bulge inched upwards slightly. Terrell realized that all the lines were slowly moving upward, like strings being drawn toward the top of the glass. A dozen thin black horizontal lines were embedded in the glass – no, he realized they also moved upward. The whole visual presentation was in motion, slowly creeping up the pane to vanish at the top.

Nortin pointed to the horizontal black lines. "The space between each of these represents one hour of time, what the commoners often refer to as one candlemark." He waved to a large hourglass on a stand at one end of the pane. "Of course, our measurements are much more precise than a candle. We fit twelve hours at a time on the glass."

Terrell peered closer and saw that the closely packed lines bent aside when one bulged, so that there was always a little space between lines. "This is an amazing device. You can literally track every user of magic in the city with it?"

Nortin nodded proudly. "We can track everyone drawing from the City Node."

"How do you tell them apart?"

"There are labels magically embedded in the other side of the glass which can only be seen from that side, and only with our inspection goggles. After enough practice we learn to recognize many individuals by the texture of their lines, which are more specific than a face. That's how I recognized Mage Red's line. Keeping accurate track is the main job of this office. The mages wearing white badges do the initial count, then after a shift the black-badged mages repeat their count to be sure it is correct. The Mage Guild complains quite loudly if we charge them for more power than they think their members actually used, so maintaining verified documentation is crucial for resolving disputes."

Terrell pointed to eight short yellow lines just beginning to creep up the pane. "What are these?"

"This morning's newly confirmed batch of priestesses," Nortin explained. "An hour ago we granted them their first access to the node. These eight are all students at the Collegium who weren't born here, since the ones native to Aretzo already have their own lines." He pointed to an adjacent white line that turned yellow at the same point where the new lines began. "Such as this student, who was born here."

Terrell looked searchingly across the huge pane. "I see. Priestesses are marked in yellow and mages in blue. Why was that woman's line white before?"

"She only had three or fewer talents and wasn't capable of exerting a significant draw on the node. Her Collegium education will develop her latent talents so that she can do more. If she weren't able to improve, she wouldn't have qualified for the Collegium in the first place."

"You look at different groups of magic-users during the day? How often does the display change?"

"Every quarter-hour it shifts. Five hundred users slide off the display and five hundred more slide on."

162

"I see." Terrell thought for a moment. "The color of these lines is assigned by this office?"

"Yes. When one achieves status as a mage or priestess, we assign a line in the pane to that person, and the color of the line identifies their status. The orange lines are visitors to the city, mostly mages but some priestesses, who are allowed to draw on the Node through temporary licenses. We bar visitors from access if they don't buy a license."

One of the subordinate mages muttered "Got you!" and manipulated something on the crystal's other side. A thin blue line abruptly turned orange and winked out.

"What was that?" Terrell asked sharply.

"A counterfeiter, Highness," Nortin explained. "Someone unlicensed but masquerading as a legal mage, generally to avoid paying the Crown fee."

"Does that happen often?"

"At least fifty times a year, Highness. A lot of them are like that one, a foreigner visiting for a few days and trying to do magic on the cheap, without getting the temporary license to draw on the Node. That results in two lines that seem to belong to the same owner, which eventually attracts our attention. So we catch them no matter how clever they are, and then we cut them off like that one."

Terrell raised an eyebrow. "How long do they usually get away with it?"

"One or two days, for most; it can take a while for us to cross-reference and discover the deception. The restrained ones can get away with it for several tendays or even half a season by just dipping into the node briefly every few days. Really clever ones have managed a whole year, but we always catch them in the end."

"Are they punished?"

"If we can figure out who they are, Highness, but that's difficult. We usually don't try for the brief ones, they just aren't drawing enough power to matter. Or to be worth the expense of chasing them down. The serious draws we can trace more easily, and since they're fined proportional to what they stole, they're worth going after." The mage grinned smugly. "We usually have to make an example of one of them every year, sometimes twice. Four years ago we caught a trio of Fehdarans running an unlicensed magic shop out of a warehouse by the Serpentine. They were selling their services only to departing foreign ships, which meant they didn't show up anywhere in the customs or tax records. They were very clever, shifting their draw to different forged identities at least twice every day. It took thirteen tendays to pin them down, but we still got them." He and the mages on the other side of the glass all preened.

Terrell smiled. "Glad to hear it. What happened to them?"

"Your judge for the Harbor sentenced them to five years at the Royal Mint, stamping depleted silver into coins with manacles on their ankles and eating porridge three times a day." Grins through the big crystal celebrated this bit of justice. "They're still there, probably counting the days to their release, when they get put on an outbound ship and sent home with empty pockets."

"Good work," Terrell told the mages, meaning every word of it. He pointed to the crystal pane again. "You mentioned blue, yellow, and orange, but what are the other colors?"

"Green is the Gwythlo Druids, who have a special allocation – there aren't very many of them. Purple is the city's own systems." He pointed to a purple band wider than Terrell's head. "That one is the Harbor's draw, if you look closely you can see the separate draws within it for the different mages who manage ship traffic. Other purple lines mark the water system and the sewer system, the Gray Fort, the protection spells on the city's exterior walls and gates, the Navy Yards, and the Admiralty, but they aren't on the glass at the moment."

"And the Palace?"

"Those spells drink from the Hill Node, not the City Node, including this Office." He waved at the length of the crystal pane. "To track them too, we'd need a second glass."

Terrell estimated the relative width of the purple bands and suppressed an exclamation of surprise. A tenth of the total outflow from the Aretzo Node was dedicated just to running the city and his government. *Mage Blue claims the priestesses are inefficient; I wonder if my own people are part of the problem?* He set the thought aside for later.

Terrell surveyed the length of the crystal pane. A thick white band in the newly arrived section caught his eyes and he walked over to examine it more closely. It was made of very thin white lines packed so closely together that they could barely be distinguished from each other. Terrell didn't see any bulges, all the white lines appeared perfectly straight. The band was nearly three feet wide and the mage examining it on the other side was not calling off names or numbers. "What is this?"

"Those are ordinary citizens with minimal talent who are getting close to the threshold of true mage talent. If they successfully achieve it, we try to track them down and issue them a license. And collect their tax, of course. Some are too poor to pay it and they are firmly instructed to not use more than their basic talents until they can pay, or to apprentice to an established mage, or to join the Hierarchy. Registered apprentices and postulants for the Hierarchy get a free year to prove that they can actually do spell work, and to establish their draw capacity, before we tax them. Most new talents choose that path, since working as a mage or priestess is a better life than most."

165

Kirin must have been registered when Chisaad took him as an apprentice, Terrell realized. *Have they been tracking his use? Or does he even* use *the Node the way regular magic users do? For that matter, does this tracking device even work on him? I should talk to him about this some time, and the mages as well, but I don't want to draw attention to him just yet.* "And the ones that don't?"

"They must either have a source of income to pay the tax, or not use their talents, or leave the city."

"Really?" Terrell looked at him in surprise. "Do any do that? Leave, that is?"

"A few. Young merchants sometimes simply move to another city where their families have business. They usually operate there as permanent guests while running that branch of their family business." Nortin pointed to several orange lines in the giant pane. "We mark permanent guests' lines in a darker shade of orange, and they pay a slightly lower fee. Your great-great-grandfather wanted to encourage trade, you see, so he made it advantageous. As it still is."

Terrell measured the width of the white band with his hands, did a quick estimate and said, "Wait. This can't be all of the minor talents in the city. Shimoor told me there were more than a hundred and fifty thousand of them."

"True, Highness, but most aren't normally tracked on the glass. If we showed them all you couldn't tell them apart." He called out a warning and all the duty mages stepped back and took off their spectacles. Then Nortin did something and the huge pane changed into a solid sheet of glowing colors, much of it white. "That's what it would look like if we displayed everybody. Even with our enhancement goggles it's difficult to tell one line from another. Display everybody and the lines all merge into a blur." He reversed whatever he had done and the glass reverted to its earlier pattern. The duty mages put their spectacles back on and returned to work.

"That flood of white lines is the general background use by people who aren't licensed mages or any other category but who have one to three Talents able to draw on power," Nortin continued, much more relaxed than he'd been when Terrell arrived. "We don't actually track them, Highness. Their lines aren't even identified or labeled, unless they attend the Collegium or a mage school or become apprentices or postulants. Or if a white line grows big enough to easily see apart from the others. That means a new mage or priestess has developed enough talents to require a license. It happens two or three times a tenday. The line size is deceptive since each line thickens at a slower rate than the actual increase in power consumption. There has to be a minimum width of a line for us to even see it. Measured by consumption, all of the white lines together don't add up to as much power as the Harbor draws, but they represent more than three-quarters of the city's people. They're pretty constant, too, essentially about five parts in a hundred of the Node's available supply, day in and day out. Which is a lot of power, but it's so finely divided that there's no efficient way to tax or regulate it, so we don't try."

"And red?" Terrell indicated the lone thick line that pulsed bright crimson. It was almost lost in the overall mass of color.

"Oh, that's Madame Ymera and the allocation for the Red Street, Highness." Nortin's voice sounded embarrassed. "We, ah, monitor that, but we don't ever touch it."

"Why not?" Terrell thought the mage might be blushing.

"She can tell if we do anything to her allocation, Highness, just like the Council mages and the higher Priestesses can. She sends tart notes to us if we disturb it. Very tart. Acerbic, even." The mage was definitely blushing now, and some of his subordinates displayed smirks or outright grins.

"I see." A centuries-old sorceress might have an impressive grasp of the way language could be used to puncture the vanity of a male target. Terrell allowed his own grin to show.

They had been slowly walking down the length of the long pane as they talked. Now Nortin stopped at the end. Terrell realized that the last few finger-widths of the pane were empty of lines, though the other edge had been populated right up to the end of the glass. "What's this?"

"The reason that I asked you to come here this morning, Highness," Nortin answered. All the confidence had fled his voice. "Let me show you what we observed early this morning. I saved it and will repeat it now." He cast a complicated spell.

A thick black line started at the top of the crystal and ran downward through the empty space like a slow-moving lightning bolt. It pulsed for a moment, then faded out.

"What was that?" Prompted Terrell.

Nortin looked frightened. "Your Highness, the night mage first saw it last night and told me about it when my morning shift began. It happened again about three hours ago, just after he left, then again a candlemark before you arrived – that's the instance I captured to show to you. Nothing like it ever happened before in the four years I've worked here, Highness. I was looking in the Directives when you arrived." He pointed to a thick book on a stand set a little aside from the crystal pane. "The notes in there are the chief touchstone we use for managing the flow of power. But there's nothing about a black line running contrary to time!" Under his breath Nortin muttered in a despairing tone, "Chisaad understood this thing better than I ever will."

One of the mages on the other side winced hard enough to be seen through the glass. Nortin's eyes got big as he realized what his mouth had said.

Terrell commented distantly, "Mage Nortin. Remember that he was a traitor. That said, I note that you are quite disturbed by this manifestation. Please explain why."

The mage gulped and said, "Highness, the lines move upward and disappear off the top. That line ran the wrong way."

"Top to bottom," Terrell realized. "That's what you mean by 'backwards across time,' wasn't it?"

Nortin squirmed a little. "We don't know, which is disturbing enough. But the power draw wasn't *out* of the Node. It was upwelling power being drawn back down *into* the Node. That's why there's a gap here at the end that hasn't filled back in – a gap that wasn't there before. A slice of the city's available power supply has been denied to us." He did something that caused the gap to split into three, separated by thin black vertical lines. "This shows the three separate instances where it happened. The right side is the first, the left is the newest."

Terrell felt a chill on his spine despite the warmth of the big room. "The oldest is smallest, the newest is four times as wide."

"Yes. We've pinned this section of the display in place and have been watching it, but the active user lines have not reoccupied those spaces, the way they do when a magic user leaves town. Or not yet anyway. We're losing bits of the city's power supply, and we don't know how long they'll be gone." His voice went low as he whispered, "And each time it happens, it's gotten worse."

Lost power means lost revenue, Terrell thought. *Too much lost revenue and I can't pay Osrick's tribute. He won't take that well at all.* "This is cutting into the amount available for use?"

"Not yet. We have several tons of depleted silver stored in the basement under this office, its original power consumed by the Navy. We store surplus node-power in it at night and parse it back into the city during the peak demand periods of the day. We can do that twenty to thirty times before the silver become too depleted to take a new charge and gets retired to make coinage. The buffer's big enough to handle more than ten times this black draw."

"But not twenty?"

Nortin's face grew even more worried. "Maybe twelve to fifteen such incidents, if they don't get any worse, Highness. After that the stored power will be gone and spells will start failing, unless we c-cut off some users to reduce d-demand."

His stutter's back. Terrell nodded gravely. "I see. We have an alarming pattern. Marking it this way and informing me were both well done, Mage Nortin. Now I must prevail upon you to see that your associates are fully informed of these happenings. Tell them, if it occurs again, I want to be informed as promptly as you alerted me this time. Also, send messengers to the Temple Collegium, to my scholars, and anyone else who knows about the history of the node. If this has ever happened before, I want to know about it, and know what was done last time. Now I need to go deal with Chisaad's tower. I'll expect you to have at least the beginnings of an answer for me when I return."

Nortin's relief showed in the way he almost prostrated himself as he bowed. "Yes, Highness!" he promised the floor.

The eight members of the Council of Colors arrived then as planned. Terrell collected them and left the Glass Office. Pen walked by his side down the long corridors leading to the Clerk's Gate and the streets that led to Chisaad's house. A dozen Palace Guards closed in around them as an escort. The tramp of their feet echoed off marble walls.

In a voice pitched for Terrell's ears alone Pen asked, "Do you think that black line could be him?"

Terrell shook his head slightly and answered the same way. "I doubt it. He's been living in Aretzo for years, and they just noticed this black mystery last night. If his presence or actions made such a startling disturbance in the crystal, it surely would have been noticed before this."

Pen didn't look quite satisfied but subsided into silence again.

I hope I'm right, Terrell thought privately. *Because I don't want to consider what I might have to do if that black effect really is due to my twin brother. The City can't survive chunks of its power supply simply disappearing. If I lose even a quarter of that revenue permanently, I can't run the kingdom and still pay Osrick's Tribute.*

If I fail Osrick, he'll think it's a deliberate betrayal. Then he'll kill me.

CHAPTER 20: INQUISITORS

Just before Evening, Second Day of the New Reign.

The sixth bell was still ringing over the Inquisition's headquarters as Dona Nivera DuNimes, First Inquisitor, stood up to leave her desk. Before she took a step, her investigator Dona Celia DuVigo DiCerat barged in and announced, "New information in the DiUmbra case."

Dona Nivera sat down again and beckoned her subordinate to a chair. "I'll make time for that. Speak!"

Dona DuVigo did, laying out evidence she had gathered and filling the gaps with reasoning. The First Inquisitor was impressed.

"Very good research, Celia. I can see you have a theory that ties all of this together. Propound it for me."

Celia DuVigo took a deep breath, clearly aware that she was putting her career on the line. "I believe that Gerlach succeeded in summoning a demonic entity, but not the one he sought. The entity he summoned took up residence in Kirin DiUmbra, and together they killed Gerlach and fled the fire. Indeed, they may have set it specifically to cover their escape and obscure their actions. If so, it worked – when we were unable to raise Gerlach's spirit for questioning, we assumed that he had compromised himself so badly with the demon that it carried his soul off and thus killed him. Which may or may not be true but is not relevant to my theory. Somehow the boy Kirin, and the entity, then befriended or ensorcelled Pieter DiUmbra and persuaded him to give them shelter with the acrobat family, where they lay low for an unprecedented ten years."

Dona Nivera looked down her nose at her subordinate. "Let me play opposition against this theory. Every precedent we have says that no human could have survived such a drawn-out possession, and no being of chaos could have resisted feasting on the host and the people around it for so long."

DuVigo's mouth drew down in a pained grimace. "I know. But bear with me. Kirin DiUmbra became a successful acrobat, and regularly performs as the Imp Malik and dances with shadows."

"Yes, yes, his Troupe has become famous for that illusion," Nivera commented. "And the girl's exquisite levitation talent, too."

"The levitation appears to have been real, but the illusion – may not have been an illusion at all. He may really be host to a Living Shadow, displaying it in plain sight literally for years, and everyone attending has always assumed it was mere illusion. Safe, inconsequential, a trick – instead of a demonic devourer of life and magic."

Nivera raised her eyebrows. "That's an astonishing accusation you ask your opponent to believe so close to dinnertime. If he has a Shadow, and long experience with Shadows indicates that they are neither portable nor capable of self-denial, how do you explain his survival? Why didn't it just eat him?"

"He has to be able to control it somehow. Perhaps through a radical new talent."

"Ah, the perennial excuse when something lacks explanation – a new talent!"

"Remember that Chisaad took him on as a charity apprentice?"

"A remarkable departure from the former Royal Wizard's normal habits," Nivera conceded. "Implying that he saw something unusual in the boy."

"Exactly. Only he didn't inform the Council of Colors of just what he saw. Given the fight that the mages have picked with us over the Aretzo Node, and their desire to have him take their side, they evidently didn't risk annoying him by asking about the boy, though they surely must have been curious. Which may have served the Shadow's needs perfectly."

"You still have a tissue of conjecture, not a supported theorem."

"Then let me add this. A message construct arrived from Sulmona this morning with a bizarre report. I had my husband send questions back immediately, in the name of the Inquisition. Just after the fifth bell this afternoon, those questions were answered."

"What did you learn?"

"Kirin DiUmbra killed Duke Darnaud in a vicious melee in the courtyard of the Sulmona Palace two days ago. He was brought there from somewhere in the Duermu lands by one of the Ilvars flying a carpet. The report is clear that DiUmbra rode with Prince Terrell, who was reportedly afflicted with a nasty mind-dominating spell centered on a silver spike driven into his head. They both claimed it had been done by Royal Wizard Chisaad and that Chisaad was scheming to usurp the Throne. The Prince was wounded during the fight, and while Baron DiLione protected him, DiUmbra removed the spike and killed the mind spell."

Dona Nivera lost her poise as opponent and leaned back in her chair with a thump. "What in the name of all that's holy?"

"I know, it reads like a mad melodrama, but look." DuVigo spread the message transcript in front of her. "The story is attested to by the Sulmona Temple's ranking Healer, who was in the middle of it. She examined the spiked device and questioned both His Highness and DiUmbra, as well as several of the Gwythlo soldiers while treating their wounds."

"I begin to suspect where you might be going with this, and while this tissue of speculation astonishes me, I confess that I don't *yet* want you to stop talking. Explain how your theory relates to the message from Sulmona – and with our newly chosen King-who-goes-by-Prince. You said DiUmbra killed Duke Darnaud in a fight?"

DuVigo leaned forward to tap the message transcript. "According to the local Inquisitor, who is at least competent at reporting if not particularly inspired in her work, DiLione arrived nine days ago bearing Prince Terrell's appointment as Hand."

"Which we knew about." Nivera waited.

"The Temple has had a bad relationship with the Imperial Administrator, Gwynned, for the past fourteen years. Our agent had to ferret out what little she knew of goings-on inside the Sulmona palace through indirect methods."

"I know, I've seen her reports." Nivera scowled. "If there hadn't been so many worse problems elsewhere, we'd have done something about that by now."

"She reports that DiLione and a company of Silbari soldiers arrived, took control of the palace, and began questioning everybody using the two Truthtellers that Her Holiness loaned to the Crown. Gwynned refused to talk, and it was plain to everybody that he thought someone would save him. Then Duke Darnaud arrived in disguise, with a company of Gwythlo soldiers masquerading as caravan guards. He lured DiLione out into the courtyard, where he attacked the King's Hand with overwhelming force. DiLione should have died, despite his sword, but Terrell and DiUmbra intervened."

Nivera raised a skeptical eyebrow. "That must have been interesting."

"Spectacular may be a better word. When they arrived on the Ilvar mage's carpet, the two of them literally threw themselves into the fight."

Both of Nivera's eyebrows twitched this time. "Brave move, that – and nearly suicidal if they really were facing an entire company of Gwythlo troops and their military mages."

"It would seem so. But I want to draw your attention to a particular event during that fight." DuVigo turned a page and tapped a new section of the transcript. "While DiLione and the Prince and a couple of Silbari soldiers were fending off the attackers, DiUmbra threw up a massive bank of darkness behind them, like a wall to protect their backs."

"Really?" Nivera's skepticism didn't quite ring true even to her, and she shifted uneasily in her chair. "You mean he cast a large illusion? Or was it this Shadow you claim he carries?"

"I suspect the latter – though evidently some thought it merely an illusion at first." Dona DuVigo made the Sign Against Evil and continued, "The Truthtellers and our local Inquisitor questioned several of the Gwythlo soldiers who were caught *inside* the darkness. They report being utterly blinded and afflicted by a terrible draining cold, much like the chill air of a high mountain pass. Some lost their orientation so completely that they couldn't stand. They also report that Kirin DiUmbra moved through the darkness as though it didn't affect him, slew several soldiers, and battled Darnaud, ultimately killing him too. Then, and note the choice of words, the darkness flowed like smoke as it went into DiUmbra's back and vanished."

Nivera's own back prickled with sudden, shocking fear. "It really wasn't an illusion. Your mad theory – and until this moment I confess I really have thought it mad – might be right."

"It *clearly* wasn't an illusion,' DuVigo answered forcefully. "It had temperature and was as opaque from the inside as from without. An illusion wouldn't have either of those features. He has a Living Shadow under his control, and it dwells inside him. He used it against Darnaud's soldiers when they attacked him at the Sulfur Serpent Inn, and one of them died without a mark on his body. He used it in the courtyard at Sulmona and eight men died – admittedly with mortal wounds, but who can tell if the bleeding killed them or if some, or all, of their lives were consumed to feed the Shadow?"

"The report said some men were covered by that Shadow yet survived? That's rare – Living Shadows are usually deadly."

"DiUmbra's control may be good enough to choose who it kills and who it doesn't – indeed, his control *must* be that good, since it hasn't killed him."

"This is still speculation," Nivera ground out. "I cannot prosecute a case on speculation, the Judicial Branch will laugh at me. Give me facts."

"You've got several already. Consider these in the light of my theory. Dona Keldra experienced a spectacular magic malfunction during the DiUmbra troupe's performance at Millago's mansion, and as a result they ended their famous play early. Chisaad was present at that party and shortly after he chose Kirin DiUmbra for a charity apprenticeship, no explanation as to why. Chisaad was known to associate frequently with our ex-Governor, Ap Marn, who sold a boy into slavery who was probably this Kirin. Granted, as Royal Wizard Chisaad had to spend time with the Governor, but he spent a lot more of it after Prince Terrell arrived. Then barely a season later, Duke Darnaud accused this Kirin's adoptive father of murder in a suspicious circumstance. Then the Prince sentences the man to an unusually harsh term in the Sulmona mines. The next night Darnaud and Boerga attempt to murder this Kirin in his home and do murder his wife. Not two hours after that both priestesses at the Temple of Heavenly Peace – the DiUmbra family's temple – are murdered as well. The next morning Duke Darnaud accuses Kirin DiUmbra of doing it as part of a blood magic ceremony. The prince, who later turns out to have been replaced with an astoundingly lifelike golem, does nothing about all of this, despite substantial unrest in the Old City, a request for orders from the Watch, and the accusation itself. Does any of that add up to an answer in your mind?"

"A mad plot against the Crown," growled Nivera. "Involving Darnaud, Chisaad, Ap Marn, and probably Boerga. That's what Prince Terrell has proclaimed."

"Now consider what role Kirin DiUmbra played in all this," DuVigo continued implacably. "He disappeared after the murders and was not seen for days. The next report we have of his whereabouts comes from Sulmona, where he and Prince Terrell suddenly appeared riding on a carpet flown by an Ilvar Mage. The two of them immediately leap into a fight where Kirin DiUmbra spectacularly uses something that looks like a Living Shadow to save DiLione and incidentally kills Darnaud and some of his men. The Prince is wounded by an arrow during the fight, and something even stranger happens as a result. Whatever it is, DiUmbra plays a key role in it. Then the next morning the Prince and a stranger who must have been DiUmbra fly here on a carpet flown by none other than the Master of the Air himself, just in time to attend the King Choosing. Chisaad is burnt to ashes during it, and Terrell is chosen King, but the stranger is flown away by the Master before the Choosing formally begins. The Master flies toward the Old City, leaves his passenger somewhere, and departs back north. A few hours later Kirin DiUmbra, who had been four hundred miles away in Sulmona only the day before, fishes a tortured body out of the Charcoal Canal, and tells me a lie about where he's been."

She took a deep breath. "Time and again he does something bizarre, often in concert or conflict with powerful people, after years of seeming harmless and insignificant. He cannot be scryed, he can't be investigated magically by mage or priestess, he's an astounding cipher – but one that was held and likely tortured by a blood mage for two whole days. If I am right, he has carried a lesser demon within himself for a decade and reached such a rapprochement with it that it serves him in some not-so small, and sometimes deadly, ways."

DuVigo leaned forward, hands on the desk, and stared at her superior. "A young man with a unique talent who was surely tortured by a blood mage, a young man who the most powerful mage in Silbar found fascinating and yet tried to have killed. A young man whose soul may have been feeding a demon for a decade! A Prince who says Chisaad kidnapped him and put a simulacrum in his place that our own healers could not tell from the real man. Perhaps still cannot tell apart – and after whatever Kirin DiUmbra did atop the Hill of Sight, that prince let him leave with no acknowledgement. Why?"

"Disturbing questions," Nivera growled. "Something very strange is going on at the topmost levels of the men's side of our society."

"Exactly." DuVigo folded her hands and stared frankly at Nivera eye to eye. "Shall we women stand aside and do nothing about it?"

"No," answered Nivera. "Whatever you have planned for tomorrow morning, cancel it. I'm making us both an appointment to see Her Holiness before breakfast. If you are right about this Kirin DiUmbra, we dare not let him roam around free without knowing whether he is possessed – and knowing what influence over our new King he may be wielding."

CHAPTER 21: TERRELL

Evening, Second Day of the New Reign.

Terrell's stomach reminded him that it was past supper time. Around him Chisaad's tower bustled with excited members of the Council of Colors. Terrell held up a preemptory hand. "Enough arguing, Mages. Give me your best estimations. Mage White, you first."

"Chisaad's teleporter is still functional," the elderly Mage reported. "It appears that it only works between two fixed points that have been connected by some means that we don't yet understand, but once we replicate that means then I see no reason why dozens of points could not be connected to it, enabling rapid transfer about the kingdom. However, the power draw on the City Node to operate it appears alarmingly large. Unless that expense can be brought down to a more reasonable level, I fear there is very little practical use for it."

"It is activated by a word, one which I unfortunately do not know," Terrell told him, remembering what Kirin had said about the device during their arduous journey through the wildlands. "It's probably connected to at least two counterparts, one in Chisaad's office in my Palace and another in the ruined temple in Silbariki." Assuming Chisaad had repaired whatever damage Kirin did to it to delay pursuit. "I'll want you to figure out how he cast the one in the palace without setting off any alerts. I also need to send a force to Silbariki to take control of that one and properly shut it down and obliterate it. I dare not leave such a major magic unsupervised and operational when it draws on that corrupted node. Are you willing and able to undertake both missions?"

White looked sorely torn. "I have difficulty riding horses for any length of time these days, Highness, but if I could borrow Shimoor's riding litter, and take enough silver to be sure of protecting my journeymen and my guards from the creatures that lair in those ruins, I would be willing to undertake the effort."

"Done," Terrell answered. "I'll write out your authorization and dispatch orders in the morning. You'll receive a reward commensurate with the danger."

White looked pleased by that.

I wonder if the guards that Darnaud left there already tried to come back through it? Terrell looked around the room but there were no signs of anyone being here recently. *I'll have to send someone to arrest them too.* Belatedly he remembered that Darnaud had no heir of his body, so his duchy would ordinarily pass to his next-of-kin – which would be Duke Madoc Swansea DiCerai, and then a female cousin in Gwythlo, and then Terrell himself. *Madoc already has a better fief than Darnaud's, and certainly won't want Guglione for himself or his eldest son, though he might want it for the younger one. But I can't have such a major city ruled by a child! Non-royal women can't inherit territorial fiefs in Silbar, so I'll need to decide who to bestow it upon. Later.*

He returned his attention to the business at hand. "Mage Red."

"Two of Chisaad's golems are still working at keeping his house clean," Mage Red reported. He was a balding fifty-year-old, one that Terrell recalled was famous for his fascination with complex spells. The Council had put him in charge of maintaining the Navy Yard's construction spells, as there were few things more complicated than a warship. Only the prospect of examining Chisaad's secrets could have drawn him away from his normal tasks. "The insect-like cleaning golem is relatively simple and has been known to us for years. The more sophisticated greeting golem is at least an order of magnitude more complex, but not sufficient to deceive any competent mage or priestess even at first glance. The incomplete one in Chisaad's workroom is more complex still, and some of the spells anchored in it are extraordinary. May I examine it in detail, Highness?"

"Does that mean you want to take it apart?" Terrell asked.

"Don't do that!" Mage Green interrupted, aghast. At just under forty years old he was the youngest member of the Council, with an impeccable lineage and what Terrell recognized as a stubborn streak wider than the Bazaar. "We can analyze the spells in place if we're patient, but once you break it, we'll never figure them out!"

Red drew himself up in righteous annoyance. "I am the best forensic spell analyst in all of Silbar! I bloody well *will* figure them out even working from tiny scraps of spells!"

"I do not doubt you," Terrell quashed the argument. "But I want that spell suite mapped in detail before you attempt any direct tinkering. We only have this one partial example of the spells that Chisaad used to fool people into thinking his creation was me. My highest priority is figuring out a way to guard against a repeat, which means we must know how that trick worked. The Throne blasted the fake me to scraps, so this is the only sample we have left. I cannot afford any errors in this, Mage Red, and you are human and therefore vulnerable to error. I will not risk that." He turned to Green. "You will both work together on the mapping, then Red will do the dismantling."

Red looked mollified and Green looked excited, so Terrell decided to count that as a victory. "Mage Orange?"

"Highness, there are so many partly-done projects in this tower that we could spend a tenday just cataloguing them." Orange was so excited that his halo of gray hair quivered like a live thing. "To name three, I saw an advanced form of lens maker, a clever improvement on locator devices, and most important of all, a brilliant new method of lead separation. If applied to the Varone mines, whose production has been shrinking as they cope with ever-larger amounts of lead in the ore, that ought to wring substantially more silver out than the realm has gotten in decades."

Terrell perked up at that. "Increased silver production would satisfy my second priority. Can you figure out how to implement that one swiftly?"

"I already have," Orange boasted. "I have a cousin who works with the Varone refineries. Between us we could have their existing process revised in less than a season, and additional silver flowing before Midwinter with no increase in mining effort."

That would be too late to pay Osrick this year. *But it'll put me well up on next year's tribute.* "If you are successful, I'll pay you and your cousin each a five percent production royalty on the volume of improvement."

"Gladly, Highness." Orange bowed low, which didn't quite hide his glee.

Terrell didn't mind; harnessing human greed to serve the Kingdom's need was a king's most important job. Some of the other mages favored Orange with covert glares, but Terrell pretended not to notice. "Mage Yellow?"

"Chisaad's protection spells are all still in force and extremely sophisticated," Yellow reported unctuously. "It would take all of the Council acting together to pierce them and spy on the doings inside this tower. I dare to suggest that this means nobody else succeeded in doing so either. So long as you leave them operating, they should protect his secrets

184

for several more years. Time enough for us to thoroughly examine everything in here and catalogue it as you asked, Highness. But Chisaad was Acting Royal Wizard for eighteen years, and a prolific experimenter and note taker. It's going to take a tremendous effort to analyze all this material. I recommend that you assign several master mages to conduct the effort and appoint one of the Council to oversee it."

"I want to second my colleague's recommendation and add my own," Mage Purple interjected in a squeaky voice utterly at odds with his hulking appearance. "Chisaad kept secrets well, but there are extensive notes tucked away all over this tower. We need dozens of scribes in here to transcribe them all and put them into a systematic order. But those scribes cannot possibly be secured well enough to stop them from whispering about what they read. Every mage in town, and half the Hierarchy too, will want to pore over something or other. With such demand, there is no way to keep them all out. There would be bribery, family pressure, and forty degrees of seduction applied to extracting information. Instead I recommend that you welcome all the magic users of Aretzo and Silbar in, and spend your efforts on keeping the process orderly, since secrecy is hopeless."

Yellow's face didn't change but Terrell sensed the spike of resentment that he almost concealed. *Yellow sees those as manageable problems, especially if he's the manager.* Terrell resisted the temptation to smile. While Mage Yellow's ambition was understandable and to be expected, this was an issue that men might well kill over. From the look on Mage Blue's face he had also thought of that and was trying to signal Terrell not to choose hastily.

Purple makes a novel point, Terrell thought. *And a politically astute one, as Blue seems to know. There's no way to be sure what else in here might be as important as the silver refining idea. Wide access will put lots of mages at work finding whatever is to be found as quickly as possible. That will result in quicker applications and higher tax revenues, as well as win me more loyalty and less resentment, than a narrow favoritism.* His promise to Mage Orange now looked prescient, a useful guide to conducting business for the realm. *Chisaad must have kept the silver refining a secret because he knew Ap Marn would steal most of the increase.*

"I agree with your recommendation, Mage Purple," Terrell finally said. "But I will appoint a committee of three. You, Mage Yellow, and Mage Blue are assigned to implement it, and will make decisions collectively – and report them all to me the same day. Talk to my Mayordomo about borrowing some Palace scribes and see if the Hierarchy will spare a few as well. Put them to work in tandem so they can watch each other. When it is sorted out, you three will have first choice of interesting paths to follow, with the same financial split as I promised Orange. Then all the rest of the Council will each get to choose something. After that we'll open whatever else is here to competitive proposals from the larger body of mages."

From the look on Blue's face this was what he had hoped. Purple looked pleased and Yellow annoyed-but-accepting, so Terrell turned to the eighth and last man. "Mage Black?"

Black harrumphed. "You asked me to find any notes specifically mentioning Chisaad's apprentice. I've found a few in a thoroughly warded drawer in that desk." He pointed to a massive piece of furniture squatting in one corner of the tower room. "They don't appear to be encrypted. Other notes in the same drawer are definitely encrypted, those will require some tedious work to translate. The few hints I found in the first batch make me quite curious about the encrypted ones, particularly a mention of designing some tests for the apprentice, this young Kirin DiUmbra. Everything after that was encrypted."

Terrell sensed a subtle shift in the other mages' attention. Their general air of excitement had come to a quivering sharp focus at the words *Chisaad's apprentice.*

They know there is something highly unusual about Kirin, he realized. *I made a mistake by not telling Black to keep this in confidence between us. Now the other seven will badger him to share his findings — and whatever their rivalries, these men have worked together successfully for years. I must quell their interest immediately.*

"Mages," Terrell said in a louder voice. "Attend to my words."

Their attention shifted with gratifying speed. Terrell sensed Pen move behind him and heard the slight snick of Irreneetha being drawn a few fingerwidths from her sheath. *Good — this is the right moment for a little intimidation.* He took a deep breath and did his best to watch all of them as he spoke.

"You are all aware that Chisaad's former apprentice, Kirin Sule DiUmbra, has an unusual talent. You may also be aware that he returned to the City with me on a carpet flown by the Ilvar Master of the Air. DiUmbra did a great service helping me escape from the captivity imposed upon me by Ap Marn and Chisaad. In exchange, I granted him freedom from his indenture to the Royal Wizard and the right to pursue, or not pursue, further magical studies *at his own discretion*. All of you will refrain from attempting to influence him further except as he agrees. If he chooses to pursue magery as a profession, and chooses to study *with* one or more of you, he has license to do so and you have my blessing to teach him as best you are able. And if he chooses not to, but stays an acrobat, that also is his privilege, and you will refrain from badgering him. Any arrangements, with any of you or any other mage in this city, are to be strictly voluntary on his part."

Terrell turned back to Mage Black. "I assign you to continue gathering and translating all of Chisaad's notes concerning Kirin DiUmbra. You will provide them, and the translations, to me, and only me. I will then decide which information should be disclosed widely. You will consult directly with me, and only me, on any issues you discover.

You will have the freedom to pursue this investigation anywhere within Chisaad's tower, but all material other than that concerning Kirin is to remain under the control of the committee that I just appointed, which is to be headed by Mage Blue." Terrell broadened his attention to include the whole Council of Colors. "This is my decision."

Black glanced at his colleagues and answered, "We hear and obey, Your Highness."

Terrell watched with a sinking heart as eight smiling mages nodded like marionettes.

And I can believe that for as long as I want to fool myself. They'll obey until temptation overrules their wisdom.

Before that happens, I'd better figure out what I'm going to do about Kirin.

~ ~ ~

When Terrell returned to the palace, his path lit by mage lamps as the night settled in, he found Nortin so agitated the mage was wringing his hands. "Highness! It just happened again! Look!" He pointed to a new gap between the lines inside the glass. "That's four times!"

Terrell frowned at the huge pane. The four vacant bands added up to a tiny fraction of the whole, but they didn't look to be going away – and the new one was as wide as the three previous bands combined. *What did Shimoor call that? An exponential increase. That's bad.* "Are you dipping into the reserve power yet?"

"No Highness, in fact we're beginning to pour surplus power into the buffer," explained Nortin's evening compatriot, who had recently arrived and who everybody referred to as 'Silk'. "Most mage workshops have shut down for the evening, the draw on the City Node is dropping and there's plenty of slack in the flow." He looked sidelong at the glass monitor. "If those vacant bands fill in overnight, it won't even make a ripple in our typical consumption. If they stay the same, we'll still be well within the buffer's capacity, though it's rather annoying to waste some of it replacing such losses. If the gaps multiply until the reserve is drained . . ." Silk shrugged with a helpless expression on his face. "Then we are in new and uncharted waters, Highness."

"I sent messages to the Temple Collegium and to your library and your scholars," Nortin added anxiously. "They're here now and they have reached a preliminary conclusion."

Terrell looked to the assembled group of scholars that Nortin beckoned to join them. It was composed of two men and a woman. "Share it with me."

A middle-aged priestess with a matronly figure answered first. "Highness, we believe that the spirit that sleeps deep inside the Aretzo Node is being prodded to awaken."

An elderly scribe from the royal library, thin as a rail and gray from head to toe, added, "Each flicker of loss to the Node's manna-flow represents an increase in the sleeping wight's awareness, and thus its mana consumption."

A beardless scribe with a rotund frame finished with, "Once it becomes fully awake, Highness, it will be able to divert the Node's power to its own purposes and leave the city to starve."

Terrell swallowed a vulgarity and made himself take a deep breath before he spoke. "How is this prodding being done?"

"We do not know, Highness," the priestess answered. "Our strongest suspicion falls on a blood sacrifice, due to the speed and arrhythmic pattern of the power draws."

"You mean a blood mage is doing this?"

"Not quite, Highness," the eldest explained. "A mage or a priestess is surely doing it, but not to attract a demon familiar such as blood mages typically seek. Instead a sacrificial victim's pain is being poured quite expertly into the wight itself, to break the spells that bind it."

"I thought the sleep spells on it were unbreakable!"

"Not easy to break, certainly, but not impossible either," the rotund scribe answered. "Azerin and Zablock's struggle over Silbariki provides us with a particularly horrible example of the consequences if anyone is so mad as to try what we suspect."

Oh no. Terrell remembered the slimy touch of the corrupted node under the ruined city. "That nightmare under Silbariki was caused by my ancestors?"

"One of them, at least," The elder librarian said diplomatically. "The wights that dwell in the mana streams flowing out of our world can be manipulated by various means, and those means shape their subsequent behavior. Our Silbari ancestors chose to lull our wights into slumber, where they cannot be a threat to anyone and consume relatively little of the mana flow in which they dwell. If instead one were to addict a wight to human pain and suffering, or feed it demons, it changes, becomes more active in the service of the controller, but also consumes more of the mana flow around it. Such a wight can be used offensively, as is done in the north; I believe you experienced one of those on your journey south to claim Silbar?"

"Ah! That's how Klairveen made those monsters to attack us!"

"Exactly, Highness," the rotund scribe agreed, nodding his head till his triple chins quivered. "But such an awake and active wight shares comparatively little of its mana stream with human users. Instead it tends to consume much of the power itself, though it can be bound to use that power in the service of a human master."

"Or Mistress," the priestess drily observed. "That binding is what the Druids do in the north lands. We of the Hierarchy deny them that choice here in the south."

"A Druid is trying to awaken the Aretzo wight – and enslave it to her will," Terrell realized. "Is it Daugala, the Chief Druid?"

The priestess shook her head. "We doubt it very much, Highness. She is a capable manager, but neither powerful nor skilled as a spellcaster. Someone more talented than Daugala is doing this."

Terrell rubbed his forehead and cursed silently to himself. "You mean Boerga."

"We very much fear so," agreed the priestess. "My colleagues in the Hierarchy have been searching for her since your decree of Banishment was announced, but at present we have no idea where or how she is piercing our guardian spells. No one should be able to do that. Even the Hierarch herself could not do it alone, it would take most of the Temple's Inner Circle to cast such a spell."

"Do you have any inkling of her location?"

"We do not. She has found a way to hide from us magically as well as physically."

"Nortin! Silk!" Terrell turned to the mages. "Have your crew seen any sign of her in the glass?"

"No, Highness," Silk replied regretfully, while Nortin shook his head and again wrung his hands together. "We cut her line off from access to the node many days ago, and it has not returned."

"But she could be counterfeiting another mage." Terrell resisted the temptation to curse aloud. "Wouldn't she have to draw a lot of power from the node to penetrate the protections? Look for the largest power draws and check to see if they are really coming from the mages they are supposed to!"

"We t-tried that already, H-Highness," Nortin answered miserably.

Silk added, "So far, nothing. If Boerga is active within the city, she's either using stored power from silver or sulfur, or is utilizing another source."

"Such as blood magic," Terrell realized. "Which will addict the wight to destruction."

"Not immediately, Highness," the plump scholar interjected. "It has slept long; it will not wake rapidly no matter what she does."

"But every death or demon she sacrifices to it will poison it a little more," the priestess warned. "At some point the corruption will become irreversible, and we do not know where that point is. If the wight is corrupted before it fully wakens, the chaos of its rise will be severe. Not just lost access to power for spells, but distortions manifesting in normal spells too. Each day the people of this city cast more than a million spells and minor magics. Consider what might happen if healing suddenly becomes hurting and repairing becomes breaking?"

Terrell visualized the Harbor magics gone awry, ships smashing into piers and sinking. Worse, fire protection spells igniting what they were meant to protect. Aretzo burning.

"What can we do to forestall this?"

"I notified the Hierarchy of our deduction as soon as my colleagues and I reached it," said the priestess. "By now the priestesses in the Sonorium will have begun spells to lull the wight back to sleep. That should delay its awakening at least a little while."

192

The older scribe spoke up. "We will search the records to see if there is another way to help."

"Good." Terrell nodded curtly. "Go and do your best. The survival of this city may depend on your efforts."

The three bowed and left. Terrell noticed that different mages were on duty behind the glass pane, the earlier ones evidently gone to rest. "You should get some sleep, Mage Nortin. I want you rested and ready for tomorrow, when we may need to try whatever choices the scholars and priestesses discover tonight."

Nortin gratefully bowed and departed, and Terrell did the same after a long searching look at the glass. Pen followed him like a shadow, as always. When they reached the domed hall before the bridge that led to the Royal Apartments, Terrell abruptly turned aside.

"Open it," he ordered the guards at the Hill Door. They hastened to obey.

Pen gave him a dry look. "You want to climb the Hill in the dark?"

Terrell's stomach chose that moment to rumble again, and he sighed. "Not particularly, but I have a feeling that I'd better not put this off. And you're the one who nags me about getting more exercise."

Pen said nothing more but simply followed Terrell onto the Five Hundred Steps. Full night had fallen over the city, Madness was aloft and near full while Calm hadn't yet risen. Pen drew Irreneetha and her white light helped illuminate the steps as they climbed. Terrell had to stop on the seventh landing for a breather, staring over the city while he panted. Temples rang the ninth bell and the rumble of heavy delivery carts full of stone, brick, and tile, banned from the city during daylight hours, echoed from the streets below.

He used his magesight, and again the city was almost too bright to look at. Tens of thousands of magic users; hundreds of thousands of spells. Boerga could be hidden anywhere.

My city, Terrell thought, letting his sight fade. *My people. My duty.*

He returned to climbing.

At the top, the Stone Throne gleamed whitely in the moonlight. Irreneetha's light seemed wan and pale compared to it, and Pen sheathed her. Terrell strode across the little plaza and paused with one foot on the dais that supported the snowy marble chair.

It hasn't yet been two full days since I became King, he thought. *And already I face a challenge that may presage a disaster for the realm.*

Terrell took a deep breath and sat in the seat. Previously it had seemed just a little too large for him, on the verge of being outright uncomfortable. It seemed even more so tonight.

I AM NOT HERE FOR YOUR COMFORT, the Voice informed him drily.

I'm beginning to realize that. What are you? Terrell asked directly.

YOUR KIND CALL ME A SPIRIT.

Do you dwell inside the Hill's node?

FROM YOUR POINT OF VIEW, YES.

And from yours?

I LIVE EVERYWHERE IN SPACE AND TIME, IF I CAN BE SAID TO LIVE AT ALL.

Live at all? What did that mean? Terrell reminded himself not to get distracted. *Tell me about the wight that sleeps within the City Node.*

IT IS OLDER AND MORE WEARY THAN I. IT CRAVES SLEEP.

Is it being awakened?

YES.

By Boerga!

THAT NAME IS ASSOCIATED WITH HER ESSENCE.

Where is she?

NEARBY, AS YOUR KIND MEASURE SPACE.

I need to find her!

THEN YOU MUST SEARCH THE CITY.

Can't you tell me where she is?

I DO NOT PERCEIVE SPACE AS YOU DO. YOU MUST FIND HER YOURSELF.

Terrell swallowed his irritation; at least it was talking to him. *About the wight in the City Node – how is it being awakened?*

BY FEEDING IT HUMAN SUFFERING.

Terrell's gut tightened as he remembered Kirin's memories of being tormented by Gerlach. *Blood magic?*

THAT TERM IS ASSOCIATED WITH THOSE ACTIONS.

Is this what happened at Silbariki?

THE DETAILS WERE DIFFERENT, BUT THE RESULT WOULD BE SIMILAR.

Terrell remembered the monsters stalking those ruined streets. The Aretzo node was three times the size of the one under Silbariki. He imagined Aretzo equally devastated, the works of ages crumbled into mud and ruin and its people dead or fled. *I cannot let that happen! But how do I stop it?*

STOP FEEDING PAIN AND SHAME TO MY SIBLING.

To do that, I need to find Boerga.

YOU ALREADY HAVE EVERYTHING YOU NEED TO DO SO.

It really wasn't going to be more helpful, Terrell realized. Whatever motivated it, the spirit in the throne clearly did not think like a human being. *Very well,* he thought at it angrily. *I will find her and stop her.*

The spirit evidently did not regard that pledge as needing a response. Terrell got up and headed for the Five Hundred Steps, Pen dutifully following behind him. At the top step Pen drew Irreneetha again to light their way, and Terrell glanced back at the Throne gleaming in the moonlight.

WE SPIRITS ARE CLAY MOLDED BY YOUR HUMAN MINDS, the spirit unexpectedly volunteered. WHEN THE KILN OF YOUR CHOICES HARDENS US INTO THE PATTERNS YOU CHOSE, THAT FIRING CANNOT BE REVERSED. ONLY CONTAINED, OR BROKEN. CHOOSE WELL.

I will, Terrell answered firmly. *And . . . I thank you.* He turned his face to the long descent, and supper and bed. Tomorrow promised troubles aplenty.

CHAPTER 22: BOERGA

Evening, Second Day of the New Reign.

The crows came straggling back by ones and twos throughout the evening. By the time the eighth bell rang from the city's temples all seven were back at Boerga's rooftop aerie. Two had completely lost their control spells and only the company of their mates brought them to her.

That answers two questions, Boerga thought glumly. *They can follow him, and he can detect them when they do. And kill my spells.*

She replaced the vanished spells on the two – that required replacing the silver rings since the magic had been completely stripped from the original metal. Then she left the birds to feed and descended the stairs to the basement again, thinking.

I don't dare follow him myself. I'm too conspicuous in this city without the Herdae disguise, but a Herdae wouldn't loiter around watching someone. Gorsyn wouldn't be as obvious – except to DiUmbra, who would probably be able to see his disguise spells instantly. Now that he knows someone is spying on him, he'll be alert for any watcher.

Her subterranean sanctum was richly aromatic with pain and fear. Gorsyn was busy washing and dressing himself after another round of raping the sacrifice. The halfbreed had been bent over a crossbar in the rack for further humiliation as well as Gorsyn's convenience. An angry red welt circling the lad's neck showed where her brother had expertly applied the leather semi-garrote to increase the victim's fear and pain.

Now tears dripped even as fresh blood runnelled down the half breed's legs to drip on the floor.

"Clean that up," Boerga told her brother.

He reached for a bucket and sponge with a discontented grunt and got to work.

While he labored, she wrapped the silently weeping youth in her aura. His nerves were already burning with pain and rage and fear, a delicious brew to feed to the wight. She healed him just enough to stop the bleeding – it wouldn't do to lose him at this point. Then she expertly jabbed several of his pain centers to force him to scream, which made Gorsyn laugh and added to the youth's humiliation. The rack, and Gorsyn's brutal handling, had dislocated his arm-joints. She opened herself to the halfbreed's pain and luxuriated in it.

Then she also opened her magesight to the currents beneath the Skin of the World.

Demons surged and clawed at her. They fought each other to break through. Fanged mouths snapped at her, every one of them ravenous for the tempting bait she held out to them. Heedless of her preparations, the spirits of chaos sought her soul with a lust beyond the mortal, while the veil between the worlds slowly thinned.

Very close – I'll have one of them before morning. My demon traps are ready.

Idly she prodded fresh pain from the sacrifice until he wept thin cries of despair. She thought about traps, which lead to the subject of bait.

"Of course!"

Gorsyn looked up as he polished a bloodstain off his boots, and said with lazy, sated detachment, "What is it, sister-mine?"

"Instead of chasing DiUmbra, we'll snare one of his abundant kin!" she declared. "That will lure him to me on my terms."

His wife, she thought, *would have been perfect for that, if Darnaud hadn't killed the bitch.*

But there were plenty of others to choose from. One of the younger ones would do well – first she could use him as bait, and then as a sacrifice right next to DiUmbra. Two strong young men of that lineage would make an excellent meal to feed to the awakened wight, and thus bind it to her.

"How?" Gorsyn asked eagerly.

"You're fetching the third halfbreed tonight?"

He nodded, looking pleased. "Yep. Got a spy inside the Mercenary's Guild, checked his assignments. When he gets back from the job he did today, I'll let him eat and drink to dull his senses, then when he's relaxed, I'll ensorcel him to follow me here. Nice and peaceful as any lamb headed to slaughter."

"Good, but afterward you and I will seize another prize." She explained the plan.

Gorsyn gave a happy chuckle. "Two sweet victims for me? Such a treat you offer, sister! I'll get right out and be back with the first as quick as I can."

Boerga grunted in satisfaction as he hurried away. Gorsyn could be counted on to work hard and reliably to earn his pleasure.

Once she had all the power of the Aretzo Node at her command, the halfbreed Prince and the yellow bitches could also be fed to the wight. Gorsyn would enjoy degrading women as much as men, and there were enough of them to last for years.

CHAPTER 23: KIRIN

Night, Second Day of the New Reign.

Nightfall. The seventh bell died away as Kirin left the Sulfur Serpent Inn. Sevan had wanted to come with him.

"I'm stronger than you are," he'd argued. "And bigger. Trouble will stay away from us if we're together."

His wife Carlai's face showed just how much she disliked that idea, so Kirin hastily turned him down. Stett intervened to side with Kirin, and while Stett and Sevan argued Kirin ducked down the back stairs. He got safely out of sight before Sevan reached the back door.

Kirin visited three more women on the list of Merrias, with increasingly hostile responses. He finally realized that the alleys of the Old City were darker than ink to ordinary folk, and having his pale bruised face appear at their doorways just plain scared them. Searching for baby Grigor was useless after nightfall.

After reluctantly accepting that, he wandered, wondering whether to start looking for Boerga again. But there were too many people awake and using magic. The tenements and occasional private houses still glowed with busy spells. He would have to kill an hour or more before the city's glow died down enough for him to see clearly.

A pair of laborers made their way home from work late. Hands on their belt knives, they stared nervously from side to side in fear of footpads. Kirin avoided them and cut across one of the loops of the Serpentine. A tramp of booted feet, a clink of metal on metal, and he rounded a corner to find an armored man with helmet, sword and familiar battered shield making his way homeward.

"Aeddan," Kirin called from the other end of the alley. "Wait up for me."

The mercenary guard paused with a surprised grunt, shield half-raised in reflex. "Kirin?" he asked tentatively, his sword at the ready. "That you?"

"In the flesh," Kirin agreed, and hurried into the moonlight so that Aeddan could see him. "You on a job?"

"Done now, and on my way to get a beer and some supper. Care to join me?"

"I already ate, but I've got a couple lepta burning a hole in my purse. Where do you drink?" The DiUmbra men rarely went farther than the tavern on the Serpent's ground floor.

"The Knotted Strings. It's right across the street from my building. Watch your step through this patch ahead, the pavers are busted." Aeddan felt his way along in the dark, feet sliding over the broken stones.

Kirin stepped over the holes and kept even with him without comment. On the other side Aeddan picked up the pace and took them through two more alleys before they regained the broad Serpentine. The moon of Calm was a thin crescent newly risen above the eastern horizon while Madness dwindled as he sank toward her. The shadows of masts and bowsprits patterned the Serpentine's cobbles as the winding street rounded the inland end of the Charcoal Canal. Kirin suppressed the ugly memory of Rian's body when they crossed the little bridge over the north fork.

The Knotted Strings had an open door indifferently covered by a big curtain of dangling strings. Each strand had been knotted in four clusters of four knots to honor the Great Seraphs. The room inside was surprisingly large and boasted two dozen rough plank tables. Aeddan appropriated one and called to the bartender, working in a corner behind a half-wall. A three-branched oil lamp hanging on a chain from the middle of the ceiling hosted sputtering flames that barely lit the room. Kirin pulled a stool over and sat across from Aeddan, who'd found a stubby bench.

An ancient brown crone brought full mugs and a bowl for Aeddan, with coarse flatbread to shovel up the dubious contents. Those appeared to be mostly fish cooked into mush, with lentils and beans and enough garlic to kill a small animal. Aeddan wolfed it down like a starving man. Kirin nursed his beer, which at least was passable, and looked around the room. He noticed two more halfbreed men in the far corner. Their voices were quiet as they bargained over a knife in a leather sheath on the table between them. A quartet of halfbreeds in the opposite corner finished their meal, lit a taper from the lamp, and began dicing by its smoky light. Someone else snored in a chair in a third corner, hat pulled down over his face.

"A lot of the halfbreeds in my apartment building spend time here," Aeddan volunteered around a mouthful. He swallowed and added, "Only place in this part of town that will serve our kind."

Kirin pointed to the bargainers. The younger looked to be about his own age but the other boasted at least three times the years of either himself or Aeddan. "Are they mercenaries too?"

"Kaghar is; he lives on the floor below me. The old guy he's trying to buy from used to be, but he's a used weapons dealer now. He's got a room somewhere around here but does all his deals from that table. I've heard that his mother was the bartender's mother's sister." Aeddan pushed his empty bowl aside and took a long drink from his mug. "Ahhhh, that filled up a hole. I had an orange on my way to the guildhall this morning, but nothing since."

"Were you working for the same client all day?"

"Yup, a Fehdar wine merchant, I've worked for him before." Aeddan swigged his beer again.

"Didn't he feed you at midday?" Kirin didn't know much about the life of mercenary guards but had heard they were hired by the day, generally from sunrise till whenever the client went to bed. He took a pull from his own mug.

Aeddan snorted. "Fat chance with that one. He squeezes every dhoba till it squeaks." Then he shrugged philosophically. "At least he pays on time, and the place where he usually has lunch with his merchant buddies keeps a bench outside for guards like me to wait on. Today they even gave me a mug of decent ale to drink. I call that a good day."

"Showing off your low standards again, Aeddan?" said a mocking voice. Kaghar had left the weapon seller's table and paused by theirs on his way towards the door. The young mercenary moved with a lithe prowl that showed off the two knives at his hips.

"You don't do all that much better, Kag," Aeddan amiably replied, waving his mug.

"Enough that I don't need to share a room, and can buy me a woman every tenday," Kaghar boasted, while surveying Kirin up and down. "Who're you, stranger? Family throw you out?"

Kirin resisted the temptation to bristle at the young mercenary, who stood no taller than himself and had sandy brown hair and slightly pointed ears. "No. Name's Kirin DiUmbra." He didn't offer his hand.

Kaghar stared closer. "DiUmbra? You one of the acrobats?"

"Yup."

"Huh. What's a pretty boy like you doin' slumming with Aeddan here?"

"That'd be my business," Kirin answered evenly, liking the young mercenary less with every word. Kaghar had the edgy pushiness of someone looking for a fight, which was the last thing Kirin needed right now.

Kaghar smirked at them both, leered at Aeddan. "You sellin' a little on the side, Aed? Or buying? I thought you was a dedicated Sathist!"

Kirin's back stiffened and his Shadow stirred under his heart. He pressed it back down despite the temptation to show up this overconfident punk.

Aeddan scowled. "Don't be a bigger prick than you have to be, Kag. Kirin's a friend."

"Close friend, eh?" Kaghar giggled. "You two have a fun night together!" He strolled off before Kirin could think of a retort.

"Sorry about that," Aeddan offered quietly. "Kag's a nasty bastard sometimes."

Kirin swallowed his anger. "No worry," he managed, and then the clue dropped like a brick and he stared at Aeddan. "Oh."

Aeddan sighed but didn't flinch from his gaze. "Yeah. He's right about the dedicated part – I vowed myself to Seraph Sath last season. I wondered if you'd guessed."

Kirin remembered the Sathist section of the Sulfur Street Baths, run by the religious order devoted to the warrior angel who ruled the bodily love of men for other men. Seraph Sath served under Father-Seraph Haroun's command in the wars of heaven. The married men in the Bath's main section sometimes made rude jokes about the rumored practices of the Sathists, but the ones he'd seen swimming in their section of the pools had behaved with ordinary decorum and looked like any other former soldiers. "No, I didn't guess. You're the first halfbreed I ever got to know. There aren't any others in the acrobats' guild." He hesitated for a moment, staring at the young man he'd begun to think of as a friend. "Are you trying to woo me, Aed?"

Aeddan twisted his mouth in a bitter smile but didn't look away. "I swear by the One God above, I hope I have more decency than to flirt with a man who's mourning his wife." He pointed at Kirin's freshly scarred sideburns. "I didn't intend to make any moves on you. And if I did without knowing it, then I'm ashamed of myself. I just want a friend. Rian was a good friend, even though he didn't incline to Sath, but now he's dead."

"Jerril?" Kirin asked curiously.

Aeddan shrugged ruefully. "He's a decent roommate but we're not really friends, we just share a place to live. And he's pining for some girl he wants to bed, though she's full blood and won't give him more than a distant 'good day.' Poor fool. I hope he's home by now and snoring in his own bed instead of staring at her window. Last time he did that the Watch beat him up and threw him out of Cliffside."

"I understand how he feels," Kirin answered slowly. "Maia was the best part of my life. Every night I spend without her, I ache so bad, sometimes I wish I was dead just to be with her again. But we had a son together, and now he's missing, left with a wet-nurse whose family names I don't know."

"Aha! That's why you were looking for a woman named Merria."

Kirin nodded. "Yeah."

Aeddan took a drink, then looked at him shrewdly. "So that's why you're out on the streets tonight?"

"I was, but it's too late to pester people in their apartments. Now I'm looking for somebody else."

"Want help?"

Kirin wondered what Aeddan would think of his Shadow, quickly decided he'd rather not risk finding out, and shook his head. "No. I can handle it, and it's better done alone."

"Your choice." Aeddan gave him a dubious look — the mercenary was half a hand taller and two stone heavier than Kirin, his strength brawny rather than sinewy. "You got any practice walking around Aretzo in the dark?"

"No," Kirin admitted. "But it's not like it's hard."

Aeddan snorted. "Not hard to get your throat cut either. There's some out there who'd do it just for fun. Don't forget whoever grabbed Rian."

"That's who I'm looking for," Kirin told him.

"Dung on a plate! Kirin, are you crazy? It's gotta be someone with a powerful magic talent, to have taken Rian. You move well, but I can tell you haven't got much practice as a fighter."

"True, but I've already got too damn much practice killing men." Kirin scowled. "And it wasn't a man who killed Rian, so I'll have to defeat her another way."

Aeddan's face struggled with incredulity, then the last phrase caught the mercenary guard's attention and his eyes widened. "You said 'her.' You know who killed Rian?"

Kirin sighed. "Dung. I gotta learn to watch my mouth better."

"Do you?" Aeddan insisted, hunched over the table and staring at Kirin. "Don't leave me guessing, tell me the truth."

Kirin twisted his mouth like he'd bitten a lemon. "All right. I can't swear to it, but let's just say I've got a really strong suspicion that Boerga had a hand in it."

"Boerga? You mean that nasty Druid that Prince Terrell banished? I heard about her in gossip at the Merc Hall."

"That's the one. Madame Ymera traced her magic on Rian's body."

"Madame – Holy Humping Harlots, Kirin! Ymera and Boerga?" Aeddan stared so hard Kirin thought his eyes might pop out. "You keep crazy company!"

Kirin shrugged. "There's been a lot of craziness going on around me lately." *And inside me,* he thought but carefully did not say. He could feel his Shadow stirring under his heart.

"Craziness? You're talking about the most dangerous witches in the city!"

"Yeah, I know finding Boerga is going to be tough." Kirin made a dismissive gesture. "But I've got pretty good magesight, and strong magic users like her shine like a torch even when they're sleeping. Once people go to bed and the city quiets down, I can do some serious looking."

Aeddan gave a small snort. "You think she's gonna do you the favor of sleeping in front of an open window? She'll be behind stone walls for sure, else the Prince would already have found her and arrested her." Then, when Kirin didn't answer, Aeddan added in a whisper, "Oh. Father Haroun defend you. You've got a way around that too, don't you?" His eyes had grown enormous.

Kirin hoped they didn't fall out of his head. Aeddan, he decided, was a little too smart. "Aed, I can't talk about this anymore. I need you to trust that I know what I'm doing."

The young mercenary stared at him for a long minute. Kirin stared back and forbade himself to fidget.

"There's more to you than my eyes can see, isn't there?" Aeddan finally said.

"Yeah. Please don't ask." Kirin held out his right hand.

Aeddan hesitated, then took it in the Warrior's Grip and solemnly shook it. "All right. But, if you find her, remember he was my friend. I wanna know what happens."

"I'm just going to tell Ymera where she is. They can fight it out, and believe me, the Witch Queen of the Red Street will collect your blood-price for you. All right?"

"It's a deal." He let Kirin's arm go, then swigged the last of his beer. "Gonna be hard to sleep."

"If I succeed tonight, I'll tell you in the morning," Kirin promised. "But odds are it'll take me more than one night – Aretzo is big."

"Ain't that the truth."

They got up and made their way out into the black night. Kirin caught a glimpse of glowing spells as someone ducked into Aeddan's tenement, possibly frightened by the sudden appearance of two men of unknown character and obvious armament. Aeddan clapped Kirin's shoulder with a rough fist, squeezed once, and turned for home without another word.

Across the city, Temple bells rang the ninth hour as Kirin hurried off into the Sump. Before he rounded the next corner, his Shadow covered him head to toes in a moving blot of darkness.

He wandered through streets and alleys like a black fog. Tapers burned in tenement rooms, a few even lit outdoor balconies where folk lingered to enjoy the evening cool. His Shadow made the walls translucent to his eyes, let him see parents soothing ill children to sleep. Men and women coupled with happy abandon in their own beds, rousing

208

memories of Maia that stabbed his heart. He averted his eyes from their pleasure and sought for darker forms of magic.

Ten thousand spells kept flies out of windows, drove rats out of buildings, mended cracked pottery and lit lamps. They did nothing to stop his vision but in their sheer exuberant numbers they overwhelmed it. Neighborhood Temples were bonfires of power where Priestesses healed the sick. Under the streets, spells pulsed as they shoved water up into fountains and pushed sewage out into the harbor against the tide. Aretzo was a giant tangle of magics twining from the rooftops down into the very foundations of the city. He strained his magesight until he could even sense the enormous Node under the city, for the first time seeing it as a separate thing from the streets and buildings.

That only made the cacophony worse. The sheer power in the city hurt like staring into the suns. He closed his magesight entirely before it overwhelmed him and leaned against a six-foot-high garden wall. Overhead the branches of somebody's apricot tree rustled in a passing breeze. He rubbed his aching eyes and thought. The farther he tried to look through his Shadow, the worse the confusion. Maybe he needed to see less, rather than more?

This time he barely peeked through the Shadow. The building across from him gradually went transparent, until he could see all the way through the back wall. He stopped there, stared at it for a moment. Nothing but ordinary household magics. The tenement next to it was the same. He shifted a few steps up the alley and did it again on the other side, studying one building at a time. A glassblower's shop gave him pause; even at rest the magics used to manipulate the glass were strange and beautiful. Then more tenements, occasional houses, more shops, bakeries, a candle maker, and on and on. He soon got practiced enough that he could saunter slowly up a street or alley and examine every building as he passed.

Twice Kirin surprised lone men prowling near late-night taverns. He made no effort to be quiet as he walked, so both heard him approach, turned, and saw the billowing Shadow. The speed with which they fled was the most gratifying feeling he'd known since killing Darnaud.

That thought stopped him in his tracks. His heart felt like a rope tugged two ways at once. He was glad the murderous Duke was dead, glad he had avenged Maia's death so personally, but he didn't want to be the kind of man who gloried in killing. After a struggle he set the disturbing feeling aside and kept walking.

He found magic schools he hadn't heard of, odd workshops making devices he didn't recognize, an illusionist-mage putting on a splashy show in a tavern, and a few priestesses working late to do extraordinary healings after the city's distracting background magics had quieted down. But nothing resembled the horrible taste of blood-magic. The midnight bell tolled, then the bell for the first hour. At last he gave up and slumped against a piss-smelling tenement wall for a few breaths. He yawned so wide he heard his jaw crack.

And heard a frightened voice echo down the alley, saying, "Blacker than night and billowing like a storm cloud! It was headed this way, Sargent, I'm sure of it!"

Time to stop for the night. I don't wanna have to explain myself to a Watchman.

Kirin drew his Shadow back inside himself and pushed off the wall, hurried into a branch alley and hid behind a bakery's charcoal bin. Two men passed the alley mouth with only a cursory look before they moved on, one walking with the distinctive tramp of a Watchman. Kirin waited several breaths to be sure they were gone, then went back the other way, tired and discouraged. He'd searched the Sump most of the way to the north city wall and found nothing.

When he plodded back to the Serpent's outside stair, he discovered tapers being wasted as Papa and half a dozen other family members swirled about, most in different stages of undress.

"What's going on?" Kirin asked, stepping out of the shadows.

"Kirin!" Carmella gasped, rushing up to hug him hard. "Thank The One you're back! Is Attir with you?"

"Attir? No, I went alone." He patted her back as he looked around at the worried faces. "What happened?"

"We don't know," Papa said somberly. "He took a bucket down to the fountain to get some fresh water for your mother before he went to bed, just after the tenth bell." He held up one of the family's water buckets, empty. "He didn't come back."

CHAPTER 24: AEDDAN

Dawn, Third Day of the New Reign.

Aeddan muzzily swam back to consciousness. His ears were ringing, his head ached, and his arms felt like they were being dragged out of their sockets. *What in the Nine Hells? I only had one beer!*

He tried to remember what had happened. He recalled saying farewell to Kirin, remembered entering the hallway of his tenement, and remembered heading for the familiar stairs in the dark. Then a stirring sound, somebody coming down the first-floor hallway towards him, a flash of blue light in his eyes – and nothing. He vaguely remembered walking after that, but not where or why.

Dung! Somebody sorcelled me!

Then he realized he was bound upright in a wood frame. Through the light of a muted mage lamp he could make out stone walls and a stone floor, a room roughly twice as long as it was wide. Another wooden rack faced him across several feet of space and a third stood to his right, making three sides of a square. The one across from him held a naked young Silbari man, snoring. To the right another naked young man, half-blood by his skin and looking familiar –

"Aeddan!" Kaghar hissed. "You awake?"

"Am now," Aeddan muttered back, suddenly aware that he was also naked. Icy dread ran its fingers down his spine as he realized what that must mean. "Wish I wasn't."

Kaghar made a sound between a laugh and a sob. "Same here. Look to your left."

Aeddan did. Something lay on the floor where the fourth side of the square would be. It took him a moment to realize it was a man, and only a little longer to be sure the man was dead. The dull dark sheen of congealed blood painted the wrecked body and held his gaze so thoroughly that it was a while before he recognized the corpse.

"Jerril," he blurted, feeling gut-punched. *Both my roommates are dead.*

"Yeah," agreed Kaghar raggedly. "Look what's been done to him. You know what that means?"

"We're in the dungeon of a blood-mage." Aeddan kept his voice flat with an effort. He tested his leather-padded iron manacles. They were tight but not enough to cut off the blood to his fingers and toes. He tried straining against them as strongly as he could, but they didn't budge. A thick wooden rod ran across the middle of the rack right about the height of his navel and prevented him from rocking his weight forward to overbalance the device. Another one behind the small of his back did the same duty there. He gave up testing his bonds just before his wrists and ankles started to bleed and returned his attention to Kaghar. "How long you been awake?"

"I don't know." Kaghar's voice was jittery and he trembled. "Feels like more than an hour, but I haven't heard any temple bells ring. Salim take it, Aed, I haven't heard anything but you two breathing!"

Aeddan looked around, battling fear by keeping his mind busy. "Look at those stone walls – this has to be a basement. The roof is brick, and vaulted, so this is likely somebody's old wine cellar. Walls might be three-four feet thick. I don't see any windows and only the one door." Which was made of thick planks and looked like it fit tightly,

213

more evidence that this had been a wine cellar. "No wonder we can't hear anything."

He scanned the floor, which had been paved with square brown flagstones. Except over in a back corner behind Kaghar, where he spied a big circle of stone set in the floor, close to a yard across. A drain? It seemed large for that, and the stone cap looked too solid.

There was only one piece of furniture in the room. A massive wooden table stood against the wall behind Jerril's body, with polished silver instruments arrayed on it in a neat row. Some were pointed, some had blades, and a few had hooks. They, and the body, were directly in Kaghar's line of sight.

No wonder the poor bastard is shivering like a leaf in a breeze. I'm not feeling too steady myself.

Aeddan deliberately looked away from the corpse and table to study Kaghar. The mercenary had a lean whipcord build that promised deadly speed in a fight. The room was cool but not uncomfortably so, yet Kaghar shook like a man with a chill. His skin had gone unusually pale, even the tanned parts of his arms and legs and face. At first Aeddan wondered if he was hung over, but he hadn't seen Kag down more than one beer at the tavern. Then he looked closer; there was a disturbing waxiness to the mercenary's skin-tone.

"Kag, what happened while I was snoring?"

Kaghar let his head droop until Aeddan could barely see his face. For a moment the thin half-breed said nothing while shivering shook him so strongly that his rack creaked. Then his trembling lessened, and he blurted out, "The blood-mage was here, him and a Northern woman. She put a spell on me that's making me feel sick. Then he . . . told me things." Kaghar stopped talking and shivered even harder than before, with a few gasps thrown in. Aeddan realized the hardened young mercenary was straining to stifle his weeping.

Aeddan knew the common gossip about blood-mages. They would torture their victims to death to attract a demon, which the mage would snare so he could force it to supply him with power. If he failed to catch one, and the demon didn't eat him instead, the mage would just try again with fresh victims. Evidently Rian and Jerril hadn't been enough, so a triple attempt was planned. Kaghar must be designated as the starting sacrifice.

For a moment Aeddan was selfishly glad it wasn't himself. Then shame slapped down his relief and he thought about what he was going to be forced to witness. Kaghar was an irritating bastard, but Mercenary Guild gossip said he did his work honestly and didn't take too much pleasure from beating up pickpockets and footpads. He surely didn't deserve death by torture.

The Silbari man's snore broke as he began to wake up. Aeddan took advantage of the excuse to look away from Kaghar and study the stranger. He was slender and very strongly muscled with light brown body-hair that was still more fuzzy than coarse. Clearly young and new to his manhood, likely still a virgin. Aeddan felt sorry for what the youth was about to experience before he died.

Stop that! he told himself, angry to find despair already creeping into his thoughts. *We're none of us dead yet.*

The Silbari youth's head jerked up with a gasp and he strained against his bonds, then stared wildly around. There was something familiar about him but Aeddan couldn't place it.

"Don't scream," Aeddan advised him quietly. "It's unlikely to be heard, and if it is, it'll be by the damned mage that took us all prisoner. I'd rather put off meeting him as long as we can."

The youth looked around, visibly bewildered and trying to make sense out of his surroundings. He flexed against his restraints and tried to tear himself free by sheer strength.

"Don't bother with that either. I'm probably stronger than you and I can't break mine."

The youth looked at him, tried to speak through a dry throat, swallowed painfully and then managed to croak, "Where am I? Who are you two? What's going on?"

"Let's see, that would be: in some mage's cellar. My name is Aeddan and that's Kaghar on your left. I'm sorry to tell you that I'm pretty sure we're slated to be sacrificed for blood magic."

Shock and horror stormed across the youth's face. For a moment Aeddan thought he'd lose his composure entirely, but the Silbari youth fought his way through to a stunned calm punctuated by heavy breathing.

"What's your name, stranger?" Aeddan asked, hoping to keep the lad out of a complete funk.

"Attir," the youth replied. "Attir Sule DiUmbra."

Aeddan goggled at him in stunned surprise. "You're one of Kirin DiUmbra's kin?"

Attir looked surprised and possibly a little jealous. "He's my next-oldest brother. Brother-in-law. My uncle adopted Kirin when I was a kid, and later he married my sister."

Aeddan found himself grinning idiotically. *The odds of being rescued just went up!* "I'm very pleased to meet you, Attir," Aeddan told him with great sincerity.

Before Attir could reply they heard the bolt being drawn back and the door flung open. By the gasp and whimper from Kaghar, the two that entered were the blood-mage and the Northern woman. Kag hadn't mentioned that the man was also a Gwythlo, with pale skin, yellow hair, and pointed ears.

Northern man and northern woman, Aeddan thought with a sinking sensation in his belly. *Oh dung! She must be Boerga. If she's with him – we're not facing one blood mage, but two. This is gonna be bad.*

She flicked a finger and the mage-lamp brightened. The man set a bucket of water and a washrag on the table and began undressing. She casually stepped over Jerril's body and came over to inspect the three of them, starting with Aeddan. Her gaze was so cold, he felt chilled just from meeting her eyes.

Be polite to this bitch, he told himself. *Or she'll promote you to the head of the line for Hell.*

"This one will be second," she announced suddenly, then started casting something complicated on him.

That wasn't much better than going down the oubliette first. Aeddan scowled, thought about protesting or maybe even weeping to see if it would slow her down. Before he could make up his mind, the Druid finished her spell. A vast chill sucking sensation settled on his skin, soaked in and left him gasping. Now he understood what Kaghar had been feeling.

Boerga grinned at him and prodded his belly. "Plenty of life in you, half-breed trash. You'll feed the Great One for hours, maybe even days."

She turned her attention to Attir. The youth shrank from her gaze. She laughed and cast what looked like the same spell on him. "Frightened already, darkie? You've barely begun to know fear. Watch Gorsyn work and feel what's coming for you."

Then Gorsyn, stripped now, stepped up to Kaghar. A few cranks on wheels and pulling of levers had Kaghar bent forward over the middle bar of his rack. The Gwythlo mage pulled on a pair of gauntlets with odd spiky fingers. Kaghar shuddered as the torturer ran gauntleted hands over his torso and buttocks. Little red streaks appeared everywhere the gauntlets touched the mercenary's golden skin. Aeddan's own skin felt as if needles were stabbing him in the same places. Attir twitched violently.

Aeddan gasped. "You're making Attir and me feel what he does to Kaghar!"

Boerga smiled. "Tripled pain, tripled shame. Together you'll provide an excellent feast."

Gorsyn crooned to Kaghar as he took up a position behind him. "Remember what I promised you, boy?"

Kaghar bent his head up to stare desperately at Aeddan. Attir did the same, both turning to the biggest among them for guidance, solace, any help at all.

"Try to relax, it'll hurt less," Aeddan counseled, knowing how desperately inadequate his words must be for Kaghar. For all of them.

CHAPTER 25: TERRELL

Dawn, Third Day of the New Reign.

The sixth bell had barely faded as Terrell hurried through the Palace's dawn-lit corridors with Pen at his back. Fantillin, the Palace Majordomo, scurried at his elbow, saying "I summoned the Council of Colors and your scholars as you instructed, Your Highness, as soon as the duty-mage reported the latest, er, disruption. At least some of them should be here already." Fantillin gestured and the doors to the Glass Office swung open to admit the three of them.

Terrell's gaze raked the long room in one sweep. Tension filled the place like an invisible fog, clinging and hampering. Two new gaps had appeared in the giant glass, the first one twice as big as the previous ones and the newest one double that. More than a foot of the pane was now blank from top to bottom. A fading black wedge filled half of the biggest gap.

"Highness!" Mage Nortin cried, hurriedly bowing. The three scholars and four of the Council were also there, bowing like Nortin, and like him in various stages of dress. Mage Green hadn't bothered with actual clothes, just a loincloth and sandals, while Orange had simply put a belt around his knee-length sleeping smock. Red rubbed sleep out of his eyes and Blue had mismatched shoes and his hair in wild disarray. Yellow and Black hustled in moments later, somewhat better dressed, with Purple and White on their heels.

Terrell pointed at the black wedge, which had suddenly darkened and then begun to fade again. "How long ago did this one start?"

Nortin indicated the hourglass perched next to the crystal pane. "A bit more than half an hour ago, Highness. You can see how wide it is. We sent for you immediately."

"And the other?"

"After midnight, about halfway to the first bell." Nortin waved at the upper part of the gap, corresponding to a point a few hours ago on the vertically moving pattern of power-usage displayed in the glass. "It arrived as a burst, see how it pushed the adjacent lines aside? Something sudden happened!"

"A victim was surely killed by the Druid, Highness," a scholar stated solemnly. "The burst marks a sudden increase in the sleeping wight's consciousness, which I believe was driven by that murder. Then the sleep-spell reasserted itself and the death faded out of the wight's awareness, but not completely. The repeated tortures and deaths are gradually awakening it."

"Gradually? This seems shockingly abrupt. Explain." Terrell pointed to the thicker wedge, which had darkened again instead of fading. Everybody else looked at the elderly scholar so intently that the man gulped.

"I theorize that it represents multiple victims tortured at once, Highness." The scholar nervously rubbed his hands together. "Undergoing continuing torture, too, which explains why the wedge continues to widen."

Terrell shifted his gaze to the priestess, who looked frustrated. "I concur, Highness. The Hierarchy has increased the effort devoted by the Sonorium priestesses to casting sleep spells on the wight. Unfortunately, they don't seem to be having any effect. We suspect that the perpetrator has found a way to either divert or, much worse, invert our spells

220

into waking the wight instead. We're currently searching for a way to change that, but it is a slow and difficult process if we are to avoid making matters worse."

"Worse?" Pen snorted and muttered, "How?"

"Please believe us, Highness," the rotund scholar implored, deliberately ignoring Pen. "This could indeed get worse, and very quickly too, if the perpetrator can harness the Temple's own efforts to augment her own. Clearly much forethought went into this maneuver. We must not fall into a trap while trying to stop Boerga and find ourselves instead providing the wherewithal she needs."

"Yet that only makes it more imperative that we stop this sooner," Terrell declared. "Find the victims, find the torturer, and end it."

"That," Mage Blue pointed out, "Is what the Inquisition is for, Highness. They've been notified. They surely must be doing something."

The priestess shrugged helplessly. "I am not a member of the Inquisition, Highness."

Terrell wheeled to look at Fantillin. "I'm going to see the Hierarch."

The Majordomo had anticipated the command and flicked a prepared message construct into being. "When, your Highness?"

"Right now."

Fantillin gulped and sent the message.

CHAPTER 26: HIERARCH

Morning, Third Day of the New Reign.

"You've made a compelling case for indictment," acknowledged Fenecia Crasset Demorian, Hierarch of the Faith. She squinted in the early-morning light slanting through the tall windows of her office and counted the six bells ringing from the Tower of Time. She favored this room on the fourth floor of the Mother Temple for her serious work, cluttered though it was with ancient relics and modern reminders of the reach and responsibilities of the Faith. Her stomach felt the lack of breakfast, but when the Inquisition said something was urgent, she took them at their word.

The two women standing obsequiously before her were identically dressed in the black-and-yellow quartered robes of the Inquisition. "Then you'll grant our petition for his arrest?" asked the older one, the elderly Septissima who was the Chief Inquisitor and wore seven stars on her own wimple. Her most senior subordinate, First Inquisitor Dona Nivera DuNimes, stood at her superior's right with her hands folded and her eyes meekly downcast. Fenecia knew an act when she saw one. Under that bland surface, DuNimes hadn't been so excited since she won the First Inquisitor position.

I'd bet that she actually wrote this indictment, Fenecia thought sourly. *And obviously believes we must act at once. But there are complicating issues here that I cannot ignore.*

The Hierarch didn't answer the question immediately. Instead, she walked to the nearest window of her private office. It looked down three floors into a little walled garden known as the Loggia, filled with flowers under towering pine trees more than a century old. Kirin DiUmbra's sudden prominence touched on the great cleavage that ran through Silbari society.

I do not control the King, and that is a good thing, she thought. *But I am responsible to The One for tending to him and all the Twenty, to ensure we are governed as competently as may be. This possible demonic influence is too great a threat to be ignored. Such evil cannot be allowed to gain even an indirect foothold in the Royal Court. But is arresting the boy the right answer?*

"I will think upon this and give you my answer presently. Now. What word on the wight?" she demanded more harshly than she'd intended.

The Chief Inquisitor didn't stir so much as an eyebrow at her superior's tone. "We visited the Sonorium on our way here. The duty-priestesses spent all night working on the sleep spells. They confirmed to me that their efforts are being sabotaged or evaded, and they do not know how. They tell me that new efforts are under way to determine a counter and put the wight back to sleep, but they are at a severe disadvantage until they know how the awakening is being done."

It would have been highly unbecoming for the Hierarch of the Faith to roll her eyes and groan, but she nearly did it anyway. "And you?"

"The Inquisition has also had a busy night hunting for the perpetrator," the Chief Inquisitor stated evenly. From the dark circles under her eyes she hadn't gotten much sleep. "We have determined that the sabotage is not being conducted from within the grounds of the Druid's fane, nor from any other temple in Aretzo, including the Dissenters, the Purists, and all of ours. It is not coming from the home or workshop of any major Mage. We agree with the Collegium and palace scholars' collective opinion that Boerga is involved, but we have not yet located her; that search continues. And we are considering the possibility that her disruption, and young DiUmbra, may be subtly related."

"Related?"

At a slight hand movement from her superior, First Inquisitor DuNimes broke into the conversation. "Holiness, we have all underestimated Boerga, to our peril. We cannot dismiss the possibility that Kirin DiUmbra's demon may somehow be involved with her success at infiltrating the wight's protections. Wittingly or not. Clearly, she wanted to gain control of him or kill him. If she had a demon-trap ready, then killing him and taking his demon prisoner may have been her prime goal. If that demon has inhabited the boy for the last decade without revealing itself through spreading chaos, then it must have unparalleled self-discipline. The lack of such discipline has always been our chief aid in defeating demons. One able to practice strategy and patience will be a far more dangerous foe. Since she has found a way to wake the wight despite our spells, we cannot disregard the possibility that she can capture even a very wily demon. With an enslaved demon of this one's suspected capacity at her command, her ability to corrupt or even control the wight would be greatly strengthened. We do not know if that could even *be* countered."

Good Seraphs, help us all, the Hierarch prayed, horrified by the vision of the Druids in control of the Aretzo Node and its wight. For the last two decades the two faiths had been locked in a struggle for the hearts and minds of the Empire's people. The Druids had made no secret of how they wanted to end that battle – with the bloody martyring of every Silbari priestess and complete obliteration of the Faith.

She forced herself to suppress her emotional reaction and look at the situation dispassionately. All the arguments were reasonable, but incomplete. The sheer uncertainty of the situation overshadowed normal procedure. *If there is anything* normal *about a young man harboring a demon for, The One God help us, ten years! But if his presence is the key by which thrice-damned Boerga is getting at the wight, we absolutely must stop that immediately.* "Do we know if he is aware of this particular potential of his talent?"

"Alas, we do not," the Chief Inquisitor answered. "He is impossible to observe magically, and if we observe him by eye we can only do so intermittently, unless we are willing to reveal our interest by attempting to physically follow him. I have delayed that revelation because he is such an unknown. The report of him killing several men in Sulmona while inside his Shadow indicates that he can be exceedingly dangerous if he chooses. If we are to ask questions that get to the heart of this matter, we must have him under enough control that he cannot either flee or attack – or be captured by Boerga. Which means he must be under legal arrest inside our stone walls."

Either we question him directly, or we do not, the Hierarch thought. *Terrell has said that he released this Kirin Sule DiUmbra from his apprenticeship to the Royal Wizard in gratitude for the boy's help defeating Chisaad's treason. But that raises a new host of questions, none of which have clear answers. If young DiUmbra does harbor a demon, I must make sure it can neither aggravate our problems with the wight, nor be used by Boerga to do us further injury.*

She turned to the waiting Inquisitors. "You have convinced me that letting him wander free is too risky. But!" She held up an admonishing finger. "Treat this young man cautiously. He is to be held securely and questioned thoroughly, but not abused in any way. I will make a separate determination as to whether this case should go forward to trial after I have seen the results of your questioning, and after I have spoken to him myself." She scribbled her name on the order and handed it over.

The Inquisitors bowed and hurried out, triumph plain in DuNimes' stride. Fenecia sighed; zeal was necessary in that work, but it carried its own dangers. Still, better one innocent man be upset and frightened by spending a few hours under Temple arrest, than have a powerful demon in Boerga's hands.

And if DuNimes is right, what mischief has such a demon been building toward? A decade to plan, and if any creature of chaos actually can plan, it would have to be this one. Is it possible that Boerga is the tool and DiUmbra's demon is using her?

She hoped it was all a mistake, but her prudence told her otherwise. *There are too many coincidences here. Some great Power is moving behind the surface events that I can see. But for good or for ill?*

Before the door fully closed behind the departing Inquisitors, her secretary slipped in. The woman's eyes were wide, and she carried a little T-shaped stand holding a glittering purple-and-gold message construct. Only the King's secretary and the Palace Majordomo were allowed to use that pattern in those colors. Hierarch Fenecia sat in her chair and activated the spell, reading the cursive writing-on-the-air with the ease of long practice. Her heart sank as she finished the deceptively simple request for an immediate meeting.

What is the boy-king up to now? He might have heard some gossip about the Inquisition's plan to arrest DiUmbra. She absently tapped a finger while her secretary waited.

I shall treat this as an opportunity to explore his thinking.

"Send a message back immediately with my assent. I will see him alone as soon as he can get here," she told her secretary. "Have the Loggia prepared for our meeting. And bring me some breakfast."

~ ~ ~

Terrell gazed up at the frescoed underside of the enormous dome of the Mother Temple. Several devout early-morning supplicants prayed near the huge bronze brazier in the center. There an eternal fire sent a trickle of white smoke up through the ocular at the dome's top. The kneeling folk looked tiny in the vast room. A chanting priestess with a censer and two acolytes paraded through the shadows of the eight colossal statues supporting the vast curve. The morning sunlight slanted in through the eastern side of the circle of arched windows ringing the dome's bottom edge. The long beams of light reminded Terrell unpleasantly of the ruined temple in Silbariki where he'd been imprisoned. He blinked away the memory – these frescoes glowed where the sun's fingers touched, lovingly cared for and vibrant in the morning light. He was not in a dead place, but in the living heart of the Faith of Silbar.

Living, but Boerga certainly doesn't intend to let it stay that way. Nor will she leave me alive, or any other half-breed in the city. Or any Silbari Priestess able to oppose her.

Pen hovered at his elbow, one hand on the pommel of his sheathed sword and looking as solemn as if someone had just died.

"Her Holiness will see you now, Your Majesty," a gray-haired priestess announced.

"Highness," Terrell corrected her. "My half-brother the Emperor –"

"We know, Your Majesty," the priestess blandly interrupted. "This way please."

I don't get to tell the Hierarch how to talk, Terrell remembered as he shut his mouth and followed. *Or her minions.*

Pen stayed at his heels through frescoed corridors and down a flight of broad stairs until they reached an inner room on the ground floor, windowless and lit by a mage lamp. There the old priestess fixed the bodyguard with a steely gaze and, in a voice that would have been grandmotherly if it hadn't been uttering a command, said, "Baron Sir DiLione –

227

sit." She pointed to a chair. "Stay here." Her gaze made it clear that this wasn't a suggestion.

Pen hesitated. Terrell knew that, technically, the Hierarchy had no authority to order his servants around, especially his Hands. But to show good faith, he nodded and gestured to the chair. *Is this a test for him, or me, or both?* he wondered. Then, when Pen sat and the woman flicked an approving eye at him, he decided, *Both.*

She led Terrell through a short corridor and another door that opened into a shaded courtyard ringed by tall pines and crowded with lush greenery. Some plantings grew in beds under the trees, some in ceramic pots strewn about the pavement, but all had an artfully complex air that hinted at meanings in every choice the gardener had made. Four carved pillars upheld a slatted gazebo roof shading two comfortable chairs on either side of a small table that held only a bell. Both chairs had been positioned to face a round little pool where a fountain burbled. One chair held a woman dressed in flowing white robes.

"Hierarch," Terrell spoke first, and inclined his head. "Thank you for seeing me on such short notice."

"Majesty," she replied, with an equal head-bow and enough emphasis on the word that Terrell was sure the title was no more in error than the secretary had been. The Hierarch waved him to the empty chair as she said, "Welcome. Do sit. My old bones are less comfortable standing than they used to be."

More signals, Terrell thought as he strode to the chair and sat. *The Hierarch wants to establish her freedom from Osrick's whims by not-so-subtly standing on father's Edict of religious freedom. Very well.*

He had tried to organize his thoughts during the long walk across the Middle and Outer Courts and down the Processional to the Mother Temple, with squads of troops clearing his way and Pen carrying Irreneetha unsheathed and upright until they entered the holy precincts, where custom and good manners required all weapons be sheathed. Now he began with a restatement.

"Hierarch, you have been told that the banished Druid Boerga is suspected of trying to raise the sleeping wight under Aretzo through blood-magic."

"Yes, Majesty. You have been told that we are attempting to lull it back to sleep and finding the process unexpectedly difficult." She fixed him with a sharp-eyed stare. "There appear to be never-before-seen complications."

"So the scholars have said," Terrell acknowledged, meeting her stare. Her eyes were deep brown; he wondered what she thought of his own blue ones. "My mages are doing what they can to ease the drain on the Node. But if the current rate of loss continues, we will run out of stored mana before noon, and have to begin cutting back on use of magic in the city. Shortly after –" He broke off that train of thought and shrugged. "Put simply, we must find her and stop her today. I can handle the stopping part if someone can find her. Do you have a way to do that?"

"Not yet, though my people are looking for one. She appears to have either planned this well or had aid from some unforeseen quarter. Or both."

The brown eyes probed his and Terrell realized she was using some sort of passive magic on him. The crown on his head felt warm. He almost tried to block her, but if she was trying anything hostile the crown should do that for him. Instead he deliberately relaxed, acquiescing to her investigation. *I can't be surprised that she wants to know more about me,* he reflected. *Before this moment she's never met me outside the bounds of ritual.*

"If we had some idea where to look, I could set my troops to hunting for the Druid," he suggested. "It wouldn't be as disruptive to the City if you sent a number of priestesses along. But better to turn Aretzo upside-down than lose control of the City Node to Boerga."

She made an agreeable motion with one hand while never shifting her gaze from his. "Unfortunately, we face the same problem that you do. We can eliminate a few places, and have, but most of the city remains, and Aretzo is very large. If you, and my priestesses, searched ten rooms every minute, we would still be searching three days from now."

She can calculate numbers as well as I can, he thought bleakly; holding her gaze was becoming harder. "We don't have three days. Judging by the speed with which Boerga is awakening the wight, we may not have ten hours. Still, we must try."

"What is Kirin DiUmbra?"

The question was so abrupt that Terrell broke their staring contest and looked away. *Does she know he's my twin? She can't, can she? Unless the Hierarchy had a hand in keeping his survival secret? But they didn't do anything to prepare him for the Choosing, didn't train him at all, and didn't stop that horrible blood-mage from abusing him . . . and now she knows I have something to hide where he's concerned.*

Terrell met her gaze again. "I don't think I can fully answer that question, Hierarch. I don't know him well enough. He has some strange powers. He used them to save me from the ugly death that Chisaad and Ap Marn had planned for me. He offered me his life if I would free his father from Sulmona. He even gave me his own knife with which to execute him. When I refused to kill him, he saved my life again, four times. The last was on the Hill where Chisaad would surely have killed me while seizing the throne for himself. For such extreme services I granted Kirin freedom from any royal claim." He couldn't help the tinge of defiance that crept into his voice. "Honor required no less."

230

She raised an eyebrow at him. "Offered you his life? That would only make sense if he had committed a crime. What are you concealing from me, Your Majesty?"

"Nothing that endangers the kingdom." *So long as Kirin's parentage stays concealed.*

"You don't know that," she observed. "You only want to believe it."

"True," he admitted grudgingly. "Yet time after time he passed up opportunities to do me or the realm ill. Instead he did good, at great risk to himself."

"Seraph Salim is the master of betrayal, and his consort Desrey the mistress of deception," the Hierarch reminded him. "You are a young man yet, with limited experience. Are you certain you have not been too trusting?"

Terrell remembered Kirin pressing the Crown down upon his head, the sudden shocking presence of it, the staggering weight of humility in Kirin's mental voice as he declared, 'This is what I am.' *Oh my brother, you proved yourself then beyond all possible doubt. But Osrick must never know, so I cannot tell anyone — not even the Hierarch.*

Terrell's face hardened and he deliberately reached up and touched the Crown on his head. "Yes, Hierarch, I am certain. It took until this moment for me to truly understand how much he deserves my trust. I dare not tell you more."

As he had hoped, she stopped her verbal probing. All Silbaris knew that the Crown had been given to the line of Kings by the One God, who occasionally sent visions to its wearers. Terrell hoped that playing on that legend wasn't offensive to The One.

She hesitated, still staring at him and probing him magically. He endured it for two breaths, then pressed his advantage. "To the needs of the moment. I can call out my troops, but I need your priestesses to help them find Boerga and stop her blood-magic before she corrupts the wight. The sooner we begin searching, the better our odds of success. Will you aid me?"

She gave him a wintry smile. "Of course, Majesty." She lifted the bell from the table and rang it.

~ ~ ~

Terrell breathed a sigh of relief as he left the Temple complex and descended the thirty-two marble stairs toward the Processional. *Now to organize the search. And may The One be kind and our efforts yield fruit quickly!*

But the City remained as large as ever. He tried not to be daunted by the odds.

Pen strode along at his left hand with Irreneetha once more unsheathed. The bodyguard glanced back over his shoulder for a moment. The royal guards had to hurry to keep up with them both. Behind them streams of priestesses were leaving the Temple to follow. Turning back, Pen asked quietly, "Did you get all that you wanted?"

"I got what I asked for," Terrell replied tersely. "Let's hope it's enough."

He wished he had Kirin with him. Maybe his strange powers could help – and, Terrell realized, he should warn his twin that the Hierarch was much too interested in his unusual abilities.

I have to organize the search first, then I'll call him mind-to-mind. I can tell he doesn't like the experience of having my voice inside his head, but he needs to know that his hope of staying anonymous is threadbare. And I need to figure out what to do about it.

~ ~ ~

"New orders, Hierarch?" the chief of the Inquisition asked.

"No," answered Fenecia. "Continue as planned. Arrest young DiUmbra and bring him to me for questioning. Something is very odd. I intend to know what it is."

"As you will, Hierarch." The older priestess bowed and hurried away.

CHAPTER 27: KIRIN, TERRELL

Morning, Third Day of the New Reign.

Boerga wasn't hiding anywhere in the Sump, or the whole dockside district from Sulfur Street to the Navy Yards. Kirin would stake his life on that. He'd stared through every building, every rickety pier, every docked ship and small boat, and none held the glow of blood magic.

He sagged onto a bollard at the landward end of the Cinnamon Pier and thought hard. Rian's body had been floating in the Sump. The canals interconnected enough that he could have gone in the water anywhere along Aretzo's waterfront, and still ended up where he'd been found. But if Boerga wasn't somewhere close to the harbor, then how did she get his body into the water without being spotted?

The fourth bell rang. He rubbed his aching eyes. Where was she hiding?

A City Watchman strolled by, whistling while giving him a blatant look-over. It was early for someone to be here for work, but too late for even the most stubborn footpads to be out. Kirin yawned, while in the caupona behind him someone opened a second-floor window and dumped their chamber pot into the canal. Someone else banged about inside the kitchen getting ready to open for business. The combination of those mundane morning activities seemed to convince the watchman that the half-breed with the big black eye was merely waiting for breakfast, and thus legitimate enough to be ignored.

A watchman. There was something important about a watchman. Kirin scowled and thought. Sargent DiCerat, that was the one. He had said something about how Rian's body might have got into the canal –

Down the Big Asshole. Aretzo's North Sewer.

Kirin wasn't sure how large that tunnel was, but he had heard that it drained a huge swath of the City. It must be plenty big enough to carry a body. He pushed off the bollard and ran north along the Serpentine. If he started on the uphill side of the twisty water-side road, anywhere north of the Tomb, he would be sure to cross over the North Sewer somewhere. Checking every building along it would be slow, for the sewer drained a much bigger swath of the Old City than that occupied by the docks.

The solstice is twelve days away. If she's going to sacrifice Attir then, I ought to have enough time to search every building in the Old City.

It proved to be a constant struggle to follow the spell-girdled underground tunnel. It dived beneath buildings and cut long curves under the Old City's crazy quilt of streets. The sewer had an alarming number of large branches, many big enough to carry a body themselves, so he had to check every building along each branch. He persevered through the fifth bell and the sixth, gradually eliminating a swath of the Old City.

Unfortunately, as people awoke they activated more and more magics. Not long after the sixth bell faded away he had to give up, defeated once more by Aretzo's extravagance. He hid his Shadow and began asking people if they'd seen either the Druid or one of the Merrias living in the neighborhood. If he could just find baby Grigor and be sure the Druid didn't have him, he could stand to go back to his family without finding Attir.

No. Mama and Papa are counting on me. I will find my younger brother.

He rubbed his eyes and kept looking.

~ ~ ~

The cobbler's wife sniffed at Kirin's question. He suspected it was as much for his too-pale skin, bruised face, and hollow-eyed gaze, as for what he asked. But he was the one who needed the woman's cooperation, not the other way around. He choked down his resentment and tried to look pleading.

"No," she finally answered. "I ain't heard of any lost baby, or any found baby neither. No Druids and no baby. Every baby 'round here belongs right where it is." She stared down her long bony nose to show him what she thought of halfbreeds who mislaid their babies. "I can't help you."

He bowed his head and thanked her for her time, turned and found his way out. As he left, the cobbler and his two apprentices peered suspiciously at him through piles of leather and half-finished boots. Kirin clenched his jaw and said nothing. He'd lost count of how many places he'd begged for word about either the murderous Boerga or his missing infant son.

Grigor! he thought with silent anguish. *Where are you? What did Dona Abbie do with you? And Attir! Are you with him? Does the Druid have you both?* The cruel possibilities haunted his thoughts.

Outside the dark shop, autumn sunlight blinded him for a moment. He stopped to shade his eyes and get his bearings. The next shop to ask was straight across the street –

"Kirin Sule DiUmbra," said a heavy female voice. "You are under arrest."

A priestess in robes quartered in yellow and black stood on the cobblestoned street not two yards in front of him. Six golden stars winked on her starched black wimple – a Hectisima from the Temple Inquisition.

"What the –" He bit his tongue; profanity wasn't likely to make a priestess feel kinder toward him. "I mean, why, Dona Hectissima?"

She answered grimly, "You are suspected of involvement in blood magic."

He gulped. That could get him burned at the stake.

Two more priestesses similar enough to be her sisters stepped up on his left and right, triangulating him. All three held their bare hands raised palm-toward him, prepared to stun or even kill with their magic if necessary. Behind each of the three stood their mage-husbands with spells at the ready to tangle his feet and pin his arms to his sides. Behind *them* stood six armored Temple Guardsmen with drawn swords, and six more with spears.

The bottom fell out of his stomach as he realized the truth. *Somebody in the Hierarchy wants me real bad.*

For an instant he hesitated. This awesome display of power would have cowed even a swordsman with Haroun's Gift, the immunity to magic that prevented mages and priestesses from dominating the people of Silbar more than they already did. The Inquisition couldn't know how useless any magic was against him.

If Priestess' spells really were useless. He was mostly-sure that his Shadow could protect him.

But if he fought them now and won, then he'd have to run. Run without finding his infant son or Attir, without lingering to grab his few possessions, without saying goodbye to what was left of his family. If he started running now, there was a very good chance that he could never stop. The farthest ends of the World might not be far enough to escape the Hierarchy's pursuit.

Slowly he raised his hands and bowed his head in submission.

They chained his arms behind him with magical manacles and hustled him through the streets of Aretzo. At the Mother Temple they put him in a cell with a steel bar across the bronze door. It had been ensorcelled in six different ways to prevent escape. He could devour the spells with a thought, but he was dismally aware that the door had been made by simple smith-craft. The bronze and steel would still work just fine. He awkwardly sat on the edge of the bedframe, then let the Shadow within him eat the magic in the manacles. They crumbled nicely, and he flung the pieces into a corner and looked around.

The place was at least clean, with a covered chamber pot in a corner. The bedframe, a plain wooden chair, and a rough table completed the furnishings. The only light came down narrow tunnels where the back wall met the ceiling. They led up at a slant to a window a good ten feet away – he was surprised at how thick the Temple foundations were. Four of these window-tunnels had been set in a row, each one maybe a foot wide. He would not fit through any of them.

If I want out of here without revealing my Shadow, somebody is going to have to get me out. He knew someone who might. But did he dare ask him?

He forced himself to stop and simply think. To remember that shining mind that had touched his so intimately during their long trek through the desert. The prince had overflowed with eager questions, his thirst for knowledge as strong and frightening as some force of nature. But underneath there had been more, the essence of the man. Not soft, no, there was a core of steel there able to plan, and also able to kill. Kirin remembered the fight against the Duermu assassins and Terrell's blade-sharp focus on dealing death when that was the price of both their survival. But the

Prince had also been kind, especially the way Terrell's soul had enfolded and supported Kirin's own during his grieved mourning for Pieter and Maia.

He really is my brother.

The words echoed in the shadowed halls of Kirin's mind. *My brother. My brother. My brother will help me find my son, and my little brother. I am not alone.*

He took a deep breath and reached through the back of his mind for his twin brother. Outside the eighth bell began to peal across the city.

~ ~ ~

"I've called out the City Watch, every man on duty or off," Terrell told his military commanders, pacing before them in the Middle Court where he had ordered everyone to assemble. The usual traffic of petitioners and taxpayers had been crowded to the sides to make room, with grim soldiers holding spears crosswise to enforce the royal command. "They should be here in a candlemark, and they know the streets better than most of my soldiers. By the time they get here I want you to have divided the troops into patrols of six men each. Make sure at least two men with magesight are in each patrol and equip every patrol with a summoning device. You'll match the patrols to every member of the City Watch and to at least one Hierarchy Priestess, two if we can manage it. Have the Watchman lead them through his usual area. The priestesses and the men with magesight are looking for any sign of the Druid Boerga, or any unusual female magic user who is not a Priestess, or any evidence of blood magery. When they find her, the men must *not* try to seize her – Boerga will just kill them. They must try to block her escape routes and summon my battle-mages and the Inquisition priestesses, who will have the Council of Colors for support."

The five battle mages assigned to the Silbari Brigade gulped and looked hopefully to the Council. Eight decisive nods came back — there was nothing, Terrell reflected, certain to motivate a mage quite like the threat of permanently losing his magic supply.

"Make it happen," Terrell ordered his men. "Once Boerga is found, the Council will trap her and stop whatever she is doing to the wight. Then the Inquisition will take charge of her."

Two of the high-ranking mages and priestesses cast doubtful glances at each other. A couple of the married pairs rolled their eyes in a mute appeal to Heaven.

Terrell impatiently declared, "If Boerga takes control of the wight, she'll certainly use it to murder anyone who could oppose her. You'll all be on her list of prime targets, as will I. Either work together, or be destroyed separately."

That ended the hesitation. Terrell turned aside to confer with Pen as the leading magic users of Silbar began following his orders. But before he spoke a word, one of the duty mages from the Glass Office rushed up to him.

"Highness!" the mage shouted as he approached. "It happened again, only different!"

"Let him approach," Terrell snapped to the guards who had blocked the man's way. Then aside to Mage Blue, Terrell commanded, "Organize the search as I have directed, Blue, and track me while you're at it. When she's found, you are to send me a message-construct immediately." Turning to the Palace mage, he ordered, "Show me."

The duty-mage bowed so low that he nearly lost his balance, then hastily led the way toward the Glass Office. Terrell followed with Pen at his side and his ring of guards hurrying to keep up.

"Is there any way for Irreneetha to find Boerga?" he asked Pen.

Pen shook his head unhappily. "Yes, but her range is not much longer than any of the priestesses. She uses me to perceive the world around her, only augmenting my senses with her magic. I'd have to walk pretty close to the room Boerga is in, assuming she's behind stone walls, in order to find her."

"That's still better than not trying," Terrell decided. "We'll join the search."

Pen drew the soul-sword. Her white light had an angry red edge now.

At the Glass Office, the usual mutter of mages and scribes was muted to a frightened rumble. Mage Silk silently pointed to the end of the monitoring pane. Nearly a tenth of it was blank now, save for a fitful black zig-zag twitching like inverse lightning. Blood-red sparks cascaded through the emptied spaces.

Terrell hissed in fury. "She killed someone, didn't she?"

"Yes, but we fear worse than that, Highness," the scholar priestess answered. "We think she has also fed it at least one more demon, probably three or four. The corruption, and the waking, will advance faster now."

The jagged black lightning pulsed as if in affirmation and shoved a few more colored lines aside. Terrell forced his gaze away from the hateful evidence and looked at Mage Silk.

"We're tapping our reserve to fill the gap, Highness," the mage reported grimly. "It won't last another hour. I can divert some of the Hill's power to help and maybe win an extra half-hour, but the link was never meant to do that. Forcing it anyway is clumsy and we cannot divert very much through the connection. I recommend that we start right now to shut down workshops and curtail magic use. If we don't, it'll be chaos as spells fail without warning."

"Do it," Terrell ordered. "Start with the Navy Yards, Gray Fort, and city wall spells first, then the workshops, the harbor, and cut off the water and sewer system and healing temples last. Warn my people as best you can."

"Yes, Highness." Silk bowed and began issuing orders.

Terrell left the room and started back through the busy Palace corridors, his guards sweeping people out of his path by their sheer presence. They entered a courtyard paved in intricate mosaics of black and white tiles around a six-sided fountain just as the eighth bell began to ring.

Terrell?

The voice in his head was as unmistakable as it was welcome. Terrell stopped next to the fountain. "I've got to think for a moment," he told Pen, and sat on the broad stone rim. Pen took up a stance in front of him, sword facing out. The guards surrounded them both and the fountain too.

Terrell closed his eyes, stilled his thoughts, and opened his mind to that inward call. *Kirin? I'm here.*

~ ~ ~

Terrell! Kirin babbled in relief. *Thank you for answering me, Highness. Chisaad and Darnaud accused me of blood magic before they died and now the Inquisition's arrested me! I was in the middle of trying to find my little brother Attir. I think that damn Druid Boerga kidnapped him last night to do a blood sacrifice for the Solstice. Please, please, Highness, make them let me go back to searching!*

Angels and Demons! Kirin heard Terrell swear inside his mind. *She must have already ordered this before I even met with her.*

Kirin knew confusion for a moment, then caught a visual memory of the elderly woman in white and realized who 'she' must be. *The Inquisition's got me locked in a cell under the Temple. Please, Terrell, I've got to find Boerga and stop her!*

Agreed, but this is tricky. I can't give the Hierarch orders. She's my equal and not my servant. She would just ignore them, and it would make her even more suspicious.

Suspicious? Kirin caught Terrell's memory of his morning conversation. *Oh dung! How much does she already know about me?*

Very little, but she fears more. I believe she thinks your Shadow might be a demon possessing you.

Kirin cringed as a vision of the tall iron stake in front of the Temple reared up to terrify him. *Ymera says it's not, and she's seen demons before.* He sent Terrell his memory of the ruler of the Red Street telling him so, her disturbing fangs showing through her disguise spells.

Is that what she really looks like? Terrell asked, fascinated. *No wonder our ancestors bound her with oaths.*

She keeps them, too. Kirin showed him the conversation with Rian's soul.

Terrell's mind roiled in astonishment. *You can do that? Reach through the Skin of the World?*

Yeah. I don't like it, but it didn't hurt me. Please don't tell anyone else. The One only knows how many people might want me to drag up their dead to talk to. He shivered again. The mere thought of people demanding he bring them their ghosts nauseated him.

Kirin, the Council Mages are all interested in you, too. They know you were Chisaad's apprentice and they wonder what he saw in you. I can give all the orders I want but that won't stop them from prying at you. I'm sorry. I know you wanted to just be an acrobat, but I don't think the world's going to let you have your way.

Kirin remembered Pieter saying, "You've come to the attention of the powerful and that's rarely a good thing." He looked around his cell and stifled a bubble of bitter laughter.

Terrell continued in his mind. *I'll have to plead with the Hierarch to let you free, but I don't know how long that'll take, and we've already got a crisis. Boerga is waking up the wight inside the Aretzo Node. Worse, she's trying to enslave it to do her will by using blood magic.*

Iron jaws clamped on Kirin's heart. *Oh God! That's what she really wants Attir for, not the Solstice!*

Possible, maybe even likely, Terrell admitted sadly. *My scholars believe she killed one victim this morning, almost certainly after days of torture. She'll doubtless have started on another by now.*

Attir! Kirin thought with anguish, remembering what Gerlach had done to him. Attir had no Shadow to rescue him from the blood-mage's deadly intent. *Terrell, I have to stop her!*

Kirin, I already have men and priestesses out searching, Terrell tried to soothe him. *The City's big but not infinite.*

That's not enough, Kirin answered, standing and going to his cell's door. *Damn any more delay! I'm coming out to join you!*

How can you possibly get out of a Temple cell?

With my bare hands.

Kirin called up his Shadow then and broke the mental connection to his twin.

~ ~ ~

Terrell opened his eyes and gasped. "Pen – I saw – we've got to run!"

He leaped up shouting, "Follow me!" and pelted across the black-and-white courtyard. The Palace gate that led to the Middle Court lay behind the next building.

Pen followed, with guards racing in their wakes.

~ ~ ~

Kirin filled his cell with darkness and reached for the wall next to the door. The Skin of the World stretched there like something alive, flexing under his probing hands. Ymera had slit it using a claw. He didn't have any claws, but his hands were strong from years of trapeze work. He grasped at the Skin, felt it bunch like fabric. If he tore it instead –

Before his arms took up the strain, he heard the door locks click. The bar slid back with a steel shriek and the bronze slab started to creak open.

The Inquisition's come for me.

He slammed his weight against the door and threw his Shadow out into the corridor beyond.

Temple Guards recoiled in shock, endangering him and each other with drawn swords as his Shadow overwhelmed them. Two men hurled themselves against the door to slam it closed. Kirin made it out first and let them shut it after him. He dived to the floor, rolled between two attackers thrusting blades blindly toward the door, and bounced to his feet behind them. Two more guards bracketing the first four raised their swords. He threw Shadow over them too and leaped for a ceiling lamp, caught it. A blade passed unpleasantly close below his toes. Then he swung behind them and dropped to the floor, running for the end of the prison corridor. It was blessedly close, but alert guards were already slamming the exit door. A bar dropped on the far side with a loud clatter as he bounced off the unyielding bronze. He looked back - the corridor stretched barely six feet wide and dead-ended forty feet away. The six guardsmen were already finding each other by voice and touch despite his Shadow, organizing to sweep the confined space with their blades. In moments sharp metal would find him, unless . . .

No. I won't be here.

Kirin grabbed the Skin of the World by the exit door, wrenched hard, and tore it open.

The dizzying view over the Well of the World leered at him. Around and through it he saw the faint outlines of walls and floors, the shape of the Mother Temple rising about him like a ghost. He reached one arm through the rip and felt for the other side of the door as his Shadow spilled through the impenetrable bronze like a cloud. Pale echoes of guards scattered away from the billowing darkness. He groped one-handed, found the bar, willed it to move, and his straining arm flung it aside. The door swung open.

He let the gap he'd torn in the World close again, slammed through the open doorway and ran. A shove sent a Shadow-blinded guard sprawling. Echoing stairs brought him to the ground-floor level. Chanting came from a room down the hall that a discreet sign labeled 'Sonorium.' That must be where the Hierarchy fought to contain the awakening wight.

He ran the other way, his Shadow flowing around him like a racing thunderstorm.

Corridors flew past, doors, shocked faces, sudden yelps, and far too many people. Then he found a door with sunlight slanting in through a decorative grille. A twist of the simple latch as guardian spells died, and he was in a side street with the Temple dome soaring above him.

He pulled his Shadow back inside himself and ran toward the Processional.

Terrell! he shouted through his mind. *I'm out! Where are you?*

~ ~ ~

Just leaving the Middle Court, Terrell answered as he ran. Pen stuck close to his side and the three youngest of the Palace Guards kept up, the older and less fit men falling behind. Civilians and soldiers alike scattered from their path.

Meet me at Oldgate! Kirin said.

Terrell swerved across the Outer Court, dodging startled pedestrians. He cut around the Bazaar onto the Ring Road. The worn limestone arch of Oldgate loomed ahead and he slackened his headlong pace. *Almost there!*

A billowing pillar of Darkness came through the Bazaar like a giant dust-devil. Startled folk fled left and right from its path. Pen uttered an oath and stepped in front of Terrell, Irreneetha raised to fight.

"No," Terrell told him, clapping a hand to Pen's shoulder. "It's Kirin. He's going to help us." He was mildly surprised to see that his hand was glowing.

As was his whole body. His Light had surged out of his heart and filled him to overflowing. Startled pedestrians gazed on him in awe and bowed. Some knelt right in the filthy street.

Kirin leaped over one of them, landed in front of Terrell and dropped to one knee as well, his Shadow closing up around him like a garment.

"My King," he said between gasps. "I think I know where to start!"

"Tell me," Terrell commanded, aware of hundreds of eyes on them. Pen hesitated at his side, Irreneetha swaying in his hands. Her red glare had faded and now she glowed a pure white.

"Sargent DiCerat said Rian's body might have come down the Big As – I mean, the North Sewer," Kirin panted. "Last night I searched the whole waterfront looking for Boerga and found nothing. She wouldn't have risked hauling his body down to the harbor if she could just dump it into the sewer directly. We need to search buildings along the north sewer line, only I can't see enough of it in daylight!"

"I'll handle that," Terrell answered, and raised a hand to the Crown.

You, he thought, visualizing the Stone Throne, and aware that Kirin's mind could hear him. *We need your help.*

YOU TWO NEED NOTHING BUT YOUR OWN ABILITIES, answered the Hill's wight. USE WHAT YOUR ANCESTORS PREPARED FOR YOU.

What in the Nine Hells does that mean? Kirin grumbled, recovering his breath.

Terrell remembered the Sight spells attached to the Throne. They could be controlled by any member of the Royal House sitting up there. Perhaps the King using the Crown could control them from elsewhere? He reached out with his mind.

Pale symbols appeared in the air between him and Kirin. Pen started back and the crowd uttered an impressed sigh. Terrell sorted through the maze of symbols. He needed something that could look at the City's own systems. He folded his right hand around a shape like an eight-pointed star. The other shapes faded away and the star glowed. He twisted it.

The street lit beneath his feet.

"That's the Sulfur Street sewer," Terrell said aloud. "We need to find the North one and then trace it."

"Follow me," Kirin answered. He scrambled to his feet and ran under the Oldgate arch, Terrell on his heels and Pen and the Guards right behind.

Gossip buzzed through the crowd behind them.

248

CHAPTER 28: AEDDAN

Morning, Third Day of the New Reign.

The pain slackened and then stopped so abruptly that Aeddan gasped. His entire body felt abused, cut, and violated so deeply that he'd soiled himself in shock. For long shuddering breaths all he could do was hang there in the rack while he fought to win back control over himself. He had heard of torture before but never had any idea . . . and Gorsyn hadn't yet touched him, just Kaghar.

This shared-sensations spell is monstrous.

"Curse it, he's really gone this time," Gorsyn said in a disappointed voice.

"You cut his belly too deeply and nicked his liver," the Druid scolded. "He bled out too fast."

They'd been speaking Gwythlo, which Aeddan could follow well enough until the pain had robbed him of thought. He tried to pretend he was still semi-conscious while he listened.

"I warned you that you were getting too excited," she continued berating the torturer. "You should have crushed his stones more slowly, too." She added something that Aeddan didn't understand, then finished with, "Never mind, it worked. I caught two demons perfectly and the wight swallowed them whole, which is exactly what we needed. Two more will give me absolute control. Clean up the mess and then prepare the second sacrifice."

That means me. Aeddan barely managed to suppress a shudder as he feigned unconsciousness.

The Druid walked to the wall behind Kaghar's rack and began casting a scrying spell against it while Gorsyn grumbled. He freed the dead mercenary's limp form from the rack and dropped it on the stone floor with a squishy thump, then dragged the body over beside Jerril's corpse. The blood had stopped flowing from Kaghar.

His heart's stopped pumping, Aeddan saw. *He's really dead. Blessed Haroun, thank You for freeing him at last.*

Gorsyn cleaned himself, then brought the wet sponge and bucket over to Attir and then Aeddan. The torturer swabbed his nether regions, cooing softly as he worked. Aeddan kept pretending he'd passed out. The monster's touch was firm and efficient but also disturbingly gentle. Evidently Gorsyn liked to start with his victims clean, though he certainly had enjoyed degrading Kaghar in ways that Aeddan hadn't imagined. The fastidiousness was almost as creepy as the occasional little chuckles. Aeddan wished he could pass out for real, but either the spell prevented that, or he was tougher than he'd thought.

"I know you're awake," Gorsyn said in Aeddan's ear, then licked his earlobe.

This time Aeddan shuddered before he could stop himself.

The torturer laughed and ran a lascivious hand down Aeddan's belly. "You're a nice big one. I'm going to have so much fun with you!"

"Your technique needs work," Aeddan managed to growl back. "You must have had a really lousy first lover." He wished he had something in his stomach so he could throw up on the monster. If his mouth hadn't been so dry from screaming, he would have spit.

Gorsyn chuckled again. "You have no idea, little boy. But don't worry, I saved a few tricks for you. You Sath-worshipers think you know so much. You'll be much more experienced before I start with the knives."

That might delay the really damaging acts for a while. Aeddan had to hope that Kirin was looking for his brother. If he could slow down the monster, buy time by pretending to enjoy it –

No, damn it! I'm not coddling this monster.

"You've got nothing new to me," he sneered. "I saw what a pale limp little –"

Gorsyn struck him hard across the mouth. Aeddan tasted blood for real this time, not the second-hand flavor of Kaghar's torture. The monster leaned close and whispered with a fierce intensity.

"Be respectful, and maybe I'll allow you a little actual pleasure before you die, darkie. It'll make your soul an even better feast for the great wight. Imagine the feeling as you slide down its gullet! To be slowly digested, losing every memory and feature that makes you YOU! A fitting end for a wretched halfbreed pig-boy. Afterwards I'll dry and preserve your crushed stones for a memento, unless I decide to fry them up and eat them."

Aeddan's gorge rose in dry heaves.

The monster laughed as he finished cleaning up. He swabbed the floor with a mop and bucket taken from under the table, then levered up the stone circle in the corner to dump the contents. From the smell and the splash Aeddan guessed that hole led directly to a sewer. If he could get free of the rack, he'd dive in there without hesitation and worry about finding a way out afterwards.

Aeddan looked over at Attir. The boy had screamed himself hoarse and lost control of his own bodily functions the same as Aeddan before passing out. Since then he'd hung there unconscious, not responding even while being roughly cleaned. Attir hoped the second-hand torture hadn't cost Attir his mind. At least he was still breathing. The Druid seemed deeply wrapped up in her casting and the torturer was busily chuckling to himself as he worked, so Aeddan risked calling the boy's name.

Attir stirred, raised his head and stared. He didn't have the glassy-eyed look of the mind-lost, though there was a nervous tic to his left eye. Aeddan tried to feel encouraged.

"Just hang on," he told the boy quietly. "You can take this. Remember it's not real."

"It was real to Kaghar," Attir answered dully. "You know it was. When he does it to you, don't tell me it won't be real then. After he's done with you – then my turn."

There was no answer to that. Aeddan didn't want to give away his hope, but he didn't want Attir to surrender without a fight. "I've got reason to think it won't come to that," he hinted. "Just be strong and try to hold out."

"Yes," said the Druid cheerfully, evidently not as engrossed as Aeddan had hoped. "Your brother is looking for you and getting closer. I expect to trap him quite nicely, then put him in the rack next to you. Your paired souls will be the perfect meal to slave the wight to me."

Her arrogance penetrated where Aeddan's hint had not. "You'll never capture him!" Attir surged against his chains. "He'll break every spell you cast and then kill you!"

"He'll try," she chuckled. "But I know what he is. I have long experience trapping demons. He'll find me harder to escape than the foolish yellow bitches." She glanced happily at Aeddan. "Thank you both for bringing him to me."

Aeddan clamped his jaws against the reply he wanted to give. Tears began to leak from Attir's eyes.

252

Gorsyn strolled up behind Aeddan and ran both hands over his ribs. Aeddan tensed, tried to take his own advice and relax, but it didn't seem to work any better for him than it had for poor Kaghar.

"Now let's get started on you, you naive boy," the Gwythlo smirked, and began cranking the controls of the rack. "Let me introduce you to something your Sathists never taught you."

Father-Seraph Haroun, be with me and Attir now, Aeddan prayed as the mechanism stretched his arms and bent him forward. *And be with Kirin! Help him defeat these monsters, I beg you!*

CHAPTER 29: KIRIN AND TERRELL

Morning, Third Day of the New Reign.

Kirin hurled a bolt of Shadow into the air and killed the spells on yet another crow. Penghar and the Guardsmen flinched but kept following Terrell, who kept following him.

"Why are you doing that?" Terrell panted. *Answer so the others can hear you.*

Kirin glanced back over his shoulder and said loudly, "Those crows are Boerga's spies. I killed their spells so she won't know how many are with me."

Pen nodded his head as he kept up doggedly; he hadn't dressed for sprinting. They rounded another corner and pelted through a square where women washed laundry at a fountain. Some screamed at the sight of Kirin's looming Shadow, others gaped at Terrell's Light and the slender fire of Irreneetha. The men stormed past and out the other side of the square. Kirin led them through another alley to a street lined with tenements. He stopped in the middle of it and leaned over with hands on his knees to catch his breath while using his magesight. The cacophony of magic overwhelmed him again and he hastily tamped it down. He couldn't see the north sewer through Aretzo's blinding brilliance.

This is where I was when the Inquisition stopped my search, he warned Terrell even as they all gasped for air. *Can you do that light-up-the-sewer trick here?*

Terrell still had the glowing star, barely visible through his own Light. He twisted the eight-pointed shape and the pavement here lit as Sulfur Street had done. Two branch lines joined the main sewer line a scant ten feet ahead of them. Kirin's heart sank.

"Which one should we follow?" the Prince asked out loud.

"Don't know. We'll have to try all three," Kirin panted, cursing the delay in his heart.

"You needn't waste time with that, Your Highness," a feminine voice called down to them. A diminutive Silbari woman floated down out of the air in a billow of silk dress and sparkling spells. She alighted on the cobbles and flowed into an aristocratic bow directed to Terrell. "I saw the Inquisition arrest young DiUmbra in the middle of his search, so I started searching myself. I've found her for you."

"Ymera!" Kirin blurted, then could have bitten his tongue. *Dung! I'm a plebeian, I can't address her familiarly!*

He could see the lithe muscles rippling under her innocent surface-seeming, see the bared fangs as she smiled at him. Her protection spells were visibly tattered around the edges.

"In the flesh, Sir Kirin," she smirked, and he realized she was enjoying herself too much to take offense. "But I can't endure daylight much longer. That building four doors ahead on the right, go through the arched door to find a stairway down. In the basement, possibly inside a shielded set of wine cellars on the left. The stairs are alarmed and trapped. Boerga's alarms were good, but not good enough. I've cut them and left the stumps in place to fool her. The traps you'll have to handle yourselves, I don't have enough time to disarm them from outside. She's got her brother Gorsyn there too, torturing two young men while she catches another demon. Hurry, Your Highness, for the lads' sake – and all of us."

She bowed to Terrell again and winked at Kirin, then swarmed up the side of a corner building and hopped onto the parapet four stories above. Kirin caught a flash of silk and sinew as she leaped again.

"Did she jump over the next street?" Pen asked in an awed voice.

"Yes," Kirin answered, then looked at Terrell. *Can we take them?*

Terrell glanced at Irreneetha and Kirin followed his gaze. The soul-sword's glow was more red than white now as she sensed battle. "Pen?" the Prince asked.

"Ready, My Lord." The fierceness in his voice reminded Kirin that the knight's last name was DiLione.

Terrell turned to his panting guards. "Use the summoners now. Call for the Council and the Hierarchy. I want them here as fast as humanly possible." He turned back to Pen and Kirin. "She'll use her victims as hostages against us. Our first task has to be stopping her from awakening the wight. Rescuing them will be second. Pen, Kirin and I will follow you —"

"No!" Kirin broke in. "I have to go first! The trap spells!"

"Agreed then. Kirin first, Pen second. Once we're in, you two engage Boerga and I'll take out her brother." He drew his own sword. "This ends here."

Kirin let his Shadow wreath him like a cloak. Terrell's Light brightened.

Now? Kirin demanded impatiently. *Attir might be dying!*

"Now."

CHAPTER 30: AEDDAN

Morning, Third Day of the New Reign.

"Another demon," Boerga chirped happily, pinning something to the cellar wall with a gesture.

Aeddan saw a churning shape of fire and smoke writhe into being before her. A web of magical energies caged it as disturbing flashes of teeth, claws, and eyes peeked through. It made a squealing noise worse than a dying pig. Despite the pain racking his body – his arms weren't quite pulled from their sockets yet, but it was close – Aeddan flinched from the horror. Being murdered slowly and painfully was bad enough. Being eaten alive by a creature that would treat his soul like a dog's chew-toy was sure to be worse.

Boerga made a gesture and the air around the squirming thing folded over as the demon vanished. A wave of malevolent wrongness swept through the exhausted young mercenary's whole body.

She must be very close to waking it up now. Please God, make her fail.

"The next pair are almost through the Veil," Boerga added. "Hurt him again, brother."

Gorsyn's happily obliged her. Aeddan groaned and didn't try to hold it back. The worse this Gwythlo monster thought he was hurting his victim, the longer he might keep at the petty tortures. Gorsyn's embrace had started out more clumsy than painful, though the cruelty and malicious intent were clear. It had grown worse. The torturer had a talent for finding his victim's pain centers and awakening them to full-bore agony. After an hour of brutal rape, Aeddan's battered mind just wanted to keep the knives at bay at little longer.

"Silly child," the torturer chuckled. "You don't fool me." He padded over to the table where the shining instruments waited. "Time to step up this game."

Aeddan panted and risked a bleary glance at Attir. The Druid had cast something extra on him to affect the sensations pouring into his inexperienced mind. Tear-tracks silvered the young face and his staring eyes had lost focus.

Father Haroun and Mother Umana, Aeddan prayed even as he felt the trickle of blood down his legs. Something had definitely torn inside him. *Please ward Attir's mind, I beg you. Don't let them break him with humiliation. And please, Seraph Sath, send rescue, for him if not for me. For myself, I commend my soul into your hands.*

Gorsyn turned, held up a wickedly sharp little knife. "Pleasure's over." The torturer lovingly added horrifying details.

Despite his will, Aeddan's body tensed against his restraints. He screamed as his left shoulder gave way and his arm bone ripped from its socket. Attir jerked in his own rack and his scream joined Aeddan's.

"Good!" Aeddan dimly heard Boerga chortle. Through his agony he saw her fingers flashing in the mage light as smoky shapes coalesced. "Two more demons trapped! Oh mighty Obilochithlone, I command you! Awaken for me, Great Wight! Awaken and taste the feast I have spread for you!"

New pain stabbed Aeddan. He hadn't thought he could feel worse short of a knife, but this did it. *The wight – it's draining my life.*

The door slammed open and black Shadow poured into the cellar. As Aeddan's abused heart lifted in hope, Boerga shouted with delight. She made a two-handed gesture and grinned.

"Got you!"

CHAPTER 31: KIRIN

Morning, Third Day of the New Reign.

Wrapped a cloud of darkness, Kirin padded down the stone stairs into the basement. He held his knife in one hand more for comfort than need. His Shadow swept through the traps like a scythe. *Boerga's a fool if she thinks these toys will stop me!*

Pen followed, his eyes wide and Irreneetha a spike of red flame held rigid between him and the billowing darkness. Terrell trod close on the knight's heels. They hit the basement floor and Kirin swept the room with a wave of both arms. A dozen more spells died and left them in emptiness. *That was easy!*

Too easy, Terrell tersely replied. *Kirin, you said you escaped her when she tried to kill you in North Street. She's got to realize that –*

Two screams echoed faintly.

"Attir!" Kirin didn't realize he'd spoken aloud. He bounded toward a trio of doors in a stone wall. The screams had come from the middle one, which wasn't completely closed.

Kirin, wait! What if –

Kirin slammed the door open, letting his Shadow billow around him. Boerga stood on the other end of the rectangular room, hands raised in triumph. Aeddan and, *oh God!* Attir hung in racks to either side, the former bent over and bleeding.

260

"Got you!" Boerga crowed as he charged towards her. Her hands moved.

The walls to left and right dissolved. A pack of hyenas leapt into the room from behind Attir. Behind Aeddan loomed a pair of big stumps draped in vines.

Kirin threw his Shadow in the face of the charging beasts. They ignored it and bared their long white teeth at him as they gave their hideous laughs.

Dung! They don't have eyes!

They move like they can see somehow, Terrell answered inside his head. *Maybe by sound?*

They sure see me! Kirin whirled and dodged snapping fangs, slashed his knife across a too-close muzzle. The hyena yowled, then pressed forward again with a new snarl.

At the door Pen blocked the opening to protect Terrell, slashing Irreneetha's shining length across snarling attackers. Teeth and claws clattered to the floor, blood and fur splattered, but there were more still coming. Bright light outlined him as Terrell raised shining hands above his bodyguard's shoulders and lobbed glowing Light into the room. Where it hit a hyena, the beast howled and fled.

Kirin dodged another beast and stabbed the face where the eyes should be. The creature recoiled and shook its head, growling. But two others pressed him. He stepped back and back again as they forced him between the stumps. One hyena paused to sniff at bleeding Aeddan, helpless in his rack. Kirin flung a ball of Shadow at it as those teeth prepared to bite. The beast turned to him and growled, the easy meal forgotten as it responded to his challenge.

Vines rustled as he stepped on them. Something seized his left ankle.

Kirin! Terrell warned. *Those aren't plants. They're Druid-bred monsters!*

Ohhhhhh dung!

More vines grabbed his other leg, began to pull. Kirin was unpleasantly reminded of the childhood ritual of breaking a wishbone after a chicken Feast-dinner. He wanted to cut the vines, but the two hyenas pressed closer and he had to slash at them instead.

The vines began to drag his feet apart.

He sent his Shadow against the stumps, feeling for their life-force in whatever form it took. They were bizarrely alien. He struggled to fend off the hyenas while the dragging tension grew. His feet were more than a yard apart now.

The stumps had life, but a slow patient vegetable kind of life that he barely recognized. He couldn't find anything resembling a brain or heart. So he set his Shadow's fangs in both stumps and simply drank those thick slow lives, like sucking marrow out of a bone.

The vines kept pulling. Soon he'd lose his balance and fall. The hyenas pressed closer.

Abruptly the left vines went limp as the stump died. The right followed. He desperately kicked free of their clutch. Something came around the stumps and leaped on his back, throwing him to the floor. Kirin's knife scraped on the stone.

"Die now," Gorsyn hissed, his slender torture-knife groping through the Shadow to slash at Kirin's throat.

The point of Gorsyn's blade caught the stone floor before it touched him. Thin steel snapped and one sharp edge nicked the tender skin above Kirin's collarbone. He jerked at the touch and dug his fingers into the suddenly flexible stone floor, tried to heave the torturer off him.

Gorsyn dropped the broken knife and hung on. He got both hands around Kirin's neck and squeezed.

Kirin's throat closed. Intolerable pressure grew. His heart hammered. The world began to dim. A hyena snarled its laughing cry and lunged for his defenseless left arm. Gorsyn's weight pinned him to the floor, he couldn't bring the knife in his right hand across to block.

He tore the Skin of the World beneath him.

He, Gorsyn, and the hyena all fell through into madness.

Heaving carmine walls loomed around and above. A crushing sense of strain beat on him from all directions. Below, the Well of the World opened and drank cascades of gray souls, plus one falling hyena.

Gorsyn shrieked and lost his grip. Kirin tumbled with him through the ghostly space as if they had no weight. A thousand wraiths gaped greedily and reached misty fingers for their lives.

Kirin stretched and barely caught the edge of the rip, using his knife like a hook. Gorsyn flailed and managed to snag Kirin's foot. Kirin tried to kick him off, but the torturer's grip was strong. Kirin dragged them both back toward the rip, grabbed the edge, forced his head through. His weight returned, he levered himself over the slick rim as if on a trapeze.

He and Gorsyn slammed onto the stone floor. The rip in the World slid sideways, swallowed a stump-creature, and bounced upward.

Gorsyn let Kirin go and curled up into a fetal ball, mewling. A hyena whined and backed away from him. Kirin rolled desperately away from another, brought his knife up and stabbed it under the jaw. The beast gurgled and flung itself away in a spray of red.

Kirin scrambled to his feet. Boerga was only a few feet away, her eyes staring at him even as she chanted and gestured. His Shadow could reach her instantly, strip her spells and her life —

And then I'd have her inside my head with Gerlach.

Instead he hurled himself at her, his knife leading the way.

She turned the blade to dust.

He let momentum carry him into her and slammed the heel of his left hand into her chin. He felt her jaw break and saw her raging glare go blank. She toppled backward and her head bounced off the stone wall with a loud crack. He fell onto her, scrambled up again and looked wildly about.

Pen had forced his way into the room. He brandished his flaming-red soul-sword. The last few hyenas fled back into the space they'd come from. Kirin saw a bizarre tunnel made of alternating rings of dark and light. It pulsated in the air while the hyenas raced away through it. He threw his Shadow after them and the tunnel collapsed. A staggering burst of power vanished into the Shadow, that tunnel had been no small spell.

Is it over? He gasped to Terrell's mind.

Terrell's horrified voice answered inside his head. *No. Look.*

CHAPTER 32: TERRELL AND KIRIN

Morning, Third Day of the New Reign.

Terrell stared at the two trapped demons that Boerga had hung in the air near the vaulted ceiling. They were draining away through the rip in the world that Kirin had made. From the desperate thrashing as their essences dissolved and flowed away, they were not enjoying it. Then the thing that had drunk those demons like wine reared up to press through the rip.

"Is it an angel?" asked Pen in an awed voice. "Or a demon?" He held Irreneetha up like a shield. Her light had faded to a pale white, the palest Terrell had ever seen her.

She's overmatched and knows it.

Kirin snorted. "That doesn't look like any angel. What in the Nine Hells is it?" He demanded, staring dumbfounded at the solidifying shape.

"The wight that's been sleeping in the Aretzo Node," Terrell told them both, while wondering how his ancestors had ever persuaded the giant Wight to sleep in the first place. *There must be a way to do the same here, but what is it? The Throne said I already had everything I need. What do I have? Oh!*

Holy Mother Umana be with us now. Kirin, there's no time to practice this.

Then tell me what to do.

Let me lead.

Terrell pushed past Pen. "This can't be won by fighting, Pen. Help the victims. I must handle the wight myself."

He let his Light flow through every part of his body as he stepped up next to his Shadow-wrapped twin. Kirin stood there above Boerga's unconscious form, the dust of his knife dribbling from his hand to the floor.

I didn't know it would be so terribly beautiful, Terrell told him. The wight wasn't quite solid yet.

Terrible, that I can see, but beautiful?

Beautiful like a sword or a spear, Terrell answered. *Like Irreneetha, or Pen, or our mother. Or Ymera, or you. Please follow my lead, my brother. We only have one chance at this.*

Kirin gulped and nodded.

The very air twisted as the wight's entrance peeled back the edges of the Skin of the World. The vaulted ceiling arched higher and the walls bent as if in apology. The whole room stretched to admit something that could not fit into normal space.

"Obilochithlone," Terrell repeated the strange name that he had heard Boerga use. "Hear me. You have been fed a meal of pain and cruelty, and it has poisoned you."

The looming form gazed down on Terrell and Kirin through golden eyes. POISONED, it repeated, the word like thunder. A dark churning spread through the translucent body.

"You are flooded by human suffering, and thus suffering yourself," Terrell continued, watching its reactions.

SUFFERING, the wight repeated, and there was such a freight of grief in that word that Terrell and Kirin both staggered. Pen, trying to lower Aeddan to the ground gently, nearly dropped him. Aeddan groaned and Attir sobbed, which meant they were both still alive.

"I can heal you of that pain," Terrell continued. "Will you accept my gift?"

HEAL, the wight sighed like a storm. Giant hands reached towards Terrell, cupped to receive. GIFT.

Terrell held his courage tight as he stretched out his right hand to touch the flickering essence of the great wight. A sensation of fire and ice flashed up his arm and the blood-reeking wine cellar suddenly smelled of brimstone. For an instant he thought his hand had been burned away, but it was still there. Nausea and longing threatened to overwhelm him.

Then Kirin gripped his other arm. His twin's touch halved the cataract of alien sensations, gave Terrell a place and an instant in which to stand amidst the churning glory and horror of the wight.

He poured all the Light within him into the spirit's hands.

The towering wight glowed brilliant yellow. The dark shadows within it withered and vanished. A vast relief surged through him, pain eased and health regained.

Sun-bright, the giant began to shrink.

"Go back to sleep, Obilochithlone," Terrell urged it, squinting at the resplendent creature. "Rest, recover, dream again, and be at peace."

The shrinking form sank through the rip in the world and vanished. Kirin grabbed the edges of the rip, lapped them over and smoothed them shut. The ragged tear disappeared as if it had never been. The distorted cellar shrank back to its normal proportions.

"Seraphs and Angels," Kirin muttered at Terrell. *How did you do that?*

I don't know. How do you do what you do?

I don't know either, I just – do.

Same here. Someday we'll figure it out. But now we have bigger worries –

~ ~ ~

Boerga stirred at Kirin's feet as she poured her power into Healing her broken jaw. He looked down at this three-in-one tormentor; the co-author of his wife's death, certain slayer of the best and kindest priestess he had ever known, and deadly threat to his family. "Excuse me, Highness," he deliberately said in a loud voice. "One more detail to settle."

He reached down to grasp the magic in the Druid's body. As he had with Chisaad three days ago, he ripped it out by the roots. Boerga shrieked and convulsed into a curled-up ball on the floor. Kirin fought down the temptation to kick her, though it was strong, and contented himself with announcing, "She can still bite, but her fangs are gone."

He went to Gorsyn, who still lay curled like a baby, and repeated the move. The torturer barely twitched. Kirin backed away, bothered by the way the man lay there drooling.

"These monsters are multiple murderers," he told Terrell, and finished silently with, *What are you going to do about it?*

Terrell nodded sadly. "Boerga has other ways of delivering poison," he answered. "The realm needs to be rid of her, and the world is not wide enough to make us safe from her malice. As for her brother, the bodies of the dead accuse him. He cannot be allowed to torture again."

You'll get no argument from me. Kirin glared at both with loathing as he went to Attir's side. He knelt next to his little brother, who sat shivering on the hard floor. Anticipation built in his heart as Attir grabbed him and wept, stuttering nonsense in his relief. The only words Kirin could make out were, "You came!"

Kirin hugged him back, said soothingly, "I'm here, little brother. I'm here." He listened, to Attir, to Gorsyn's moans, to Boerga's vicious and tear-filled cursing.

"Sir Penghar, my right Hand," Kirin heard Terrell speak in a stern formal voice. The knight stood up from making Aeddan as comfortable as a naked torture victim on a stone floor could be. Kirin stretched out his free hand and clasped Aeddan's while Terrell pointed to the two Gwythlos. "I, Terrell the First, wearer of the Silver Crown, find these enemies of Silbar guilty of high crimes against the realm, and sentence them both to death. Carry out that sentence for me."

"Gladly, My Lord."

Boerga's cursing escalated to shrieks. "Bastard darkie! Filthy spawn of a filthy land! My sisters will dance on your grave and grind your bones to dust! We will cut your seed out of the world like the foul rot you are!" Her voice stopped with a sudden thunk. Pen stepped away from her headless corpse and a moment later a similar sound silenced Gorsyn.

"Thank you," Aeddan croaked, and passed out. Attir sighed and leaned against Kirin like a child.

Terrell, Kirin asked silently. *How do we get them out of here?*

Footsteps clattered down the basement stairs.

I think that detail is being handled now, his twin answered.

Two robed forms appeared at the door, quartered in black and yellow. They gaped at the scene – Penghar and Terrell standing over two headless Gwythlo corpses in a blood-spattered room strewn with butchered hyena parts, and himself kneeling on the floor holding a naked and cowering

Silbari youth with one arm and clasping his other to the hand of a bloodied torture victim.

I'm not exactly looking my best, Kirin realized, as the priestess' face went from shock to horror, and then fury. *Uh-oh!*

"Kirin Sule DiUmbra!" thundered Dona DuVigo. "You are under arrest for assaulting Temple Guards and escaping the Hierarchy's prison!"

Her husband Mage DiCerat threw a spell straight at him.

CHAPTER 33: TERRELL AND KIRIN

Morning, Third Day of the New Reign.

"Why did you ever think that would work?" an exasperated Terrell demanded of Mage DiCerat. "Kirin escaped from the Temple's own jail!"

Two Palace Guards had brought in a litter and, under Pen's direction, loaded an unconscious and blanket-wrapped Aeddan onto it. The dumbfounded Temple Mage and Inquisitor followed Terrell as he shepherded everyone out of the basement into the bright daylight. Attir, clothed in Gorsyn's cast-offs, leaned on Kirin, who had helped him up the stairs after destroying DiCerat's spell with a thought. Terrell caught Kirin's angry glare at the two Inquisitors but kept his own attention focused on them.

"A binding spell is our standard procedure for dangerous suspects," Mage DiCerat protested weakly, darting frightened glances at Kirin.

His wife glowered at Terrell and complained, "Your Majesty, you are interfering in a Temple prerogative!"

"No, you are interfering in mine!" Terrell snapped back, waving an admonishing finger at both of them. He raised his voice to fill the street as he continued, "Kirin DiUmbra has done all of Silbar a great service by stopping the most vicious blood mage known in decades and ending Boerga's attempt to steal the City Node right out from under us. Without him two more men would be dead and every user of magic in this city would be powerless. Show a little gratitude!"

First Inquisitor Dona DuNimes alighted from a sedan chair during this speech and joined her employees' protest. "Gratitude is not the point, Your Highness. This man DiUmbra has an appalling capacity for destruction, one that must be controlled for the good of all!"

The Hierarch herself had stepped down from another sedan chair and now swept up to her servants' side. Three frowning women and a Temple mage stood in a row to confront Terrell. "My First Inquisitor frames the problem exactly," Hierarch Fenecia declared. "Power such as he has shown cannot be allowed to wander around as it wills. That is too much risk for Aretzo, Silbar, and the Hierarchy to tolerate."

There is an easy solution to this, and a harder one, Terrell privately told Kirin. *But I will not force either one on you. We dare not reveal your birth lest Osrick turn his guilty fury on both of us. What do you want? And what will you accept?*

Aloud he said only, "Kirin?" as he turned to face him.

~ ~ ~

Kirin's stomach clenched. The Hierarch and the King were both staring at him. Dozens of other priestesses, Council mages, guardsmen, and ordinary folk were pouring into the street, all eyes on him. It made him feel naked.

He looked at DiLione, guarding Terrell's back with his soul-sword. The blade shone with a calm pale light haloing a woman's face, watching him.

She's an angel, but she doesn't look mad at me. If I were a demon, or had one in me, wouldn't she know? And pointing that out won't do me a damn bit of good. I can run – and Terrell will help me get away. Or I can stay, but at a price.

He thought about that price. Being swept into the high politics of the realm, having to watch his own back constantly, people trying endlessly to use him to get what they wanted, and an ocean of lies, lies, lies.

But I'll be able to push back. No mage can threaten me, no priestess can touch me. It won't be easy, but I'll have power of my own, power that I can use to help my family — to help everybody.

Then he turned to face Terrell, bowed, and knelt at his feet. *I choose you, brother,* he declared inside his head.

"Your Majesty," he said aloud for the crowd's benefit, placing his hands together palm to palm in supplication. "Will you accept my service?"

He had an instant of vengeful pleasure at hearing gasps from the Inquisitors. Then Terrell put his own hands on either side of his, clasped them warmly, and spoke. As he did, a knot of fear in the bottom of Kirin's heart dissolved.

"Yes, Kirin Sule DiUmbra," he answered in a loud voice that could be heard across the packed crowd. "I accept your service, and I proclaim you my second Hand, to carry my voice and authority with you in service to me and to Silbar. With the right of the Three Justices, High, Middle, and Low, and the duty to uphold the Law of Silbar wherever I send you or where you go with my leave, in your own life and in the lives of those around you. So I, Terrell the First, do declare." He released Kirin's hands, grabbed both wrists, and pulled him to his feet.

Sir Penghar's jaw dropped, as did the First Inquisitor's. Kirin caught sight of Mage Yellow in the crowd, mouth open and eyes bugged out. *I think I'll be renegotiating my family's rent,* he thought, and at Terrell's puzzled reaction, added, *Never mind, I'll tell you later.* He realized that an idiotic smile had spread across his face, but he couldn't stop it. Didn't really want to.

"My Hands," Terrell stated to the priestesses in a softer voice, "Like myself, are not subject to your jurisdiction, First Inquisitor DuNimes."

DuNimes stared back in stunned silence. The Hierarch inclined her head and a small smile fought its way onto her lips. "An elegant but short-term solution, Your Majesty. My questions and concerns remain – but you and I shall pursue them in another venue."

She turned back to her sedan chair and left. The First Inquisitor and the other Inquisition agents found voice enough to protest as they followed in her wake.

Kirin blew out a breath that he hadn't known he was holding. *That means she's still gonna watch me like a falcon, doesn't it? Waiting for me to screw up.*

I'm sorry to say that I agree about that. But at least she can't arrest you. And who knows? You might win her over with your grace and charm.

Only if I do it on a trapeze. Aloud he said, "Do I get a badge for this, Your Majesty?" Silently he added, *Breakfast would be nice too.*

For both of us, Terrell laughed privately inside his mind. *I haven't eaten today either. But we've a show to put on first.* He cleared his throat and continued in a normal voice, "Yes, Sir Kirin DiUmbra. And a baronetcy knighthood – can't have a Hand who isn't a noble. We'll settle all the details while my faithful servants of the City Watch clean up the mess here. Come, Pen, Kirin, let's go to the Palace."

Kirin looked around at the watching crowd. Attir's eyes were staring like a dried fish, the family was going to decant a hell of a story from him today. A Healing Priestess handed Aeddan off to her subordinates to be carried to the Hospital and began checking Attir over. Kirin made a mental note to ask the woman to make sure Att got back to the Sulfur Serpent when she was done.

This is going to change everything.

CHAPTER 34: KIRIN

Evening, Fourth Day of the New Reign.

"You're amazing!" Sevan the Younger exclaimed, as his wife Carlai hugged Kirin in delight.

The rest of the family crowded close, fingering the soft fabric of Kirin's new clothes and gazing in awe at the badge pinned to his shoulder. The polished silver hand on a purple field glittered in the late-afternoon sunlight slanting through the Attic windows. Kirin had already told as much of the story as he dared share with them, three times, and still their excitement bubbled over. He basked in their awe and gratitude as everybody stuffed themselves with a magnificent meal sent over courtesy of the Palace cooks. Grandmother was already planning how to stretch the leftovers over the next three days.

The news that Mage Yellow had lowered the rent on the Sulfur Serpent's fourth floor to half what it had been, and forgiven all rent on the Attic entirely for five years, had brought great rejoicing to the DiUmbra clan. They celebrated loudly and there was much oohhing and aahhing over the fine bottles of Cerrai's best red wine that Prince Terrell had sent for this occasion. Kirin was hugged and pounded on the back until he thought he might fall over. The DiUmbra's guests, who included several members of the Talliber acrobatic troupe, looked enviously around the attic practice room. They agreed that their daughter Joli could definitely benefit from some time practicing with the DiUmbras, and Stettir DiUmbra's boy Habbir would fit in well with the Tallibers. A temporary swap of offspring was arranged, and nobody

275

needed to say that both families hoped it would eventually result in two marriages. Joli herself looked shyly at the younger men of the family, her gaze lingering on Attir the longest.

Attir blushed and found an excuse to drag Kirin aside into the men's changing room for a moment's private conversation.

Kirin looked at the little washing space, remembering the events of two days ago. It seemed an eternity since then.

"I'm sorry I picked that fight with you," Attir said contritely, meeting his eyes without flinching. "I was jealous of you."

"And I'm sorry I was jealous, too, of your growing skill," Kirin answered readily. "You really are as good as I used to be. If you and Joli can work as well together as Maia and I did, you'll outpace us by next year."

"About that," Attir said wretchedly, eyes downcast now. "When those two had me in their torture chamber . . ."

Kirin looked at him keenly. "Were you raped, Att?"

"Not – physically," Att mumbled, then looked up at Kirin again. "But Kaghar was, and Aeddan, and – *her* – spells made me feel it. Every bit of it, like it was my own body being cut and –" He broke off and shuddered. "I keep expecting blood in my chamber pot. Last night I dreamed about it and woke up in a cold sweat."

Kirin chose his words with care, and prayed they were the right ones. "When it happened to me, it was real, not a spell-seeming."

Attir showed no surprise. "Sevan told me, and Father confirmed it but told me never to tell you that we knew about Gerlach. I don't know if Maia ever knew."

"She did," Kirin confirmed, relaxing into the knowledge that his family had known all along and loved him just the same. "I told her, before we were married but after she, ah, seduced me in that garden. Your sister and I were very happy in bed together, many times, Attir, and what had happened to me didn't matter to our happiness. What happened to you won't cripple you either, as long as you don't let it. Maybe Joli will choose you, maybe she won't – that's between you two. But sooner or later some woman will choose you, and as long as you don't keep bringing the ugly memories to bed with you, they'll fade until they have no power over you anymore."

Attir smiled then and hugged him; Kirin was mildly surprised to realize that the younger man was slightly taller than him despite his year advantage.

"Thank you, my brother," Att said into his ear.

"You are welcome, brother," Kirin answered, then released him. "Now go back to the party and celebrate."

"You coming too?"

"No, I need to go show off my fine new clothes to Aeddan. The healers said he should be awake tonight. You go enjoy yourself at the rest of the party."

Attir nodded solemnly. "Tell him what I told you, please?"

"Gladly."

~ ~ ~

The Healing Priestess pursed her lips and frowned, unimpressed by the awesome power wielded by a newly-minted King's Hand. "Do not keep him awake long."

"Hasn't he already slept for half of yesterday, last night, and most of today?" Kirin pointed out reasonably.

Outside the Mother Temple's Hospital, the eighth bell echoed in the young night.

"Yes, and that's not nearly enough," she answered in typical hard-nosed Healer fashion. "He needs to sleep as much as possible while his body recovers."

"I promise," Kirin pledged, holding up both hands palm-out.

As soon as she stepped aside, he ducked through the curtain over the doorway into Aeddan's tiny hospital room. A west-facing window in the whitewashed walls boasted real glass panes. They showed the final glow of the departed suns fading behind the Bright Mountains. Stars already filled the moonless sky. A mage lamp on a night-table had been turned down but threw enough light to trace the hollows in Aeddan's battered face and the bandages on his repaired right shoulder. The half-breed mercenary lay in a generous bed under a warm blanket and seemed to be dozing. But his eyes opened and he turned his head when Kirin sat down next to him.

"You look like you've been dragged through three rings of Hell,' Kirin told him cheerfully.

Aeddan smiled weakly. "Feels like it was six. Maybe all nine." He squinted. "Is that thing on your shoulder what it looks like?"

"Yup." Kirin puffed out his chest proudly. "The badge of a King's Hand. A Left Hand, as His Majesty gleefully pointed out when he stuck it on me four hours ago. Because I'm so damn sinister, heh heh heh."

The right side of Aeddan's mouth twitched up in the ghost of a grin. "Funny, I don't think of you that way. And aren't we all supposed to call him 'Highness' so the Emperor won't get a burr under his saddle?"

"I figured I'd better start the job as I mean to go on," Kirin explained in a self-deprecating way. "Respectfully."

Aeddan barked a laugh, then winced. "Hell and damnation. I feel like I've been cored like an apple."

"You damn near were. You lost a lot of blood before they got your ass knit back together, but the Healer says you'll make it back up quickly."

"Yeah, she told me too. Said I'll recover fully, and everything will work and feel the same as it used to. I mean, I'd just started learning how to enjoy being Sathist." Aeddan grinned despite the pain behind his words. "To have to switch to celibacy now would be damn hard."

Kirin converted a bark of laughter to a cough and said, "I knew you were a strong man, Aeddan, in your head and heart as well as your arms. But listen to the priestesses, please; this isn't something you can just shrug off overnight."

Aeddan's defiant smile faded. "She warned me there would be dreams."

Kirin nodded. "Dreams and nightmares. They'll keep coming back for years, too, though they fade over time. Maia helped me learn that I could give and receive pleasure without having to remember what happened when I was young."

Aeddan stared at him solemnly. "You too?"

"Not as bad as you got, or for as long, but yeah."

Aeddan was silent for a while, staring at him; Kirin let him. Finally the young mercenary said, "So much more to you than my eyes can see. Thank you, Kirin. Maybe sometime we could talk about – healing."

"Whenever you need it, my friend. One more thing; you're gonna have to switch jobs."

Aeddan looked panicked. "Are they throwing me out of the Mercenary Guild?" Getting any other job would be difficult for a half-breed with neither family nor special skills.

"No, you're being snatched out and promoted. By Royal Fiat, His Majesty King — excuse me, Prince — Terrell the First has appointed you to his Palace Guard. After you make a full recovery, of course, and train back up until you can fight a kitten and win, oh, at least three times out of five. Meanwhile you'll be on sick leave with half pay." Kirin mentioned how much silver dhoba per tenday that pay was.

Aeddan looked nicely stunned. "How did you *ever* —"

Kirin smirked. "Rank hath its privileges. Asking for a favor is one of them. Just remember, you'll have to prove yourself to the rest of the guards. They may spew dung on you at the start, for being a Sathist and having pale skin and pointed ears. Though with me around to rank the lot of them, and Terrell having blond hair, they might not be too harsh about that last part. And you'll be the junior man for a while, so expect to get all the dirty jobs."

Aeddan snorted, winced a little, then said, "That'll be just like joining the Merc Guild was. I can handle it — and I won't be the newest Guardsman forever. Or the only halfbreed."

"I don't doubt it." Kirin grinned at him, then let his face turn serious. "Attir told me you helped him stay sane. Saved him from despair after they killed Kaghar and made you both feel it. Gave him strength even while they tortured you, showing him that it could be borne."

Aeddan's expression turned grim and for a moment he closed his eyes. When he opened them again, he shrugged carefully and said, "You'd have done the same."

"I hope so," Kirin told him soberly. "Thank you for that, Aeddan Soldierson. My family says, when you're healthy and have holiday leave, they'd be honored to have you at our feast-table with us. Your mother too, if she wants to attend."

Tears filled Aeddan's eyes. He had to clear his throat before he could whisper, "Thank you."

Kirin took his hand in the Warrior Grip, held it for a long moment, then released him and stood up. "I better go before the Healer throws me out. See you around, Guardsman."

"You too, Hand."

A familiar voice that smelled like cinnamon whispered in Kirin's mind as he left the room. *That was well done.*

I hope so, Kirin answered soberly. *He'll serve you and Silbar well, and also serve all the other halfbreeds by showing them there's a chance.*

As will you. A warm chuckle followed Terrell's words. *And I. One step at a time –*

– we can walk across the world. Pieter used to say that to me.

It's an old soldier's saying. Pyrull first told it to me when I was a boy in Gwythlo. I'm counting on it being true.

It will be, for us. Brother.

Brother.

~ ~ ~

The new clothes were surprisingly comfortable, but after leaving Aeddan's bedside Kirin still felt restless. The Moon of Madness had set and Calm hung barely above the eastern horizon. He prowled the streets of Aretzo to delay his return home, for this might be the last night he spent in the Sulfur Serpent. Tomorrow Terrell wanted him to start knight's training at the Old Order Chapter House in Southgate.

Me, a knight! And a King's Hand!

Despite his strutting show for Attir and Aeddan's benefit, it still seemed unreal. He wished he had Maia by his side to give him her wise counsel, and to share his triumph.

His hands went to the ritual cuts he had made in his sideburns. He could tear his way through the Skin of the World into the afterlife again, but it was far too late to find her spirit and speak to her as Ymera had done. Her soul had surely gone down the Well to judgement. He ached at her memory.

Maia. I will miss you all the rest of my life.

Kirin ducked through an alley in the Old City to cut through a disreputable neighborhood of sailor's flophouses and workshops near the Navy Yards. He walked down a narrow ribbon of moonlight.

A footpad loomed out of the shadows. "Give me that purse at your belt and you don't get hurt, halfbreed dandyman," he sneered, mismatched knives glittering.

Kirin sent his Shadow out to overawe the fool. The footpad gaped and fled, blundering into walls and potholes. With any luck he'd sprain an ankle and the streets would be a little safer for a while.

I can do something about that now, he thought. *I have power.*

But learning how to use it was daunting.

He shook his head and compressed his lips in determination. *I don't know how to be a knight. But Terrell says I have to learn. All right then, I'll learn. I swear by Father Haroun and Mother Umana, I'll be the best damn knight the City's ever seen!*

"Wither do you wander, Sir Kirin?" asked a pleasant contralto voice – from the parapet two stories above his head.

Kirin looked up to see Ymera silhouetted against the stars. She stepped off the edge and floated down in a swirl of silk, landing lightly a few paces away, and sank into a graceful curtsey.

He remembered his manners just in time to bow to her from the waist, the formal acknowledgement a knight owed to a Baroness. Then he frowned at her.

"You called me 'Sir' – you did it yesterday too! How did you know Terrell would knight me?"

"I didn't." She smiled, fangs showing. "But it was the logical solution, the only wise one, and our new king is wise beyond his years. As, it appears, is his new Hand."

"I don't feel wise," Kirin muttered. "I feel like a green stick tossed in the fire, wondering whether I'll burn or explode."

Without quite meaning to he found himself walking beside her down the street. She moved like some jungle cat, lithe and powerful beneath the concealing silks.

"I anticipate neither ending for you, though I doubt any soothsayer in the realm can predict your fate accurately." She gave him an enigmatic look, then in that abrupt way she had of changing the subject, asked, "May I show you something?"

Kirin glanced suspiciously at her. She was still the most powerful witch in the city, and terrifying in her own physical self, too. "Show me what? And how?"

"Physically show you, by leading you there. It is only a short walk away, across the Processional."

She hadn't answered the 'what' question, he noticed, but he agreed anyway.

They strolled uphill, both surefooted despite the darkness, and left the Old City, crossing the Processional back into a better neighborhood behind the Street of Jewelers. The Watch patrolled these alleys regularly and were notably unforgiving of anyone out of place.

But I'm not out of place anymore — Terrell gave me the right to go anywhere in the city outside the Sacred Precinct, he realized, and stood a little taller.

Ymera stopped him next to a brick garden wall. A gate at his elbow didn't quite fit the frame. A mage lamp in the garden beyond sent a sliver of light through the gap.

"Look," she whispered, pointing with one claw even as her other hand cast a spell over the houses to left, right, and across the alley. It settled like a dampening rag and the night became quieter.

He put his eye to the narrow opening and looked inside.

A woman in a silk robe sat on a cushioned rattan chair, holding a baby to her breast and smiling beatifically down at it as the child nursed. Kirin was about to look away, embarrassed at spying on her privacy, when a man's voice called from the house.

"Merria?"

No, he thought, frozen. *It can't be.*

The woman turned a little to respond, but Kirin didn't hear whatever she said. He stared at the baby in her arms, now revealed by the lamplight. The familiar curve of cheek and brow, curling dark-brown hair grown thicker in the past twenty-odd days, baby-smooth skin almost as dark as most Silbari children.

Dark enough to pass, he thought. *Most people won't even suspect he's really one-quarter Gwythlo.*

The man came outside in a matching silk robe. He bent to kiss the woman, then gently touched the baby's waving fist. Little fingers curled around the adult one. The man smiled and said, "He's a strong boy!"

"Yes," the woman answered proudly. "Our little Ezead."

Kirin remembered hearing that the name meant strong one. With the suddenness of infants, the baby fell limply asleep. A tiny snore wafted into the night air, achingly familiar. *Grigor snored exactly like that.*

Kirin's heart throbbed painfully as the woman got up and tenderly carried the baby into the house, protectively shepherded by the man carrying the mage lamp. The family dressed well and had luxuries the DiUmbras could only dream about when Kirin had been growing up. *Does he know he's not the boy's body-father?*

For a moment a sick jealousy reared its head inside Kirin. Why should this family have the happiness that he'd lost? He had money now, he could hire a wet-nurse and raise Grigor to be an acrobat like his father and grandfather before him. Papa and Mama would dote on the boy. These strangers had no right to his son!

Then memory stepped up and slew the green-eyed beast.

Pieter wasn't my body-father either. And he did know it. And along with my new wealth and power comes deadly danger. I told the Mage Council this afternoon that I would hold them personally responsible for my family's safety, but I know damn well that they're still only human beings. They can't keep everybody perfectly safe, not while selfish bastards out there in the world plot and scheme against me — including some of them. But it's the best I can do for the rest of the family. What is the best I can do for Grigor?

A door closed.

Kirin looked at Ymera, still whipsawed by emotion. "How did you know?" he whispered.

"Dona Abbithana had a cousin, wife to Pernod DiBellun. You haven't exactly been subtle in your search the last few days, so I had a pretty good idea what to look for. I entered her dreams and asked her to remember who her priestess-relation might have helped to deliver a baby." She pointed one clawed finger at the garden and the house beyond.

"Then . . ." Kirin hesitated, dread rising. "Someone else could find him by asking her too."

"No. I erased the memory before I left her dreams." She revealed this terrifying feat as casually as his family might talk about an aerial somersault. "She'll not remember it again. Only you, and I, know now."

If that was true – Kirin fought down the sudden hunger in his Shadow. It oozed out around him anyway.

She stepped back and said drily, "I do hope you feel enough gratitude to refrain from killing me."

Ashamed, he drove the Shadow back under his heart. "No! I wouldn't – I won't *be* a monster, even if I am one."

She gave him a weird smile then. "I see that we're both no strangers to controlling dark impulses. What do you want to do next?"

He leaned against the gate and stared at the empty garden. It looked well-tended, an orange tree and a fig tree both still showing some autumn fruit.

Maia. What would you have wanted? But she couldn't answer him. He had to make the choice alone. The right choice for his son.

The son of the King's Left Hand. Somebody will try to use him to get at me, sure as maggots crawl. But nobody else knows where he is – and Ymera's leaving the choice in my hands.

He took a deep breath and made his decision.

286

"That family has money and means to care for him, and their lives are a lot safer than mine is going to be, or ever was," he told her quietly, though he was sure the spells she had spread around them would prevent anyone else from hearing. "Nobody's going to try to burn a gem-polisher at the stake as a demon."

He shivered a little; the Inquisition wasn't done with him, only stymied for a while. "And, maybe, they even have enough love."

This time her smile was astonishingly tender. "I think you can gamble on that last item with very little risk. I will watch over them for you, if you wish. Consider it my residual payment for the way you collected my vengeance from Boerga for my guardsman's murder."

And a way to keep him in her debt at the same time, he realized. She gave him a tiny nod, evidently expecting him to think exactly that.

A weird feeling of understanding passed between them then. *Maybe it's because we're both creatures of the darkness . . . but we won't let it own us.*

He nodded back to her and bowed deeply. She curtsied again, then leaped for the roof across the alley. A soft clatter on the tiles and she was gone.

The hardest thing he'd ever done was to walk away from that back gate.

But he made a note of the house – fifth from the east end of the street – and resolved to learn the family's names. To keep an eye on them, in case they ever needed the kind of help that a King's Hand could provide. And he walked a little straighter, his Shadow flowing around him like a cloak and his badge of rank glittering in Calm's moonlight, through the night streets of Aretzo. The few folks at large got out of his way, bowing as they went.

He had people to serve and protect, the will to do so, and even a hidden ally of sorts to help. And now, thanks to his secret brother, the means.

Finis

Cast of Characters

(in order of appearance)

DiUmbra Family

(Note – Umbra was a city on the coastal plain that was drowned thousands of years ago when the sea rose. The family traces its lineage to there, and the right to use the noble-male 'Di' prefix derives from that ancient connection.)

Kirin Sule DiUmbra – Age 18, adopted son of Pieter Ille DiUmbra, husband of Maia Sule DiUmbra (deceased), father of Grigor Sule DiUmbra; real name Ryghar DuRillin DiGwythlo, twin brother of Terrell (elder by two minutes).

Milli Ille DiUmbra (nee Bidorian) (Grandmother) – Age 66, wife of Grigor Ille DiUmbra.

Sevan Sule DiUmbra (Sevan the Younger) – Age 19, older brother of Maia Sule DiUmbra & Attir Sule DiUmbra, son of Sevan Sule (nee Ille) DiUmbra & Carmella Sule DiUmbra (nee Sabior). Kirin DiUmbra's brother-in-law. Married to Carlai, one daughter and two sons.

Sevan Sule (nee Ille) DiUmbra (Sevan the Elder) – Age 42, father of Sevan the Younger, Maia, and Attir; son of Grigor Ille DiUmbra (a/k/a Grandfather) & Milli Ille DiUmbra (nee Bidorian) (a/k/a Grandmother), husband of Carmella, older brother of Pieter (and a sister who is not named in these stories).

Grigor Ille (nee Sorle) DiUmbra (a/k/a Grandfather) – Age 65, father of Pieter Ille DiUmbra and Sevan Sule (nee Ille) DiUmbra, grandfather of Sevan Sule DiUmbra & Maia Sule DiUmbra & Attir Sule DiUmbra, older brother of Gerghar Sule (nee Ille) DiUmbra.

Carmella Sule DiUmbra (nee Sabior) – Age 42, mother of Sevan the Younger, Maia, and Attir; wife of Sevan the Elder.

Gerghar Sorle (nee Sule) DiUmbra (Uncle Ger) – Age 42, eldest son of the younger brother of Grigor Ille (nee Sorle) DiUmbra, father of 3 sons (Habbir, Mellar, Berrin) and 2 daughters (one married, not a part of this story). Married to Silla Sorle DiUmbra (nee Nunes).

Silla Sorle DiUmbra (nee Nunes) – Age 39, wife of Gerghar DiUmbra, mother of Berrin etc.

Berrin Sorle DiUmbra – Age 6, youngest son of Ger and Silla.

Attir Sule DiUmbra – Age 17, younger brother of Maia Sule DiUmbra & Sevan Sule DiUmbra, son of Sevan Sule (nee Ille) DiUmbra & Carmella Sule DiUmbra (nee Sabior). Kirin DiUmbra's brother-in-law.

Habbir Sorle DiUmbra – Age 16, eldest son of Ger and Silla.

Others

Inin Ilvar – Age 58, Wizard and the Master of the Air – Age 50, leader of the Ilvar clan.

Dona Nivera DuNimes DiGallipo – Age 53, First Inquisitor for the Sacred Office (the Inquisition).

Murror DuVaya DiGuile (Mage Yellow) – Age 46, member of the Council of Colors.

Boerga – Age 38, Druid Chaplain to the Gwythlo Brigade, banished from Silbar for fomenting strife between the Gwythlo and Silbari militaries.

Daugala – Age 50, Chief Druid of Silbar, appointed by Klairveen, the Chief Druid of the Gwythlo Empire.

Gorsyn – Age 32, mage and torturer, brother to Boerga.

Ymera – Age 250+?, Baroness and Madam of the Red Street.

Eumita – Age 56, Chief of Staff for Madame Ymera.

Rian Smithson – A young halfbreed man in Aretzo. Dead at age 18.

Prince Terrell DuRillin DiGwythlo – Age 18, Prince (King) of Silbar, son of Emperor Brion ob Gwythford and Queen-Empress Shyrill DuRillin DiGwythlo (nee DiSilbari), brother of Ryghar DuRillin DiGwythlo (a/k/a Kirin DiUmbra).

Sir Penghar DuVerhys DiLione (Pen) - Age 18, Baron, bodyguard to Prince Terrell.

Irreneetha – a magic sword inhabited by an angel. Also the name of the angel.

Cadoc Ap Marn – Age 55, former appointed Gwythlo governor of Silbar in the Queen's absence.

Merria Cadie Rodum - a fishwife.

Aeddan Soldierson – Age 18, a halfbreed mercenary guard and Sath worshipper.

Watchman Kobbir DiJulin – Age 30, a member of the City Watch with excellent magesight.

Sargent Melghar DiCerat – Age 44, Sargent in the City Watch.

Dona Celia DuVigo DiCerat – Age 43, Investigator for the Inquisition.

Mage Marik DuVigo DiCerat – Age 42, husband of Dona Celia, a staff mage for the Inquisition.

Dona Sharra Pereto Lumin – Age 59, new priestess at the DiUmbra's neighborhood Temple.

<u>Dona Seraphina DuVigo Abnellambra</u> – Age 63, Dona and Hectissima of the Temple Hierarchy, Healer to Prince Terrell.

<u>Duke Roan Gryffud</u> – Age 61, Duke of Anagni.

<u>Sir Gellir DuRicci DiSolera</u> – Age 64, Baronet and formerly Duke of Lonigo.

<u>Sir DiNivir</u> – Age 65, Baronet and formerly Baron of Cosenza

<u>DiMaritus</u> – Age 45, manager of Mage Yellow's firestarter workshop.

<u>Bassir Goya Mareo</u> – Owner of the Sulfur Serpent Inn, forced to sell out to Mage Yellow because of debt.

<u>Nortin DuBir DiTellio</u> – Mage on duty in the Glass Office, managing the magic flow in Aretzo.

<u>Fantillin</u> – Age 48, Mayordomo and senior servant of the Royal Household in the Aretzo Palace.

Mage Blue – Age 59, Chairman of the Council of Colors (Aretzo Mage Guild governing body).

Mage White – Age 64, Member of the Council of Colors (Aretzo Mage Guild governing body).

Mage Orange – Age 58, Member of the Council of Colors (Aretzo Mage Guild governing body).

Mage Red – Age 55, Member of the Council of Colors (Aretzo Mage Guild governing body).

Mage Green – Age 46, Member of the Council of Colors (Aretzo Mage Guild governing body).

Mage Purple – Age 56, Member of the Council of Colors (Aretzo Mage Guild governing body).

Mage Black – Age 67, Member of the Council of Colors (Aretzo Mage Guild governing body).

Kaghar – Age 18, halfbreed mercenary guard.

Fenecia Crasset Demorian – Age 64, Hierarch of the Faith.

Joli Melgara Talliber – Age 17, young acrobat, future wife to
Attir Sule DiUmbra.